FIRST

Storm in a teacup

L.W.King

Under the oaks publications.

DEDICATION

For the land, sea and sky, a constant inspiration!

CONTENTS

STORM IN A TEACUP

CHAPTER 1

1952

She slumped at the kitchen table as Abe walked out of Carrie's room sobbing, at that moment, she knew that she had gone. An incredible feeling of loneliness exploded throughout her entire body, she was in *that* place again! It took her back to the time when she was forced to witness her three-year-old brother, who was so cruelly snatched away from her, his face was pushed against the carriage window as he wept.

Then she was taken back as she sat beside her mother's bedside as she had for the past two years, nursing her twenty-four hours a day, and then watched as her very last breath left her body. That feeling of complete isolation was with her yet again, she thought as she cried yet more tears.

Abe put his hand on Peggy's shoulder, in a vain attempt to console her, it would never be enough, Peggy thought to herself, as Abe wept genuine tears of sorrow. She could not bring herself to begin to console him, she was far too absorbed in her grief, she did not lift her head from the table, even though Abe was now inconsolable.

William had never felt so awkward, he had no idea what to do to help either of them. He placed his hand gently on Peggy's shoulder, but she shrugged him off, so he walked to Abe and put his arms around him, Abe wept so forcefully that William struggled to stay standing as he supported him.

Peggy lifted her head, wiped her tears away, and then walked through to the hallway, putting on her coat and scarf.

"Where are you going, Peg?" William asked anxiously, he had never seen her so distraught.

"I need to fetch Dr Clarke," she said quietly.

"No, I'll go," William replied, in the hope that she would agree, he needed to get out of the cottage and take in some fresh air, he was thinking to himself as he awaited Peggy's reply. There was no reply, all he heard was the front door close shut. Abe wiped his face and attempted a smile.

"Would you like a cup of tea or something?" William asked awkwardly. Abe shook his head and walked to the lounge and straight to the sideboard, opened the cupboard door, and took out a bottle of brandy, pouring himself a large one. William stood in the doorway shaking his head.

"It will still be there when you are sober," he sighed, still shaking his head. Abe drank the contents of the glass in one, wiped his mouth and poured another.

4

"What will?" He asked as he again gulped the brandy down in one mouthful.

"The heartache," William replied as he looked at the floor.

"William, you have no idea," Abe said as he poured his third and final drink.

The front door closed, which broke the awful silence. William heard Peggy and Dr Clarke walk to Carrie's room. Abe looked at William, then got up and walked to join them.

Peggy scowled as Abe walked to the bedside, he reeked of alcohol. On seeing Carrie's soulless body he gasped, the stark realisation, that she was most definitely no longer there.

The following morning Peggy woke early, she had slept hardly a wink, she rubbed her eyes, yawned, put on her slippers, and walked down the stairs. She walked into the kitchen and put the kettle on. While she waited for the kettle to boil she opened the back door and inhaled the fresh air deep into her lungs. The sun was shining, it was a beautiful day and ordinarily, Peggy would have embraced it wholeheartedly, but this was no ordinary day, this was the first day of her lonesome journey, she thought to herself until the whistling broke her thoughts.

He walked through the gate, up the path, around the side of the cottage and kissed Peggy on the cheek, then he walked into the kitchen and poured the boiled water into the teapot. Peggy smiled at the cheeky robin that had landed on the fence, singing its beautiful song, sighed, and walked into the kitchen.

"Do you want some porridge?" William shouted as she walked back inside. Peggy shook her head, even the thought of it made her stomach turn cartwheels.

"No thank you, but help yourself," she said sarcastically and tutted as he stirred the oats and milk in the saucepan. She sat at the table, nursing her cup of tea, as William sat opposite her slurping his porridge. Twice she looked at him in disgust, she already felt nauseous, and he was not helping.

"Aren't you going to be late?" She asked as she walked to the kettle and filled it up.

"For what?" He asked as he scooped his spoon around the bowl scraping the final remnants of the porridge.

"Work William!" Peggy huffed, she just wanted to be alone, she needed time to gather her thoughts, she wanted to walk through the meadow fields, smell the wildflowers, and listen to the birdsong, all with no words to distract her attention.

"I have taken some leave, I want to take you away for a couple of days," he said and smiled, Peggy frowned.

"I canee go anywhere, in case you have forgotten, I have Carrie's funeral to arrange," Peggy said through gritted teeth and slammed the fresh pot of tea down onto the table.

"I spoke to Abe last night and Michael called around this morning, they are taking care of the arrangements," William replied as he placed his bowl into the sink.

"Over my dead body, they are!" Peggy roared. "All those two did was cause her heartbreak, no I will make the arrangements!" Peggy fumed and stormed up the stairs to her room, mumbling to herself as she did. She slammed her bedroom door shut and threw herself onto her bed, burying her face in her soft pillow, to mask the sound of her sobs. She felt so lost, so helpless, so alone. She felt her bed move, as though someone had sat at the bottom. She quickly lifted her head and looked, Carrie was sitting at the bottom of the bed, she was smiling, it was the happiest that Peggy had ever seen her.

"My dearest Peggy, you must not allow grief to overwhelm you, you should be happy in the knowledge that I am happy, I have reunited with the people that I loved and lost, you need distraction child, let Abe and Michael take over, go and find your brother," Carrie said as she gently stroked Peggy's hair away from her face.

"But I don't know where to begin," Peggy said and sniffed as she dried her eyes.

"Start by researching Hamilton House, that is where he was taken, Tilly wrote and told me. It is in Hammersmith," Carrie said as she slowly vanished. Peggy grabbed the writing pad from her desk and quickly wrote the words Hamilton House and Hammersmith down onto the paper.

She washed and got dressed then walked back down the stairs, just as William walked out of Carrie's room.

"Hey, you have no business going in there!" She shouted angrily. William blushed with embarrassment.

"Oh, Abe asked me to fetch this," He said and held up the Grimoire. Peggy frowned, now she was furious.

"Did he now!" she scorned as she snatched the Grimoire out of William's hands and marched into the kitchen, slamming the Grimoire onto the table in front of Abe, who was sitting having a cup of tea. It hit the table with such force, that tea spilt all over him.

"Peggy! For goodness sake! That is sacred!" He shouted angrily. Peggy let out a loud laugh.

"That's a joke, all that book did was bring Carrie heartache and misery!" Peggy shouted.

"What on earth has got into you!" Abe yelled.

"I listened Abe, she spoke, and I listened about all of the backstabbing, the dishonesty, the lying, the cheating! I heard it all and now I'm fucking angry!" She roared, Abe hung his head in shame.

"I'm sorry," he barely whispered.

"Rightly so!" Peggy said and filled her cup with stewed tea, screwing her face up as she took a big gulp.

"Peggy, come on, let's go away for a few days, a change of scenery will do you good," William said gently, softening Peggy's anger, she then realised how horrible she had been to him, and her expression changed to one of great shame.

"I'm sorry that I have been so unbearable William, you have been such a strength to me, and I have behaved so badly," she said as she gently touched his face, tears stinging her already sore eyes. He put his strong arms around her and held her close to him, Abe still looking at the floor.

The back door opened, and Michael walked through, stopping in his tracks when he felt the awful atmosphere.

"Sorry to interrupt," Michael said awkwardly as the three of them looked at him. "It's just that, er the Elders have sent their condolences and asked whether you would like them to lead the funeral ceremony at one of the sacred sites, it is a great honour," Michael stammered. Peggy smiled and nodded as she thought about Carrie and what she had said to her earlier.

As she and Willian wandered through the fields of wildflowers, hand in hand, they said not a word, just took in everything around them. They stopped at a boundary wall.

"So, any ideas where you would like to go? William asked as he lifted Peggy up and sat her on the wall. She thought for a moment.

"Could we go to London?" She asked hopefully, William screwed his face up.

"Why London, it's supposed to give you time to recover and reflect, you are not going to be able to do either of those things there are you?" He replied.

"But I could begin the search," she replied sadly, William frowned.

"Search, search for what?" He asked.

"For Robert, my brother," she sighed. William then nodded.

"In that case Lassie, sure we can go to London, come on let's get you home and packed," he said as he lifted off of the wall and they walked back to the cottage.

William had gone home, and Peggy was left by herself to pack everything for the following day. She was going through her wardrobe, taking things out, looking at them, and then throwing them onto the floor. She didn't know what to pack. She had never been to London before, but she knew from all the magazines that it was the fashion capital of Britain, she was thinking to herself as she threw yet another dress onto the *no* pile.

She walked into the bathroom and began to run the bath. She sat on the edge of the bath thinking how grateful she was that Carrie had paid McFadden's to fit the new bathroom, only a few months before. Sitting in the kitchen in the tin bath was never fun or relaxing!

With the bath finally full of warm water, she walked back to her bedroom, grabbed her nightdress and gown, and took them back into the bathroom.

By the time she had had a long soak and used the curling irons, Peggy checked the clock, it was nearly ten and she hadn't eaten. She walked down the stairs and bam! It hit her again, the realisation that she was alone, that Carrie was no longer there, and never would be again. She walked into Carrie's bedroom and stripped the bed, she sat in the chair, the chair where she used to listen to Carrie tell her sad story, and the tears began to well in her eyes again when there was a loud knock on the back door. Slowly and hesitantly she walked through to the kitchen, and again it knocked.

"Who is it?" Peggy called out abruptly.

"Peggy, it's Molly," she heard. She quickly unlocked the door and opened it as Molly, Carrie's oldest friend flew into her arms and held her so very tightly.

"What are you doing here?" Peggy asked once they had cried and hugged for the longest time.

"I'm going to stay with you for a while, you know, keep you company and help you with probate and things," Molly replied as she sipped from her steaming cup of tea.

"Oh, but William is taking me to London tomorrow, just for a few days," Peggy replied, not wanting to waste Molly's time, all the time Molly was nodding.

"Yes I know, that will give me a chance to go through some of Carrie's things, and sort some bits out," Molly said and smiled. Peggy smiled, she was so happy for Molly to be there.

"Now would you like me to make myself a bed up on the sofa, or shall I sleep in the spare room?" Molly asked as she took her empty cup to the sink and washed it out.

"The spare room is already made up, I changed the bed linen after you left," Peggy said.

"Well Peggy, I shall bid you goodnight and see you in the morning. What time are you leaving?" Molly asked.

"William is coming here at seven, we are going to walk to the station," Peggy replied.

"Walk, nonsense, I will drive you both," Molly said as she tapped Peggy on the shoulder and walked towards the stairs.

Peggy woke to the wonderful aroma of bacon cooking, she looked at her watch, it was six. She jumped up and quickly dressed, she had laid her clothes out before going to bed. She put her make-up on and then walked down the stairs. Molly was in the kitchen cooking bacon. "Smells lovely, I'm starving," Peggy said as she kissed Molly on the cheek and opened the teapot lid.

"I dread to think how long it's been since you have eaten properly," Molly sighed and then handed Peggy a plate full of crusty bread, piled high with bacon.

"Thank you," Peggy said as she took her first mouthful of food for the first time in days, her stomach grumbling gratefully as she swallowed.

"Now, when in London, make sure that you keep your purse close to you at all times, it is still rife with pickpockets," Molly said as she put a cup of tea on the table for her.

"I will, thank you, Molly," Peggy said gratefully, with a mouthful of food, making Molly laugh. The back door opened, and Michael walked in and smiled when he saw that Peggy was for once eating.

"I understand that you are going to the big smoke," Michael said and smiled as Molly passed him a bacon sandwich. Peggy looked at him wearing a confused expression.

"He means London, that's how it is often referred to, oh that reminds me," Molly said and hurried up the stairs, quickly returning with a pretty floral handmade scarf, which she passed to Peggy.

"At certain times in the day, the smog is dreadful, make sure that you cover your mouth and nose with this," Molly said and then gave Peggy a demonstration. Peggy smiled and nodded.

"What's smog?" She asked as she finished her food and sipped at her tea.

"It is damp air that mixes with the smoke from the chimneys and factories. It looks like fog, but it is filled with toxic gas," Molly said as Peggy looked at her in horror.

"Wear the scarf and you will come to no harm, here is one for William," Molly said and passed Peggy another scarf, this one was tartan, making Peggy laugh.

"I'm sure he'll love it," Peggy said and chuckled as the back door opened and William walked in.

"Hello, Molly!" He said joyfully, everyone loved Molly, well everyone, except Michael!

"Hello sweet William," Molly said as she passed him a bacon sandwich.

"Lovely," he said and smiled as he sat at the table and tucked in, all the while Peggy explained the smog and scarf thing to him, he grinned when Peggy showed him the tartan scarf!

Molly dropped them both at the station as promised, which freed up enough time to pop into the station café for a cup of tea and a bun. Peggy was secretly excited, she had never been out of Scotland, let alone all the way to London, what an adventure, she was quietly thinking to herself, whilst looking out of the café window, watching swathes of people from all walks of life, rushing onto the platforms to board their trains to wherever. There was a voice speaking on the loudspeaker, breaking Peggy's chain of thought, as William quickly finished his tea and stood.

"Come on, that's our train," He said as he grabbed Peggy's hand and pulled her up from the chair as she laughed, he seemed so nervous.

They had been on the train for hours and in that time Peggy had read some of her book but found it so hard to concentrate, there was so much to see and to think about, William, on the other hand, had spent the majority of the journey dozing in and out of consciousness. She was watching out of the window, the countryside whizzing by when she felt eyes on her. She looked at the empty seat opposite her and saw Carrie sitting smiling at her.

"This is where your life begins my Peggy, enjoy every second," Carrie whispered as she vanished from sight, Peggy nodded.

"I will I promise," she said as William looked at her in bewilderment.

"You will what?" he asked sleepily.

"Oh nothing," Peggy sighed as she turned her gaze back to the window and continued to watch the landscape change, she realised that they were close to London as the countryside began to disappear, replaced by giant buildings, the sky slowly disappearing from sight, swallowed by huge soot-stained towers, and foreboding black bricked factories. Butterflies began to jump inside her tummy as the whistle blew and the train pulled into a huge station, full to the brim with people.

CHAPTER 2

They scrambled off of the train, Peggy was struggling with her suitcase, and William stood on the platform shaking his head. "Peg, pass me the suitcase," He huffed impatiently.

"No William, I am more than capable of getting off of a train!" Peggy said angrily, she hated that folk always assumed that she was helpless, she thought to herself as she threw the case onto the platform and jumped down off of the train.

The station was huge, and Peggy had never seen so many people in one place before, it was overwhelming. William grabbed her hand as they raced towards the ticket collector, who examined their tickets and then allowed them to exit. The stench of the fumes hit them both the moment that they stepped out of the station. Peggy looked at William in bewilderment. "Where do we go now?" She asked.

"My dad told me that there is a decent boarding house near Marble Arch, so I suppose that we should head there," he said as he read from a scrap piece of paper that his dad had scribbled on.

"What way is Marble Arch?" Peggy asked. William looked around and then shrugged.

"I don't know," he said anxiously. Peggy huffed and shook her head, from the corner of her eye she spied a policeman walking just up ahead. She ran up behind him and tapped him on the shoulder, he turned and glared at her.

"Er, excuse me, constable, could you tell us the way to Marble Arch?" Peggy asked as William caught her up with both of their suitcases. The policeman looked them both up and down as people barged into them both as they walked past, Peggy glaring at every single one of them, desperately wanting to shout at them for their rude behaviour!

"Ah, you're from Bonnie Scotland!" The policeman said, now smiling.

"Aye sir," William said and lifted his cap. Why he insisted on wearing it Peggy would never know, she said that he would look ridiculous, and he did, but still, he wore it.

"Why Marble Arch?" The constable asked.

"My dad said that there was a good boarding house there," William replied, the constable nodded.

"Ah, I see," He replied and smiled. "If you walk past Trafalgar square, just there, you see where the lions are," he said as he pointed, William nodded. "Follow the red road, go past Buckingham palace and the arch is just up from that," He continued.

"Thank you very much, constable," William said awkwardly.

"No problem," The policeman said then continued to walk in the same direction as them.

Peggy looked at the enormous statues of the lions, and then up at Nelson's column, she was in awe. "Oh my goodness William look," she gasped and pointed.

"Aye they're very nice, but we need to get a move on Peg, come on," he said as he struggled through yet another swathe of sightseers.

Eventually, they found the boarding house, even though William had lost Peggy twice, she was so busy looking at everything, dawdling behind, both times when William turned and couldn't see her he went into a fit of panic!

William rang the bell of the boarding house and then stood back. After a while, a stern-looking woman answered, looking them both up and down. William explained that his father had recommended it, and who his father was, the woman's expression finally softened. "So you'll be wanting two single rooms then?" She asked as they walked into the hallway behind her.

"Aye, please," William said and smiled.

"And for how many nights?" She asked as she looked at the huge book on the desk.

"Er, three," William replied and looked at Peggy, who was looking around and admiring the fancy wallpaper.

"You have to pay upfront," The woman said and handed him a card to fill in.

"Up front?" William asked, feeling slightly confused.

"You pay now," the woman replied slowly as though she was speaking to a small child.

"Oh!" William said and smiled as he took out his wallet and handed the cash to her. She counted it three times and then looked at them both.

"Well come on, follow me, I haven't got all day!" She huffed as her large legs struggled to climb the stairs. She stopped at the first door, "This is your room dear, the bathroom is down there, the last door on the right," she said and looked at Peggy. Peggy smiled at her as she opened the door, as Peggy stepped into the room the woman huffed.

"Right, come on," she said to William and rolled her eyes as she walked up yet another flight of stairs and led him to his room. "This is a respectable establishment, I won't have no hanky panky, do you hear," She said as she opened his door, William nodded in spite of the fact that he didn't have a clue what she was talking about.

Peggy threw her case on the chair in the corner of the small but light and airy room and walked to the window, she pulled the lace net curtain back and watched in amazement at the number of people that were walking past, all of them oblivious to anything around them. Then it dawned on her, Carrie grew up in this vast metropolis, all alone and only a child. A veil of sadness swept over her as she remembered when Carrie told her just how hard and frightening it was for her. She jumped when the door knocked.

She opened the door and a now capless William stood on the landing. "Well, come in," Peggy said and laughed.

"I'm not allowed," he whispered, making Peggy laugh more.

"What do you mean, who says that you're not allowed?" She asked as she laughed.

"Mrs Bloomer," he said and blushed, Peggy roared with laughter.

"That's not really her name, surely?" she asked. William was nodding his head frantically.

"Come on, let's go sightseeing and have dinner," William said impatiently.

"But, but I'm not dressed for dinner," Peggy replied and looked down at the outfit that she was wearing.

"Come on, we'll get fish and chips and eat them in the park," William suggested, he just wanted to get out of the watchful eye of Mrs Bloomer! Peggy smiled.

"Come on then," she said and smiled as she picked up her hat from the chair and walked out to join him.

They were sitting in St James's park with their newspaper-wrapped fish and chips, Peggy was lost for words, it was as though they were in a completely different place, she was thinking to herself as she took in the serenity of the park the majesty of the beautiful swans gliding past on the river, and the cheeky pigeons that were on the beg for fish.

"How's your fish?" William asked as he stuffed more fish into his mouth. Peggy nodded.

"Aye, it's lovely, not as nice as Mr Donald's though," she sighed as she thought about the chippy back home.

"Aye, he's cheaper and his fish is bigger," William said, making Peggy chuckle. Peggy was so full that she fed the remainder of her fish to the hungry pigeons, much to the disapproval of William who was happy to eat her leftovers, but she insisted that the pigeons needed it more!

Once their food had gone down, they walked arm in arm along the river, which was lit up by the beautiful street lamps, the city had quietened a little, and at certain points, it was even quite peaceful, Peggy was thinking, even though the stench of the river was becoming unbearable.

"You know something?" She asked and looked at William who stopped walking and leaned against the wrought iron railings.

"What?" he replied.

"All the young men that have walked past us," she sighed.

"Barged into us, don't you mean," William interrupted, Peggy chuckled.

"Aye, all the young men that have barged into us, any one of them could have been my Robert," she continued, William frowned.

"I hope not Peg, the majority of people that we have encountered have been really rude," William sighed. What if her Robert was the same, you know, they had grown up in completely different surroundings and circumstances, she might not even get on with him, she thought as a shiver ran down her spine.

"We will get on won't we?" she asked desperately, William, who could not read her thoughts looked at her in bewilderment.

"What are you on about Lassie?" he asked, Peggy then realised that she was thinking out loud, and chuckled.

"Robert and us, I was thinking, I hope that we get on," she said anxiously.

"Sure we will, the same blood runs through his veins that runs through yours and Carrie's, I'm sure we will all get on just fine!" William said and kissed her. Her stomach flipped when he did, it always did, how she loved his very bones!

There was a loud rap on the door, making Peggy jump from her sleep. "Who is it?" she asked sleepily.

"Breakfast will be served in five minutes, if you are not in the dining room when it is served, you will have to go without!" Mrs Bloomer shouted sternly and then Peggy heard her heavy footsteps walking up the next flight of stairs, where she rapped on William's door.

She reluctantly swung her legs around and climbed out of the incredibly comfortable bed, she had had the best night's sleep ever despite the traffic and the late-night revellers! She washed her face over the small vanity sink in the corner of the room, then looked at her outfits, which one would she wear? She was thinking to herself as she laid them both out on the bed. She picked up the pale blue two-piece and held it up against herself as she looked in the mirror. She shook her head and then picked up the beige one, doing the same thing again.

"Not that one Peg, I much prefer the pale blue one," she heard. She recognised that voice, she looked around the room and then saw her standing, looking out of the window, it was Jo!

"You always did," Peggy said and laughed as there was a tap on the door.

"Who is it?" Peggy asked as the silhouette of Jo slowly vanished.

"It's me Peg, who is in there?" William asked sternly, Peggy opened the door.

"Nobody why?" she asked, a little taken aback by his mannerism.

"I heard you talking to someone!" He huffed.

"Aye, it was Jo," Peggy said and smiled.

"Jo, Jo who?" William asked as Mrs Bloomer walked up the stairs and looked at them both. She glared at Peggy who was still in her nightdress.

"I thought that I had made myself perfectly clear when I said that there was to be no HANKY PANKY" She roared.

William began to stammer as he explained, Peggy slowly closed the door, then quickly dressed, and met him outside of her room, Mrs Bloomer was now back down the stairs. William glared at Peggy. "You can explain yourself over breakfast," he sneered through gritted teeth as he forcefully grabbed Peggy's arm and marched her down to the dining room. She desperately wanted to shrug him off but didn't want to make a scene, so she quietly sat down at the table that Mrs Bloomer had ordered her to sit at.

"Once they had been served their breakfasts, William leaned across the table.

"So who is Jo?" he snarled.

"I don't know who you think that you are talking to, but you do not own me or control me, William," Peggy snarled back. "When I said that I was talking to Jo, I meant Molly's daughter Jo, you know the Jo that was murdered, my best friend JO!" Peggy's whispers became louder, so much so, that other diners were now looking at them both. William flushed with embarrassment, turned, and smiled at all of the people staring at them, whispering about them, then turned his gaze to Peggy.

"Look, sorry Peg," William whispered and attempted to hold her hand, which she pulled back rapidly and glared at him. She looked down and began to eat her boiled egg.

"Where should we start today?" William asked cheerfully, as though nothing had happened, Peggy put her spoon down and looked at him.

"Hammersmith, I already told you yesterday," she muttered.

Once breakfast had finished, Peggy went back to her room to put on her make-up and grab her jacket and scarf, leaving William downstairs with the dreaded Mrs Bloomer! Peggy chuckled at the thought of how awkward he would be and if she were to be completely honest he deserved it after the way he had behaved! She walked slowly down the stairs and chuckled inside as she saw that William was red-faced and quiet. She took his arm, and they walked down the steps onto the vast pavement, which was teeming with people.

They caught an underground train to Hammersmith which absolutely frightened the life out of both of them, and then walked through the busy streets, dodging people as they did. They had seemed to walk for miles, just going around in circles trying to find Hamilton House. Peggy was fed up and tired, she was about to suggest going back when she saw a newsagents, something was telling her to go in and ask, which she did.

As she walked through the door a small bell rang. She walked over to the counter where a jolly-looking man was putting unread newspapers into piles. "Can I elp ya love?" He asked cheerfully.

"Aye, would you happen to know where Hamilton House is?" Peggy asked politely, the man chuckled.

"If you go down to the bottom of this road and turn left, keep walking til you reach a turning called Chesson Road, walk up there til the road splits into two, Amilton house is just on the corner," he replied and smiled.

"Oh thank you very much, you are most kind!" Peggy said and smiled.

"If you don't mind me asking, what's your business there," The man asked.

"Oh, I'm looking for my brother, he was taken there many years ago," Peggy replied awkwardly as William, who had opted to wait outside, opened the shop door, and walked in.

"You won't find im there now love, it's a bookmakers," The man said and laughed.

"A what?" Peggy asked.

"Bookmakers, you know gee gee's," he replied, now totally confusing her. She blushed with embarrassment and looked at William for help.

"What are Gee gee's?" William asked, making the man roar with laughter, William frowned as he felt as though they were being ridiculed.

"Sorry mate, no," the man said as still, he laughed. "It's where people put bets on horses," he tried to explain in terms that they would understand. William nodded and looked at Peggy.

"How long has it been that, er book thingy?" Peggy asked.

"Cor Blimey! Now there's a question, ang on let me fink," he said as he thought. "Yeah that's it, Mr Philpott, a right villain brought it, cor must ave been 1921. He turned it into a bookies about five years ago, had to go legit see, the old bill was after im," The man said and smiled. Peggy nodded, not really having a clue what the man was saying.

"Well, thanks for your help," William said as he took Peggy by the hand and walked her out of the shop.

"What was 'is name?" the man shouted as William closed the shop door, the ringing bell masking the sound of his voice. The man shook his head, then went back to piling his newspapers.

"Did you have any idea what he was saying?" Peggy asked William as they followed his directions.

"Not a clue, maybe they will be better understood in the betting shop," he replied, Peggy nodded and pointed as they had reached Chesson Road.

They both stood outside staring at the huge building, which was once Hamilton House, and now a bookmakers, which was full of people smoking. As she walked in she had to use her scarf to cover her face, the smoke fumes were unbearable, and William stood close behind her.

"Excuse me?" Peggy shouted to the lady behind the counter, it was so noisy in there. The lady nodded in acknowledgement, "Do you have any knowledge of a young man named Robert wells?" Peggy asked.

"A" the lady said as she held her hand to her ear.

"ROBERT WELLS, DO YOU KNOW HIM!" Peggy shouted over all of the noise, the lady shook her head.

"No sorry love never heard of him," she shouted.

"HE USED TO LIVE HERE IN THIS PLACE!" Peggy shouted. The lady shook her head and then turned her attention to a customer wanting to place a bet.

"This is useless Peg, let's get out of here," William said, Peggy shook her head, she couldn't hear him.

"LET'S GET OUT OF HERE!" He bellowed, Peggy nodded, and they turned and left.

"Och William, what am I going to do? I'm never going to find him!" Peggy said despairingly as they walked back towards the underground station.

"I'm sure that we will, it was never going to happen straight away was it?" William said as he wrapped his arm around her shoulder. "Let's go and get changed, go out for a slap-up meal and then pictures afterwards," William suggested, making Peggy smile.

She put on her pretty floral dress, with a silk shawl, she was pleased with the outfit when she looked in the mirror, she walked down the stairs, to where William was waiting for her in the foyer. "Oh Peggy, you look beautiful!" He said as his eyes lit up.

"Thank you," She said and smiled as she stood beside him.

"Remember, the door gets locked at ten-thirty, if you're any later you'll be locked out," Mrs Bloomer shouted from behind the desk.

"Aye, we know," William sighed as he and Peggy walked out of the door and laughed.

CHAPTER 3

It was the first time that either Peggy or William had eaten in a real Italian restaurant, and neither of them had a clue, about what to order. William played it safe and had a pizza, Peggy on the other hand decided to be a little more daring and ordered Spaghetti Bolognese. The waiter brought their meals to the table and once he had placed them both down, he held out a bowl, gesturing for Peggy to take some, Peggy, being so polite, did just that and sprinkled it over her meal, William was already tucking into his pizza, two slices down, tomato sauce already forming a circle around his mouth, Peggy chuckled.

The waiter left the table, and William looked up from his plate and looked at Peggy. "What was that?" he asked with his mouth full, Peggy shrugged her shoulders and then smelt her hands, and as she did she wore an expression of great disgust. She held her hand out for William to smell, which he did, he too screwed his face in utter disgust.

"Urgh, smells like my Dad's feet when he takes his boots off Peg, you're not going to eat that are ya?" William asked and took another chunk from his slice of pizza.

"I don't really have much choice, do I? It's that or starve," she said as she frowned, trying her hardest to move whatever it was, off of some of the spaghetti.

"You can always share my pizza," William said half-heartedly, hoping that she would say no. Peggy chuckled and shook her head as she looked at the solitary slice that was remaining.

She wound the spaghetti around her fork and placed it into her mouth, she was pleasantly surprised when she tasted it, it was delicious. William watched her with great anticipation and bated breath.

"Mmm, it's delicious," she said once she had swallowed her mouthful. She wrapped some more around her fork and passed it to William, "Here, try some," she said. He screwed his face up and then frowned.

"Peggy that's not good manners," he scowled, making Peggy laugh.

"You're too scared! And in any case, it is seen to be romantic if you try one another's food," she said and ate the forkful that William turned down.

"Aye and where did you hear that rubbish?" he asked as he pushed his empty plate away.

"Magazines, they all say the same, oh and the book that I am reading, they eat from one another's forks," Peggy retorted.

"Well, I think that it's disgusting, using someone else's cutlery, that has their germs on," William scorned and frowned.

"Well you don't say that when we kiss, we share our germs then," Peggy said and laughed as William turned three shades of scarlet.

"Peggy, stop it now!" he said and looked around at the other diners, not one of them was in the least bit interested.

"Come on, hurry up, or we will miss the last film," he said and looked at his pocket watch. Peggy looked at her wristwatch, it was ten past eight, and she was nowhere near finished.

"We'll never make it to the pictures now, the last film is at eight forty-five, and we won't get back to the boarding house before ten thirty," Peggy said as she ate another forkful of her tasty meal. William huffed and then began fidgeting, Peggy rolled her eyes, and then placed her fork into her half-eaten bowl of food. She wiped her mouth on the crisp white napkin, then frowned at William.

"Well come on then, if you're in such a hurry let's go," she said loudly and angrily as she pushed her chair back and stood up. William looked at her wearing an expression of shock, he then walked to the counter to pay, while Peggy walked to the coat stand and grabbed her shawl, wrapping it around her shoulders. She was so angry, William paid, and they both walked outside into the busy street.

"Well, if we canee go to the pictures, what are we going to do?" William asked as he looked up and down the street.

Peggy shrugged her shoulders, then stood awkwardly as neither of them said a word. After a few minutes, Peggy's patience was wearing thin, she huffed and began walking in the direction of the boarding house. William was walking behind, keeping a close eye on her as she weaved in and out of the way of the many people using the same pavement.

She raced up the steps of the boarding house, flew through the door, not acknowledging anyone or anything, ran up the stairs, and into her room, slamming the door shut behind her.

The following morning she woke at five thirty, she wanted to go home, she hated London and William was behaving like a pig, she was thinking to herself as she threw her clothes into her suitcase, luckily she had the train tickets. She washed and dressed, then walked to the small writing desk and wrote William a note.

I have gone home, I hate it here, and I hate the way that you have behaved!

Goodbye, William.

She placed the note and the train ticket in one of the envelopes that were provided on the desk, licked the gummed edge, sealed it, picked up her case and quietly left the room. She handed the envelope to Mrs Bloomer, who was sitting behind the desk, listening to the radio.

Mrs Bloomer raised an eyebrow as she took the envelope from Peggy. "Going somewhere are you?" she asked. Peggy leaned over the desk,

"That's none of your business," she whispered, grabbed the handle of her suitcase, and struggled out of the door.

She finally made it to the station in one piece and looked at the timetables trying to find out what time her train was leaving and what platform it would leave from. It was no use, she could not make hind nor hair of the thing. She shook her head and walked towards a cheerful-looking older man, who was taking tickets at one of the platforms. She placed her heavy case on the floor and smiled.

"Excuse me, sir, do you know what time the train to Edinburgh leaves?" she asked.

"Yes my dear, the next train to Edinburgh leaves at seven forty-five, platform 2," he replied in a Scottish accent, making Peggy smile.

"Thank you very much, you have been most helpful," she beamed and then looked at the platform numbers.

"Platform 2 is down the stairs," he added and winked. Peggy smiled and made her way to the staircase.

She boarded the train and sighed as she looked out to the platform where many other people were boarding the train. There were businessmen, older women and men, a few young couples, couples saying goodbye, and as she watched, tears formed in her eyes, she loved William so much, but my goodness, she had seen a side of him that she did not like or wish to be near, she thought as she wiped the tears away.

The whistle blew, signalling that the train was leaving the station when she heard a familiar voice shouting on the platform. She looked out of the window, and there he was looking through all of the windows as he ran along the platform. Peggy quickly sat back, in the hope that he would not see her, she did not wish to spend the entire journey sitting in silence, while he scowled at her, she was thinking to herself, when his nose pressed against the window of her compartment, "Please Peggy, I'm sorry," he mouthed as he then ran to the door and boarded the train.

Six long hours later and one station change, Peggy was relieved when the train finally pulled into the station. She stood up and reached to grab her case from the luggage rack above. William quickly jumped up and grabbed it before she did.

"I'll take it for you," he said and smiled a sad smile, they had hardly said a word on the journey home, giving Peggy time to think about what it was that she wanted from life, should she be happy living a simple life in Scotland with William, or would she be happier somewhere else, experiencing all different types of things, travelling to different shores, meeting people from all walks of life, these and many other thoughts had drifted through her mind as she watched the changing landscape.

She walked out to the telephone box and called the cottage phone, Abe answered.

"We weren't expecting you home until tomorrow," he said when he heard Peggy's voice.

"Could you please ask Molly to collect us," she asked quietly.

"Ah, Molly has gone to the solicitors with Michael, I could come and get you," Abe replied.

"Ok, thanks," Peggy sighed and hung up the receiver. She turned to William and smiled a small smile.

"Abe is coming to pick us up," she said and sat on her suitcase.

The car journey home was quiet, Abe read the situation very quickly, so he said very little until they pulled up outside William's parent's farmhouse. Abe jumped out of the car and opened the boot so that William could grab his case, Peggy climbed out of the back and got in the front as William tipped his cap and walked away from the car.

"I take it that things didn't go according to plan?" Abe said as he drove the winding track towards the cottage.

"Aye, you could say that" Peggy sighed as she looked out of the window.

"No joy with Robert then?" Abe asked, trying to break the awkward silence,

"Who?" Peggy asked, then could have kicked herself, she was so wrapped up in her woes that she had completely forgotten about the reason why they travelled there in the first place! "No, no luck," she replied, then looked at Abe and frowned.

"Did you just ask that for me, or for you?" she asked as she screwed her eyes up.

"Oh Peggy, come on, I am not that callous, of course, I was asking for you, Abe said and chuckled.

"You could have fooled me," she scorned and climbed out of the now-parked car.

She threw her case onto the bedroom floor and flopped on her bed, she was so angry, but with whom, William for acting out of character, Abe, for well, being his usual selfish self, Carrie for leaving her alone in the big scary world, or herself, for blaming everyone for everything, for feeling so alone and helpless, for not having the ability to stand alone. She let out a loud growl when there was a gentle tap on her bedroom door.

"What?" she shouted angrily.

"Peggy, it's Molly, I have brought you a cup of tea," she said quietly. Peggy jumped up from the bed and ran to the door, quickly opening it.

"Sorry Molly, I am in a foul mood, I shouldn't have spoken to you like that," Peggy said as she gestured for Molly to go in.

"Nonsense, have a cup of tea, that will ease your troubled mind," Molly said gently as she passed the cup and saucer to Peggy. "Do you mind if I sit down?" Molly asked. Peggy smiled and patted the bed beside where she was sitting, so Molly sat, she noticed that Peggy's hands were trembling, and she then concluded that she was not dealing with the grief as well as they had all anticipated she would.

"Was it really that bad in London?" Molly asked, Peggy, shook her head.

"No, well, er, oh Molly, William was acting really strangely," Peggy sighed, Molly frowned.

"In what way?" She asked.

"Well, he became quite controlling, and I saw a selfish side to him that I have never seen before," Peggy explained. Molly shook her head, then smiled.

"You know, maybe he is struggling with it too, let's be honest here Peggy, you are no stranger to heartbreak are you? William on the other hand has never lost a loved one, or experienced anything like it, he had a good relationship with Carrie, and he is trying his hardest to be there for you, all the while dealing with his own feelings," Molly said. Peggy looked at Molly through her tear-filled eyes and smiled as she touched Molly's face.

"Thank you, Molly, Carrie will never be gone all the time that you are around," she sighed as the tears rolled down her cheeks. Molly was also now in tears. She kissed Peggy's hand, wiped her tears away and jumped up.

"Right young lady, you and I have a date in the kitchen, I was going to cook a roast for you tomorrow, but as you are back early, I think that we should cook it together, you can make us one of Carrie's famous cakes. Peggy looked at Molly wearing a confused expression, and then it clicked.

"Oh, the virility cake!" Peggy said and laughed as Molly nodded.

Abe was standing at the kitchen door when Peggy walked through. She walked up behind him and tapped him on the shoulder, he turned and smiled.

"I'm sorry," Peggy said and threw her arms around him. He closed his arms around her tiny frame and held her tightly, as he did he sobbed. After a long embrace, they separated, and both wiped the tears away. He stood back and looked at Peggy.

"I love her with all of my heart, you must believe me," he said quietly, Peggy nodded and smiled.

"Come on, we need to find the grimoire," she said, Abe looked bewildered.

"You mean, you are going to practice magic?" he asked, Peggy chuckled.

"Kind of, now lead me to the book," she said as she grabbed his hand.

That evening Molly and Peggy were busy in the kitchen, getting ready to dish up when the back door opened and Michael, followed by William walked through. Peggy blushed with embarrassment, she didn't know what to say. William walked to where she stood, "Could I speak to you outside?" He whispered into her ear. Peggy looked at Molly, who nodded, and then William grabbed her hand and led her out of the back door.

Peggy leaned up against the wall as William stood opposite her and took her hand in his.

"Peg, I am truly sorry for the awful way that I behaved in London, I havnee come here to make excuses, all I ask for is your forgiveness, please, please give me another chance to prove to you that I am not that guy, that I love you with everything that I have, and I never want to be away from you," he said in the most heartfelt way. Peggy threw her arms around his neck and kissed him passionately. When they eventually parted he looked at her lovingly.

"When this is all over, promise me something will ya?" he said, Peggy nodded.

"We can be married, be together forever," He added.

"Of course!" Peggy said, grabbed his hand and led him into the kitchen.

Once they had placed everything in the oven to warm Molly grabbed Peggy's hand. "Come with me, there is something that I want to show you," Molly said as she and Peggy walked into the hallway. Molly led Peggy towards Carrie's room and as they stood outside the door Peggy gasped, Molly gripped her hand tightly and opened the door, Molly stepped in, pulling Peggy behind her, Peggy gasped again and put her hand to her mouth.

In her absence Molly, Michael and Abe had turned Carrie's old room back into the dining room, just as it was before she became so ill that she couldn't climb the stairs. They had been in and laid the beautiful mahogany table, which had been stored in the large shed, and placed photos of Carrie everywhere. Molly waited in anticipation for Peggy's reaction, none of them sure if she would be able to cope with the change, whether she was ready for that part of her life to be removed, maybe it was too soon, Molly was thinking as she waited. Peggy said not a word, just slowly walking around the room, picking up the framed photos, looking at them and stroking Carrie's face on every single one, then she turned and looked at Molly as the tears once again rolled down her cheeks.

"It looks beautiful Molly, thank you," Peggy cried as she held her hand so tight.

"Are you sure, we were worried that it was maybe too soon," Molly said and smiled.

"No really, I love it!" Peggy said and smiled as Molly looked endearingly at the huge table, she smiled.

"The card games that we used to play there, we had such fun, she had a wicked sense of humour didn't she," Molly said as she looked at the empty chair on the end, Molly tapped Peggy's hand.

"Come now, or the dinner will spoil," Molly said as she pulled Peggy back towards the kitchen.

They had cooked roast beef which was one of Molly's specialities and the aroma that was wafting through the cottage was wonderful, they were all thinking to themselves as they walked through the hallway towards the dining room. They sat around eating delicious food, chatting about all manner of things, drinking wine, and laughing. It felt so good to laugh again, Peggy was quietly thinking to herself, when she felt a huge pang of guilt, they shouldn't be laughing, poor Carrie had just died and they were all sitting in the room in which she died, eating, drinking, and laughing, Peggy thought to herself until her eyes were drawn to the window, where, standing looking at them all was Carrie, who too was laughing at Abe's jokes, at Mollie's giggles, and at Michael's feeble attempt at humour. She nodded at Peggy and from that moment Peggy knew that everything was going to be all right!

CHAPTER 4

Peggy watched out of her bedroom window as the cars arrived to take them all to the coast, where the Elders would perform a ceremony in Carrie's honour. Peggy gulped as the van arrived carrying Carrie's coffin. She looked at her bed, the black two-piece laid out neatly. She wasn't sure if she would wear it. She wanted to wear something colourful, to celebrate Carrie's life, but the others felt that it should be a more traditional dress code. She sighed and began to get dressed in the laid-out outfit. She put on her black court shoes and looked in the mirror.

She despised wearing black and looking at her reflection, didn't change her mind. Carrie appeared behind her, she placed her hands upon Peggy's small shoulders and smiled.

"You look lovely my Peggy," she whispered. Peggy tapped her hand as the tears began to gather. "Look upon this day with happiness, rejoice in the knowledge that I have been reunited with Albert, Polly and Florence, and Peggy you know what to do when it is all over, don't you," Carrie said as her image faded, then there was a knock on the door.

"Peggy, are you ready?" Abe asked gently, she inhaled deeply.

"Yes, coming," she called out, taking one last look in the mirror, just in case Carrie reappeared, then walked to the door and opened it.

"You look very smart," Peggy said quietly as she took Abe's arm and walked with him towards the stairs.

Everyone was waiting in the lounge, Peggy looked for William as soon as she entered, he was standing with his parents, she gave him a small wave, and then was ushered out to the first car, which she was sharing with Abe, Molly, and Michael. The other people then piled into the other cars and Carrie's final journey had begun.

Before she knew it, the car stopped, making Peggy turn and look, she had spent the entire journey lost in her thoughts, thoughts of her time with Carrie, how lost she felt when she first arrived, how Carrie's silence forced her to grow strong and resilient, and the very day that she and Carrie had their first real conversation. She looked at Molly, who smiled a sad smile.

"We are here," she said quietly, Peggy looked out of the window, it was desolate. She turned her gaze back to Molly wearing an expression of confusion.

"There is nothing here, we are in the middle of nowhere," Peggy whispered. Molly nodded.

"You will understand why, very soon," she replied as they climbed out of the car.

They followed the guardians who were carrying the coffin and walked amongst sand dunes and down to the most beautiful, unexpected beach, with soft white sand. Peggy looked to the sky and was sure that she heard a hiss as the sun touched the sea on the horizon line. There was a huge fire lit on the sand and the Elders stood, solemn faced as the guardians approached carrying Carrie. They gently placed the coffin down, bowed and stood back as Henry began the ceremony, William broke with tradition, this was no traditional funeral, he thought to himself, so he walked to stand beside Peggy, as he did he grabbed her hand and held it tight.

Henry spoke about Carrie, how she had sacrificed so much for the cause, how her strength had inspired so many people that had met her or heard about her, and how much Abe, Peggy, Molly, Michael, and William would miss her. He spoke about how the Great Ones had greeted her with open arms and how her Legacy would continue throughout the ages.

When Henry had finally finished the ceremony, Peggy, Abe, and Molly were sobbing uncontrollably. The guardians then picked up the coffin and placed it onto the huge fire, Peggy crying out as it became engulfed in flames, and William trying his hardest to console her. Then she heard her words again *look upon this day with happiness…. Rejoice in the knowledge that I have been reunited….*

She wiped the tears away and then smiled as a group of musicians walked along the beach towards them. As they reached the fire, a piper played a haunting tune on the bagpipes, then the other musicians joined in to make it a merry jig, encouraging everyone present to dance and rejoice, which they all did.

They arrived back at the cottage in the wee small hours, and Peggy yawned as she walked into the cottage. Abe had gone in before and lit the fires which were most welcoming after the biting wind from the cold sea had blown all around them. Peggy sat on the sofa, William beside her when Abe passed them both a glass of brandy. "To our Carrie," he said, holding his brandy glass high in the air.

"To our Carrie," Peggy and William said in unison as Molly and Michael walked in with a tray laden with a steaming teapot, cups, saucers, and a large chocolate cake.

Peggy was cradling her brandy in her hands, thinking about the ceremony when Abe sat down beside her. "Drink it, it will warm your soul, that's what she always used to say," he said quietly as he gently nudged her away from her thoughts. She smiled, kissed his cheek, and then drank the brandy down in one gulp. "You can certainly tell that she was your grandmother!" Abe said and laughed as too did Peggy.

The following morning Peggy woke to the sound of driving rain hitting her bedroom window. She swung her legs off of the bed and pulled herself up. She put on her robe and slippers and walked down the stairs, she could hear voices coming from the kitchen. She looked at her wristwatch and jumped when she saw what time it was nine-thirty! She opened the kitchen door and smiled. Abe and William were sitting at the table in deep discussion, Molly walked through from the pantry, carrying food for the evening's dinner, and Michael was at the sink washing the dishes.

"Here she is!" Abe said happily as Peggy walked past the table to the teapot.

"Lazy bugger!" William said and laughed.

"I know, I couldn't believe it when I saw what time it was," she replied and laughed.

"We were discussing the wedding," Abe said and smiled.

"Oh, whose weddings that then?" Peggy asked and rubbed her still tired eyes, which were still so swollen from all of the tears that she had cried. William, Abe, Molly, and Michael all laughed.

"Ours you silly sod!" William said as he laughed.

"Oh," Peggy said and looked at them all.

"Well, we thought that we may as well start the planning now," William said and smiled.

"What's the great hurry?" Peggy asked, feeling slightly anxious that her future was being planned while she was in bed snoring!

"I have to leave in two weeks, I'm not sure when I will return," Abe said.

"I really would love to be there Peggy," He continued. She smiled and then looked at William.

"So when were you thinking?" She asked as she sipped her hot tea.

"Well, we have spoken to the registrar this morning and he can fit us in on Thursday," William said and smiled.

"But that's in two days!" Peggy shouted.

"Aye, and then Michael said that he will perform the handfasting ceremony on Friday, and we can have a party then, my Mum and Dad said that we could use one of the empty barns on the farm," William said excitedly.

"Handfasting?" Peggy asked and looked at Molly for guidance.

"It is the way in which people like us, promise ourselves to one another, Michael is a celebrant, so he can perform the ceremony," Molly said and smiled.

"Aye but that still only gives us three days to sort everything!" Peggy said anxiously.

"My mum and dad are happy to organise the party Peggy, all we have to do is choose what we are going to wear," William said as he pulled her onto his lap, she flushed with embarrassment as Abe and Molly roared with laughter.

"Say you will Lassie," William said and dropped his lip.

"Aye, go on then," she said as he kissed her, again she squirmed with embarrassment. Molly and Abe cheered loudly, and then each of them took turns in hugging one another, each of them with the exception of Michael, who was not one to embrace any form of human affection!

"Oh, how exciting Peggy, let's go to Edinburgh and choose our outfits," Molly squealed, Peggy smiled and nodded.

"Well, off you pop then, you can't go in your nightie," Molly said as she shooed Peggy towards the stairs.

"Yes I suppose that it's a trip to the tailors for us then," Abe said and smiled once Peggy had gone to get dressed.

"Aye, I wanted to speak to you both about that," William said as Abe raised his eyebrow in suspicion.

Peggy and Molly had been in and out of several boutiques and still, Peggy could only find an outfit for the registry office. She wanted something special for the handfasting but hadn't seen anything to which she fancied. "Let's go there and have some lunch, maybe once we have eaten, we might be easier pleased," Molly said as she pointed to a quaint café across the road. Peggy agreed and they both walked in, out of the rain. A kind-faced lady approached them and led them to a table, where they both took off their wet coats, hung them on the back of their chairs and sat down, studying the menu.

Once they had eaten their delicious lunch, Peggy looked down at her swollen tummy. "I don't think that I'll get anything to fit now!" she scorned, making Molly laugh. A young lady walked past the table, then turned back and looked at Peggy.

"I know you don't I?" She asked as she looked at Peggy, who frowned.

"Er, I er…" Peggy was lost for words, she couldn't recall ever meeting this young woman.

"Aye, you live just outside Melrose, I remember you from the dance, you certainly put that cow Jean in her place!" She said. Peggy studied her face for a moment, then recognised her.

"Oh aye, I remember seeing you there now," Peggy said and smiled, she seemed a friendly girl.

"What are you doing here in the city?" She asked as she pulled a chair up and joined them, making Molly frown, she was one for good manners, and in Molly's opinion, it was rude not to ask!

"We are shopping for my wedding outfit," Peggy said, "Sorry what did you say your name was?" she continued.

"Oh, I didnee, it's Shona," she said and held her hand out for Peggy to shake, which she did.

"I'm Peggy," she said and smiled.

"It's good to meet ya, Peggy, what's your Mum called?" She asked, making Peggy fight the laughter back when she saw the look on Molly's face.

"I am not her Mum, my name is Molly!" Molly said agitatedly as she shook her head.

"Oh, sorry," she said and tittered.

"Molly is a good friend of the family, she is going to be my matron of honour," Peggy said trying to lighten the mood.

"Nice, when's the big day then?" Shona asked as the kind-faced lady approached the table. She looked sternly in Shona's direction.

"Are you actually going to do some work today Shona?" She asked.

"Aye in a wee minute Mum," she replied and chuckled. "Wow, you havnee given yourself much time, most wedding dresses take six months to make," she continued.

"I know, but this is not a traditional wedding, it's a handfasting," Peggy replied as Molly looked at her disapprovingly.

"Oh I see, so you are a pagan," Shona replied.

"Something like that," Peggy replied as Molly shook her head.

"Well, in that case, I might be able to help you out," Shona said as her eyes glistened, Peggy frowned.

"Really?" she replied.

"Aye, one day I am going to be a famous fashion designer, not one of those fancy pants Parisian ones, one who designs cool clothes for folks like us," She said as she wore a beaming smile.

"Folks like us?"

"Aye, you know different, from the others, spiritual folk," Shona replied. Peggy smiled and nodded, Molly however still remained unimpressed.

"Look, wait there a sec, ok," she said as she left the table and walked out to the kitchen.

"I'm not sure that I like her Peggy," Molly leaned across the table and whispered. Peggy chuckled.

"I think that she's nice, full of fun!" Peggy whispered back as Shona reappeared.

"My dad owns the haberdashery up in the old arcade, he has some beautiful fabrics. If you come up there with me now and choose one, I will make your wedding outfit for you," she said and smiled.

"Peggy, I am going to pay the bill," Molly said as she stood up and walked to the counter.

"What's wrong with her, she seems a wee bit edgy?" Shona whispered.

"She has an issue with trust, especially strangers," Peggy whispered, hoping that Molly couldn't hear them.

Meanwhile, Molly was waiting at the counter when the kind-faced woman reappeared. "How much do we owe you?" Molly asked and looked at the two girls huddled together laughing and joking, it was the first time since Jo had died that Molly had seen Peggy look so comfortable around someone, she was thinking to herself.

The lady waved her hand at Molly "No need, a friend of Shona's is a friend of mine, she tells me that you are having a handfasting ceremony," the lady said and smiled, and although Molly felt awkward, she couldn't help but get a warm feeling from these kind people.

"Yes that's right, young Peggy over there," Molly said. "Are you sure about the bill, really I insist," Molly continued.

"No, no need, maybe an invite to the big day? I'm Brigit," she said and held her hand out to Molly, who shook it and smiled, she felt good energy radiating through her.

"I'm Molly and yes, of course, I will give Shona the details," Molly said.

"That's great, well, I will see you soon Molly," Brigit said and walked over to a new table of customers.

"Thank you," Molly called out to her as she walked back to the table. "Are you ready girls?" she asked and smiled. Peggy smiled, she just knew that Molly would warm to Shona, she was thinking to herself as the three of them left the café in search of the haberdashery.

Later that evening over dinner, Molly and Peggy were telling Abe and Michael about Shona and Brigit, Michael frowned and looked at Peggy.

"So, let me get this right, you are going to allow a perfect stranger to design and make your wedding outfit," he asked snootily, Peggy looked at Abe, then Michael.

"Yes Michael, yes I am," Peggy said as she scowled.

"But you have no idea who she is or what she represents," he replied and looked at Abe for backup, Abe just shook his head, he knew that Michael was skating on thin ice.

"What I do know is, Shona is a kind person as too is Brigit her Mum, and yes I trust her, and yes she is making my outfit," Peggy huffed. Michael shook his head in disbelief and looked at Abe.

"Well, aren't you going to say anything, she is your granddaughter after all!" Michael said angrily.

"No Michael I'm not, and do you know why? Because it is none of my business who makes Peggy's wedding outfit, so long as she does a good job, that is all that matters," Abe replied angrily.

"But she could compromise the guardianship, her family could be one of many, who class themselves as enemies of the guardianship!" Michael replied. Abe shook his head, and so too did Molly, who after hearing enough slammed her clenched fist down onto the table.

"I have had enough of this! So many years of listening to you bleat on about the fucking guardianship. How many sacrifices need to be made Michael, how many hearts are left to be broken, how many more? TELL ME THAT!" Molly screamed in his face as she then broke down in tears. Peggy jumped up off her chair and ran to Molly to console her. She was Carrie's oldest and best friend, and since the day that Carrie had died, Molly had been the rock that everyone leaned on, not one of them stopped to think about what she must be going through, how she must be feeling, because they were all wrapped up in their own feelings! Peggy was thinking to herself as she held Molly, stroking her hair. Michael now red with either embarrassment or anger left the room, Abe walked to the sideboard and poured them all a brandy, he handed Molly a hanky, then her glass, she looked up and smiled.

"I'm sorry," she sniffed as she dried her tears and blew her nose.

"Do not ever apologise for speaking your mind!" Abe said as he held her hand.

"I trust both of you, I trust your judgement and intuition, and if they turn out to disappoint, so what, you live and learn," Abe said as he swilled the brandy around the glass and took a long sip, Peggy began to applaud.

"Well bloody said granddad!" she said and laughed, making Molly laugh, all the while Abe scowled then he laughed too.

Michael then re-entered the room and leaned down where Molly was sitting. "Could I please speak to you in private?" He whispered in her ear. Molly sat motionless for a moment, then reluctantly nodded, she knew deep down in her heart, that he would only have to utter a few words of apology and she would forgive him, and everything would return to as it should, yet somehow, this time she yearned to stay angry with him, if not for her, then for Carrie. She stood up and followed him out of the room.

CHAPTER 5

The following morning, Peggy forced herself to get up extra early before any of the others. She crept down the stairs, walked into the kitchen, put the kettle on to boil and opened the back door. She stood breathing in the fresh, damp, morning air, when her small friend the robin appeared on the wall in front of her, digging the grubs from the broken mortar between the bricks. She looked at the sky, which seemed unusually cheerful, the clouds were white and puffy, drifting slowly in the gentle breeze, and the sun shining gently made the blue of the sky seem almost indigo, Peggy was thinking as her attention was then drawn back to the cheeky robin, who must have run out of grubs, and looked at Peggy in anticipation of her generously sharing some crumbs from the breadbin with him. She smiled. "Aye, go on then," she said as she walked into the pantry and emptied the crumbs from the enamel-coated breadbin into her hand.

The robin, happy with his feast, pecked away at the crumbs, so Peggy walked into the kitchen to pour the now boiling water into the teapot. The wind had strengthened, she noticed the branches of the trees blowing to and fro, and then the back door flew open, making Peggy jump. She walked over quickly to close it, the curtains were blowing up to the ceiling, and she jumped when she noticed a brown paper wrapped package on the doorstep. She bent down and picked it up, studying it as she did. *Peggy* was all that was written on it. She placed it on the table and looked at the loudly ticking kitchen clock, it was only six thirty, who would be around at this time, she thought to herself as she poured the tea into the cup. She blew fervently on the steaming cup, desperate to take a sip, and then began to open the package. She looked at the contents, studying them, she opened the box and slowly took them out, placing them carefully on the table, who would have given her these, who would have known that she has a secret yearning, she was thinking to herself as Molly walked into the kitchen and picked them up.

"What a beautiful set, where did you get them, Peggy? They are very unusual," Molly said as she put them back down in front of Peggy, she looked at Molly in bewilderment and shook her head.

"They were on the doorstep, the package had my name written on it," Peggy said. Molly frowned and looked at the tarot deck once more.

"How peculiar," she said and poured herself a cup from the teapot. "They are rather extraordinary," she added and smiled. Peggy picked the cards up and held them close to her body, she could feel good energy running through them, so she began to look at them one, by one. She heard footsteps coming down the stairs, so she quickly gathered the cards and put them in the pocket of her dressing gown, she really didn't feel like another lecture from Michael the righteous, she thought and chuckled. As it happens, it was

Abe, who yawned, kissed Peggy on the head and smiled at Molly as she poured him a cup of tea.

"What are your plans for today?" Abe asked Peggy as he sat opposite her at the table.

"I have to go to Shona's this afternoon for a fitting," she replied and smiled.

"Does she live nearby?" Abe asked, Peggy, nodded.

"You know that big fancy white house, just before the butchers, she lives there," Peggy said.

"Oh yes, I know the one, didn't that used to be a rectory?" Abe asked Molly, who nodded.

"Yes I believe so, Michael was friends with the reverend, Green I think his name was," Molly said as she thought, then Michael walked through the back door.

"Michael, what was the name of your friend, you know the vicar chap?" Molly asked as she smiled a small smile at him, she was still harbouring anger.

"Oh, John Green," Michael said as he filled the kettle with water.

"Yes that's it, what happened to him, you saw him not long ago didn't you," Molly asked, Michael, nodded as sadness crept across his face.

"Yes, when Carrie had that trouble with the locals, sad story," Michael sighed.

"So where is he and why isn't the rectory, the rectory anymore?" Molly asked impatiently, Peggy giggled and looked at Abe, who was hiding his smile behind yesterday's newspaper.

"Well, the very next day after my visit, the poor fellow was struck by lightning, killed him!" Michael said, wearing an almost shocked expression.

"Oh, how awful," Molly said sadly. "Did he have a family?" She added, Michael nodded.

"Yes he has a son, who is at college, training to be a vicar, I believe," Michael said as he thought.

"What happened to his wife?" Molly asked, and at this point, Abe began to tut.

"Molly, what is this? The Spanish inquisition?" Abe said and shook his head, making Peggy laugh.

"I was just curious, that's all Abe," Molly scowled, Michael chuckled.

"She died during childbirth, many years ago," Michael replied.

"Oh, I am sorry," Molly said, then got up and walked to the boiling kettle.

"Oh Peggy, if you are going into Melrose, would you be a dear and collect the order from the butchers?" Molly asked.

"Aye of course I will," Peggy smiled.

"I'll drive you into Melrose, there is someone there that I need to speak to," Abe said as he looked over the top of the newspaper.

"Oh the intrigue, is it top secret business?" Peggy asked with just a hint of sarcasm in her voice, Abe laughed and shook his head.

"Hmm, something like that," he replied.

That afternoon, Abe was waiting patiently for Peggy, who was still faffing with her hair. He had paced around the kitchen for long enough, he thought to himself as he walked to the bottom of the stairs. "Come on Peggy, I have an appointment at two," he shouted and looked at his watch, it was one forty-five! He shook his head as Peggy ran down the stairs.

"Sorry, my hair just would not play the game," she sighed.

"You are only going for a dress fitting, not strutting the catwalk!" Abe said as he hurried her through the hallway.

"Oh Peggy, don't forget to check the list off if it's young Reg, he always forgets to put something in," Molly said as she handed Peggy the list. Peggy took the list and smiled as she rushed out of the back door, for fear of Abe leaving her behind.

"I'll meet you at the clock tower at four sharp, don't be late!" Abe said as Peggy climbed out of the car.

"I won't, thanks for the lift," she said and blew him a kiss. It was the first time that she had thought of him as her grandfather, before, she always saw him as the man that broke Carrie's heart and for that, she despised him, even though Carrie didn't, she still loved him, right to the very end, and now Peggy had found a lost affection for him, except for William, and Robert, he was the only family that she had, she was thinking as she rang the doorbell to Shona's large house. She heard footsteps running down the stairs, and then the door opened. Shona smiled and invited Peggy in.

The house was beautiful, unusual but beautiful, there were intricately embroidered hangings on the walls and the plants! Peggy had never seen so many in one house, Shona led her into the lounge, where the sofas were covered with wonderful throws, and big thick heavy curtains hugged the windows.

"Would you like tea, coffee or lemonade?" Shona asked and smiled.

"Oh, I'd love a coffee," Peggy replied. Shona left the room and returned a few minutes later with a tray and two unusual cups, with no saucers. She passed a coffee-filled one to Peggy, who smiled and inspected it, making Shona laugh.

"These are unusual," Peggy said as she tasted the coffee.

"Aye, my dad travels a lot, you know to source his fabrics, he got them from Morocco," Shona said.

"I have never heard of it, is it in Scotland?" Peggy asked, making Shona roar with laughter.

"No, it's in Africa Peggy, I take it that Geography was not a strong subject for you," Shona said through laughter. Sadness crept across Peggy's face along with embarrassment as she looked down at the rugs that covered the floor.

"I didnee go to school, I had to take care of my mother, she was sick," Peggy said quietly. Shona put her hand over her mouth.

"I am so sorry Peggy, I had no idea, me and my big mouth," Shona said as she blushed, Peggy smiled.

"It doesnee matter," Peggy said and chuckled.

"But you can read," Shona said as she remembered back to Peggy adoring the fabrics in the shop, reading out the descriptions.

"Aye, we lived on an estate, and if I groomed the horses they would let me have an hour with the governess, who taught me to read and write," Peggy replied as she thought back to the stern, almost dead-faced governess, who would rap her knuckles if she dared to get a word wrong!

So after the fitting, Peggy was amazed at the ideas that Shona was suggesting, she was in awe of her talent. "How are you getting home?" Shona asked as they walked to the front door.

"Abe is meeting me at the clock tower," Peggy said as she put her head scarf on.

"Ok, well, I will bring the dress to your house tomorrow," Shona said.

"Oh, it'll have to be after twelve, we are getting married at eleven," Peggy said.

"Oh, ok, I'll see you around two then," Shona said as Peggy trotted down the steps and onto the pavement. The weather had definitely taken a turn for the worse, the wind was howling, and the clouds were now filled with rain and ready to empty over anything that was beneath them. Peggy hurried along the street until she came to the butchers. She ran inside to get out of the wind. Young Reg laughed and pointed to her scarf, which had twisted and was almost back to front.

"Windy out there is it?" He asked as he laughed.

"No, I have no idea what you are talking about," Peggy scowled and then laughed as she handed Reg the list. He took it and walked through the back, returning with a box filled with meat.

"Molly says that I'm to check it because you always forget something," Peggy said and laughed.

"Did she now!" Reg said and growled. Peggy looked at him, he was such a kind soul, with a kind face.

"I could have dropped this off tomorrow morning Peggy," Reg said as he methodically checked the contents of the box.

"We won't be there," Peggy replied as she looked out of the shop window at the pouring rain that was soaking any poor soul that was walking outside.

"Really? Are you going on your holidays?" Reg asked.

"No you daft bugger, I'm getting wed tomorrow, I thought that everybody around here knew," Peggy said and laughed. "Did William send you all an invitation?" She asked.

"No, but why would he, he knows that I am madly in love with you, and he's afraid that I will steal you away," Reg said and winked.

"I have never heard of anything so daft, well you and your folks are welcome to come, it's in the second barn on William's parent's farm, Friday at six pm," Peggy said as Reg handed her the checked box.

"Ok beautiful, I'll see you then," Reg said and laughed as Peggy left the shop.

She could see Abe's car waiting and she ran, trying not to drop the heavy box. He looked through his rear-view mirror and jumped out of the car, he ran to her and relieved her of the heavy, wet box as they walked back to the car. Once settled inside the warm car, Abe started the engine, and they began the drive home.

"You were in the butchers a while, I watched you go in," Abe said.

" I made Reg check it all, just as Molly asked me to," Peggy said as she watched the raindrops run down the window.

There was a tap on the door, Peggy opened it her hands trembling. "Are you all right?" Molly asked as she took

Peggy's hands in hers. Peggy nodded as her eyes filled with tears.

"Peggy, what's wrong?" Molly asked her voice full of concern.

"I'm not sure that I can do it, Molly," Peggy cried. Molly chuckled as she folded her arms around Peggy's small frame.

"Oh my sweet child, everyone gets the jitters, it's perfectly normal, when you see William, standing outside the registry office, your nerves will dissolve and all that you will think about, is how much you love him," Molly said as she sat Peggy on the bed, sitting down beside her. Molly passed Peggy a hanky.

"Now, wash your face and make yourself beautiful, the car will be here in half an hour," Molly said as she took Peggy's hands and pulled her to her feet. Peggy smiled and nodded, she inhaled deeply then walked over to the sink and splashed her face with cold water.

She sat in front of the mirror and looked at the sad, lonely girl gazing back. She began to apply her make up and as she did she thought about William. How from the moment she laid eyes upon him she knew that she would marry him, how he would whistle so that she always knew he was there, how kind, and thoughtful he was to Carrie when she lived out her final days, how he made her laugh. She smiled, and the sad lonely girl was no longer, she was a happy, nearly married woman, who had the rest of her life in front of her and a wonderful husband to share it with, she thought to herself.

She put on the cream two-piece and stood in front of the mirror. She smiled.

"That'll do," she sighed.

"You look beautiful," she heard, she knew that it was Carrie, and then the door knocked.

"Peggy, the car is here," Abe said. She walked to the door and opened it, Abe stood back and gasped.

"Oh my, you look incredibly beautiful!" He said and smiled.

"Why thank you, you don't look half bad yourself!" Peggy said and laughed as she took his arm.

William was waiting outside the registry office with his mum and dad, Peggy laughed as she watched him pace up and down the pavement. The car stopped and William's dad opened the door for Peggy, smiling from ear to ear as he did.

A little after half an hour they all stepped out of the registry office and as they adorned the pavement they were instantly covered in confetti, which made them both howl with laughter. They all went back to the cottage. Molly had laid out a buffet and decorated the entire cottage with flowers and ribbons, it looked gorgeous, Peggy thought to herself as William carried her over the threshold.

A little later Peggy's attention was drawn to the corner of the room, where Abe was watching her, she smiled, and he beckoned to her. She kissed William and walked to Abe.

"Follow me," he said and winked, so she did. He walked up the stairs and opened Peggy's bedroom door. She looked at him in complete shock. Her tiny single bed had gone and was now replaced with a lovely double bed, the furniture was all new. She looked at Abe.

"Did you do this?" she asked.

"That's what I was doing in Melrose yesterday," he said and smiled, Peggy held her hand over her mouth.

"Oh, I don't know what to say, thank you," she said as she hugged him.

"My pleasure," he replied and smiled. "Oh one more thing," he said, disappeared along the hallway then returned carrying Carrie's ashes in an urn. He passed it to Peggy.

"You made her happy, you will know the right place," he said and winked.

"Aye, I know exactly where to take her," Peggy said and kissed him on the cheek.

"Molly, Michael and myself have booked into the hotel in Melrose for a couple of nights, and after that, we all must return to Salisbury," Abe said. Sadness then swept over her like a tidal wave, engulfing her. These were the people that she loved that she trusted and very soon, it would be just her and William, nobody else.

"As soon as you find Robert you must promise to send word to me," Abe said as he held Peggy's small hands in his. Peggy nodded and wiped the tear that ran down her cheek away. "Hey, there is no need to cry, this should be the happiest day of your life my Peggy," Abe said as he pulled her close and hugged her tightly.

"I want to scatter her ashes in Boscastle," Peggy said when Abe finally let her go. He smiled and nodded.

"Perfect!" he said and smiled.

CHAPTER 6

When Peggy returned to the busy living room she smiled when she saw Shona chatting with William and his younger brother Wilf. She hurried over to the three of them and looked at Shona expectedly.

"Well, where is it?" Peggy asked impatiently, Shona smiled,

"I left it in the car, I wasnee sure that you would be back," Shona replied, William, frowned, not having the slightest inkling of what they were talking about.

"The dress for tomorrow," Peggy said and shook her head as she beckoned Shona out of the room, leaving William to his conversation with Wilf. They both ran out to the car, the rain had begun to fall, the drops were heavy and full, and Peggy really did not want to have to tame her untameable hair yet again! Shona opened the back door and pulled out the linen-covered dress.

"Come on, I'll just make sure that it is all good, then I'll be on my way," Shona said as she hurried back to the cottage.

Shona looked at Peggy and gasped. "Oh my goodness, Peggy you look absolutely beautiful!" She said and smiled.

"Go on take a wee look," She added and gestured to the mirror, Peggy walked over and looked.

"Oh Shona, it's perfect, such beautiful autumn colours," Peggy said as she did a twirl.

"Aye you definitely made the right choice with the Moroccan silk," Shona said and smiled, then there was a knock on the door.

"Are you decent? What are you doing in there?" William asked abruptly.

"Don't come in!" Peggy shouted as Shona quickly began to unbutton the back of Peggy's dress.

"Peggy, for crying out loud, it's our wedding day and you are choosing to spend the time with your new friend!" William said angrily. Peggy quickly slipped back into her two-piece and opened the door while Shona wrapped the dress in the linen and put it inside Peggy's wardrobe.

"I was trying on the dress," Peggy scowled as she barged past William, with Shona quickly following her. Peggy walked Shona to the door. "Are you sure that you won't stay for tea?" Peggy asked, Shona shook her head.

"No, thanks for the offer, I don't want to tread on his lordship's toes any more than I already have now, do I?" Shona said as she ran to the car. "I'll see you tomorrow Peggy," she said and waved as she jumped into her car and drove away. Peggy was now furious, how dare he! She was thinking to herself as she slowly walked up the path, she no longer cared that the falling rain would ruin her hairstyle, she wanted to delay having to be face to face with him and pretend that she was the happiest woman alive when that could not be further from the truth at that moment in time, she feared that she had just made a huge mistake! She opened the door and jumped back as William's parents and Wilf met her.

"We'll be seeing you tomorrow then Peggy love," William's mum said as she kissed her on the cheek.

"You're not going, are you? " Peggy asked anxiously.

"Aye love, but we'll see you at the barn tomorrow," she replied and walked towards the car. Peggy slammed the door closed and walked into the lounge, and into somewhat of an atmosphere. Abe was red-faced, which usually meant that he was angry, William just stared out of the window, Abe smiled at Peggy and stood.

"We are going now Peggy," he said as he kissed her on the cheek. This was becoming too much of a habit too quickly, Peggy was thinking as she frowned.

"Why, why are you going so soon?" She asked sadly. Abe scowled at William, then turned to Peggy, touching her face.

"Molly has cleared everything away, and I will be back first thing in the morning, if in the meantime you need me, here is the address and telephone number of the hotel," Abe said as he passed Peggy a piece of paper. Molly poked her head around the door.

"Are you ready Abe?" she asked quietly, Abe nodded and walked out. Once she heard the door close and watched

Molly, Abe, and Michael get into the car she turned and looked at William.

"WELL?" she roared angrily. He walked over to her, away from the window and grabbed her face in his hands tightly, squeezing her cheeks into her teeth.

"Do not EVER SPEAK TO ME LIKE THAT AGAIN, YOU ARE MY WIFE AND YOU WILL RESPECT ME!" He roared as he released his grip from Peggy's face, she tasted blood as he did and wiped her mouth on the back of her hand, she was bleeding.

"Who the hell are you?" She cried as she ran out of the room, up the stairs, and into her bedroom, locking the door behind her as she did. She threw herself onto the bed and sobbed, she couldn't quite believe that this was happening, how did she not see it, how did she not read the warning signs, when they were in London, she should have finished it there and then, she thought to herself as she wept.

"Not so sweet after all," she heard and instantly recognised Carrie's voice. Peggy looked up with her swollen eyes to see Carrie standing looking out of the window.

"I have been in that room with him and hard as I tried to get through, he would not hear me, Peggy, if I were still alive, that man would not be walking now, you must tell Abe," Carrie said angrily, Peggy wiped her tears away and shook her head.

"It's my mess, I will sort it," Peggy said and sniffed, Carrie sat beside her on the bed and sighed.

"You are maybe a little too much like me, did my story not teach you anything?" Carrie said and chuckled,

"Something was telling me from deep inside, not to do it, but I thought that I was maybe overreacting," Peggy said sorrowfully, Carrie touched her face.

"Tell Abe Peggy, tell him," she said as her silhouette faded away, leaving Peggy alone with him once more. She lay on the bed and drifted off to sleep.

She awoke to the sound of tapping. "Peggy, Peggy, please, I'm sorry, I don't know what got into me, please open the door and let me explain," he pleaded. Peggy rubbed her eyes, and looked at the clock, it was nine-thirty, she had been asleep for hours, and she then sat herself up. "Peggy love please, I need to explain," he pleaded again, Peggy shook her head.

"Why, so that you can grab hold of me again, or even better you can give me a good smack, no William, I want you to leave this cottage and I never want to see you again do you hear me!" She shouted.

"I'm sorry, I never meant to hurt you, please Peggy I promise that I will never lay a hand on you ever again!" He said as he began to sob. She felt no sympathy for him, she shook her head, she was still so angry, and she still didn't know the reason why all the guests had left so abruptly, but she needed to find out and not from him!

"Go away!" she shouted.

"Fine! I will sit out here all night if I have to!" he said and then Peggy heard him slump to the floor, she shrugged her shoulders and walked to the mirror, she looked a mess, she thought to herself as she ran her hairbrush through her now matted hair. Who would she speak to? She asked herself, Molly wouldn't say, she knew that, and she didn't want to involve Abe, which only left Michael, and for once Peggy believed that he would tell her the truth. She climbed back into bed and soon she drifted off to sleep.

The following morning, Peggy woke before the birds began their usual dawn chorus, she opened the curtain and looked out of the window, not quite sure what she was looking for. Everything was still and silent. She put on her dressing gown and walked to the door, slowly and quietly sliding the bolt across. She turned the handle and gently pulled the door towards her, she was relieved to see that William was not there. She tiptoed down the stairs and into the kitchen, where she filled the kettle and opened the back door. She crept through the hallway and peeked through the crack in the half-open door, he was asleep on the sofa. She crept back to the kitchen and poured the boiling water into the teapot, then she heard a car engine stop. She walked down the side of the cottage and smiled when she saw Abe, Molly and Michael get out of the car. She quickly ran back inside so as not to arouse suspicion. The door opened and Peggy looked up from her cup of tea and smiled.

"Were there bed bugs?" Peggy quietly asked and chuckled, Abe, sighed.

"No, we were all so very concerned about this wonderful young lady," he replied and smiled, then kissed her on the cheek. Then the door opened, and William walked out, Peggy gulped, she had no idea how he was going to react. He looked at them all and said nothing, he walked to the cupboard, took out a cup, poured himself some tea and walked towards the door.

"Abe, could I have a word?" he said as he walked through the hallway back into the lounge. Abe looked at Molly and then Michael, shook his head, stood up and followed William, Peggy looked at the remaining two.

"Well, are either of you going to tell me what happened yesterday?" she asked. Molly shook her head and walked to the sink, Michael cleared his throat.

"He told us all to leave, his parents included, and if I am to be completely honest Peggy, he spoke to his mother in a manner that I found most disrespectful," Michael said sadly, Molly nodded in agreement.

"Why, why did he want you to go?" Peggy asked, Michael, sighed as Molly looked at him and shook her head.

"He said.."

"Michael, don't," Molly shouted, Peggy looked at Molly in complete astonishment.

"No, Michael, do," Peggy said angrily.

"He said that you had angered him, by keeping things from him and that he needed to speak to you alone, when Abe refused to leave it all became quite heated, with Abe threatening him at one point, just before you returned," Michael continued, Peggy shook her head.

"Thank you for your honesty Michael, at least one of you had the decency to tell me," Peggy said as she looked at Molly disappointedly.

"Peggy, I just thought that maybe the both of you had been able to sort things out, that's all," Molly said and smiled, Peggy scowled.

"Well, for your information Molly, we haven't," Peggy said and walked outside to catch a breath of fresh air, the atmosphere in the cottage was stifling her. Within a few moments, Abe stepped out and exhaled as he did. Peggy looked at him and raised her eyebrow.

"Well?" she asked, Abe, shook his head.

"He apologised, said that he was overcome with emotion and didn't know how to process it, he said that Carrie's death had, had quite an impact on him," Abe replied.

"And do you believe him, do you think that his apology was genuine?" Peggy asked, Abe scratched his chin and looked at Peggy.

"Maybe," he replied.

"So what do I do now?" Peggy asked, she needed some guidance.

"Come away with me, join the guardianship, I will take care of you," Abe said. Peggy exhaled deeply, she didn't know what to do, part of her wanted to run, as far away as she could, but thinking about how Carrie's life had panned out when she became involved with Abe and the guardianship, she knew that it would be a bad move. She looked at Abe and smiled.

"No, I have to finish what I started," she said as the tears began to well in her eyes.

"No Peggy, no you do not! You cannot live your life with someone who dictates to you, you are worth far more than that," Abe said, tears now forming in his eyes.

"Yesterday, I made a commitment to William, and I have to see it through," she said quietly. Abe shook his head and held Peggy's face in his hands, forcing her to yelp from the wounds that were made the day before, Abe stood back.

"Peggy, I hardly touched you," he said and stared at her intently. "Open your mouth," he said, she shook her head. "Peggy open your mouth, or I will go inside and force him to tell me what is wrong with your mouth," Abe shouted angrily. Reluctantly she opened her mouth and Abe winced when he looked inside.

"How?" he asked, Peggy shook her head, "Ok, I'll ask him," he said as he began to walk to the door.

"He grabbed my face," Peggy said as the tears ran down her cheeks. Abe looked as though he were about to explode. He marched back into the cottage, where William was now sitting at the kitchen table, Abe pulled his arm back and punched William square on the jaw, knocking him off of the chair, landing at Molly's feet.

"ABE!" Molly shouted as she looked at him in horror.

"Just remember this, I have tried to stop her from going through with this, but she seems to have a misguided sense of duty towards you, if you ever so much as hurt a single hair on her tiny frame, you will get far worse than that, remember, I am no ordinary man, and wherever I am, I WILL know if you hurt her. DO I MAKE MYSELF CLEAR!" Abe bellowed into William's face as he sat on the kitchen floor, he was frantically nodding as he held his jaw, in fear that it might drop to the floor if he didn't. Peggy then walked into the kitchen after she heard the raised voices. She saw William and his swollen face and looked at Abe. He shook his head, rubbed his chin, and looked at Peggy.

"I am so sorry, my sweet, beautiful Peggy, but I cannot come and watch you make a binding with him, I respect your decision to continue, but I just cannot bear witness to that, knowing what he is capable of," Abe said and walked to Peggy, he gently lifted her chin as the tears silently fell. "If ever you need me Peggy, just think of me and call out, I will hear you," he said then bent down to William. "You do not deserve her," he growled as he then walked out of the back door, Peggy at that point not knowing that it would be the last time that she ever saw him. She went to run after him, Molly grabbed her arm and shook her head, then grabbed William by the arm and helped him to stand.

"Right young man let's get you healed," Molly said and led him into the lounge. Michael was standing with his back to the sink, the entire time, not saying a word, Peggy put her face in her hands and began to sob uncontrollably. Michael

78

walked over to where she was standing, wrapped his arms around her tightly, allowing her to release her devastation.

Molly returned and moved Michael, so that she was standing in front of Peggy.

"Now my dear, you have a decision to make, and before you do I suggest that you go in there and hear him out, then take yourself off for a while and think deeply and thoroughly," Molly said gently. Peggy nodded, slowly and reluctantly she walked to the lounge, she inhaled deeply and opened the door. William was sitting with his head down on the sofa, he looked up and smiled, then stood.

"Please sit down, so that I can explain," he said gently, she did as he asked.

"I was so overwhelmed with emotion Peg, I just didn't know how to process it, when you disappeared with Shona, I felt a little offended that you would choose to entertain your new friend rather than stand beside your husband ," he said, Peggy looked into his eyes and scowled.

"I understand that you were rude to your mum, have you apologised to her?" she asked, William shook his head.

"Well, don't you think that you should?" Peggy asked sternly.

"Aye I will, but I need to know that you forgive me Peg?" William asked.

"If you ever hurt me again, I will leave you, I made a commitment to you yesterday and I will stand by that but if you touch me again so help me, it will be the end of us, do you hear me," she said quietly, knowing that Molly and Michael were at the door listening. William frantically nodded his head. "Well, away you go then, and apologise to your Mum," she said.

"Can I at least have a wee kiss?" he asked and leaned in, Peggy turned her head so that his lips met her cheek. He pulled back and looked at her.

"You can count yourself lucky that you got that!" she said, stood up and left the room, slowly walking up the stairs and into her room, she needed some time away from others, time to think. She quickly dressed, ran down the stairs, put her headscarf on and left the cottage. She walked through the fields, the corn and wheat had been cut and all that remained were the stalks, the sad, lonely looking stalks, that was how she was feeling, cut away, then left, sad and lonely. She perched herself on the boundary wall and looked to the field beyond, she smiled at the wildflowers that were in their final bloom, it made her realise, that despite every set back, you must look forward, for what is sad and lonely now, will stand tall and proud once again. She jumped off of the wall into the field and picked a flower, placing it into her hair, this would be her reminder that there is always something beautiful that follows sadness.

CHAPTER 7

She sighed and then made her way back to the cottage. She opened the back door and walked into an empty kitchen, she looked into the lounge, then the dining room, but the house was deserted. She walked up the stairs and began to run hot water into the bath. Whilst waiting for it to run, she went into the bedroom, made the bed, and took out the dress that Shona had made for her. She hung it on the wardrobe door, stood back to look at it and smiled.

She had a lovely soak in the warm soapy water, washed her hair and then thought that she had better get a move on. She climbed out, wrapped herself in a towel and walked back to the bedroom, and as she did she very nearly jumped out of her skin when she was met with William sitting on the bed.

"I didnee hear you come back," she said as she sat at the dressing table.

"Aye, I've been back a while," he said as he polished his shoes.

"I wish that you wouldn't do that up here, it makes the room smell awful!" Peggy said and scowled. He turned to look at her and smiled, he stood and walked to where she was sitting and handed her an envelope. She took it and looked concerned, having no idea whatsoever what was inside. She took out two train tickets, and as she studied them she looked up at William and frowned.

"Where is Delabole?" She asked,

"It's the closest station to Boscastle, I have booked us a hotel nearby, you know for our honeymoon, I know that you want to take Carrie's ashes there," he replied and smiled. She smiled, then stood and gently kissed him.

"Thank you, that's very thoughtful," she said as she sat down and began to brush her hair.

"You might want to pack before the ceremony, the train leaves early tomorrow morning," he said as he took his outfit from the wardrobe and laid it on the bed.

"How long are we going for?" Peggy asked as she began to apply her make-up.

"A week, that's as much time as I could get off, you know what with the second cut of the season," he replied as he buttoned his shirt. Peggy nodded, then continued to beautify herself. After a while, she turned and looked,

"Well that's me done, how do I look?" William asked. Peggy let out a small chuckle when she looked at his pale, skinny legs that were dangling from the kilt and sporran that he was wearing.

"You look dashing!" she said and smiled. "Now hurry along, I need to get dressed!" she said as she stood.

"Peg, in case you hadn't noticed, we are married, I am allowed to see you without your clothes now," he said as he laughed.

"I know that! I just want you to see me when I am completely ready," she said as she shooed him towards the door.

"Ok, I'm going, will you be long?" He asked and dropped his bottom lip, forcing her to laugh.

"No! Oh, have you packed your things for tomorrow?" She asked as he was just about to leave the room, he looked at the case that was sitting on the floor beside the door, shook his head and walked down the stairs.

She packed her case and then finished getting ready, there was a tap on the door.

"Who is it?" She called out.

"It's me, Molly, can I come in?" she asked.

"Aye of course," Peggy called out, Molly opened the door and stood back when she saw Peggy.

"Oh, sweetheart, you look so beautiful, Carrie would be so proud," Molly said as she kissed Peggy on the cheek.

"Thank you, Molly, you also look beautiful," Peggy smiled. Molly turned a twirl and laughed.

"I cannot wait until you go down the stairs and see Michael!" Molly said and laughed, Peggy frowned.

"Why?" She asked curiously.

"You'll see!" Molly said as she took Peggy's arm, and they walked down the stairs to join the others.

Peggy chuckled when she walked into the lounge and saw Michael, he was also wearing a kilt, Peggy looked at Molly who was laughing and shaking her head, Peggy walked to Michael and smiled.

"Oh Peggy, what a picture!" he said and smiled.

"I must say, Michael, the kilt really does suit you," Peggy said and winked, Michael frowned.

"Now I think that we both know that is an absolute lie! I look ridiculous!" he said and laughed.

After the beautiful handfasting ceremony, Peggy looked around and sighed. William's mum Morag had done them both proud. Outside of the barn, there was a large roaring fire lit, and around it were hay bales with blankets draped over them, she had decorated the barn with beautiful wildflowers and heather, and the fire was a welcome blessing, as the sun disappeared leaving a crisp Autumn chill in the air. The food was wonderful, and the guests all seemed to be having the best time, and while they ate in the barn, the ceilidh band were setting up just away from the fire.

Peggy and William had the first dance, and then many of the guests joined in, dancing and making merry. Peggy and Shona were dancing, when something caught Peggy's eye from the fence, she looked and watched as a man walked away from the fence with his head down, "Come on Peg, you can introduce me to Wilf," Shona said as she pulled Peggy's arm towards William and Wilf who were sitting around the great fire.

Abe turned back to look once more, she looked incredibly beautiful, and he only hoped that she knew just how very proud of her, he was, how hard it was going to be knowing that she was here, but from that moment all ties had to be cut, for her sake as well as his, as she skipped off with her new friend, she seemed to be having fun, he thought to himself as the tears rolled down his face, at that very moment, he knew that he would never see her again, and the same gut-wrenching emotion that he felt when Carrie drew her last breath, had returned.

After a wonderful evening, Williams's dad Andrew pulled up in his horse-drawn cart, and gestured to William and Peggy, the guests cheered as they boarded the cart and drove away, leaving them to continue with the cheerful jubilations.

The alarm rang out and Peggy moaned as she looked at the small window and could not see light, only darkness, she nudged William and climbed out of the warm bed, shivering as she did, Autumn was definitely approaching fast, she thought to herself as she wrapped herself in her dressing gown and walked down the stairs.

She stood beside the stove while she waited for the kettle to boil, she revelled in the warmth that seeped out and surrounded her. She heard the floorboards creak and knew that she would be joined very soon by William, the steam was pluming from the kettle, so she poured the boiling water into the teapot and prepared the cups. Just as she had expected, William joined her in a matter of a few minutes, she smiled and handed him his cup.

"What do you want for breakfast?" she asked. William looked at his watch and shook his head.

"We don't really have time Peg, Molly will be here soon to take us to the station, we'll just have to grab something there," he said and smiled as he drank the warm amber tea, she always made it just how he liked it, he thought to himself. Peggy placed her empty teacup in the sink and rinsed it out.

"I had better get dressed," she said as she looked at the clock on the wall. William nodded as he poured the last cup from the pot, and she disappeared up the stairs.

When she returned, she smiled when she saw Molly and Michael waiting in the kitchen. She placed her heavy case by the back door and then hugged them both.

"I hadn't realised that you were coming too Michael," Peggy said and smiled. Michael frowned, this was the moment that he had been dreading.

"I'm afraid that this will be the last time that we shall see one another," he sighed sadly, Peggy frowned.

"We're only going for a week," she laughed. Michael shook his head as he looked at the floor.

"No Peggy, that's not what I meant, Molly and I have to cut ties with you now, for your own safety and happiness," Michael said, still looking at the floor, still not able to look her in the eye.

"But, but I thought that I had to contact you when I find Robert?" Peggy said as she felt the familiar sting of tears in her eyes, Molly smiled and shook her head.

"No dear, we will know, have no fear of that," she said and wiped the falling tears from Peggy's cheeks. "Come now, you don't want to ruin your make-up, dry your eyes," Molly said and smiled a sad smile. Peggy wiped her face as William stood at her side and grabbed her hand. "Right, we should get a move on, you don't want to miss your train," Molly said as she took the car keys out of her bag and struggled to fight the tears away. William picked up both of the cases and walked out of the back door, Peggy followed and waited for Molly and Michael to come out so that she could lock the door. She stood with the key in hand as first Michael walked past her, then Molly came out, "Peggy, aren't you forgetting something?" Molly asked as she stopped her from closing the door.

"Yes! Sorry Molly, thank you for everything!" Peggy said and wrapped her arms around her. Molly laughed and pulled back.

"Not that silly! That!" she said and pointed to Carrie's urn that was sitting on the side in the kitchen. Peggy chuckled, shook her head, and grabbed the urn, calling out to William not to put her case in the car.

As Michael pulled up outside the station Molly sighed and turned to look at Peggy.

"We won't walk you in, I don't think that I could bear it," Molly said sadly. Peggy gulped, nodded, and climbed out of the car, not uttering a single word as she and William walked to the station, she dared not look back, it would be too heart-wrenching, she thought to herself as William passed the tickets to the guard, who inspected them and allowed them both to go through.

She sat at the table in the empty station café and looked out of the misty window, wiping away the condensation and catching a glimpse of Molly and Michael driving away. William put the tray onto the table and grabbed her hand.

"I'll take care of you, don't be sad," he said.

"Do you promise?" she asked, he nodded frantically.

"Aye, I absolutely promise! Now drink your tea, breakfast will be here in a minute," he said and smiled.

The train journey seemed to take forever, and Peggy was relieved when the train pulled into Delabole station. As they disembarked she couldn't believe how tiny the station was, she picked up her case and they walked outside to be met by pouring rain. "Great!" she said as she looked up at the driving rain.

A car pulled up and wound down the window "Hubbard" the man shouted, William, nodded as the man jumped out of the car and opened the boot, throwing their cases inside. The journey didn't take too long, but she hadn't seen a thing except for rain flowing against the condensated windows of the car. As she climbed out of the car she gasped when she saw the hotel, it was like a castle. She turned to William and smiled.

"Go inside, you'll catch a death out here, I'll grab the cases," he said and shooed her up the steps of the impressive building. Inside, it was equally impressive, and a cheerful-faced man sat behind the desk as Peggy shook the rain from her coat and undid her scarf, shaking that too as she took it away from her head.

"Not the best of the Cornish weather," the man said in a thick West country accent.

"Och, we're used to the rain," Peggy replied and smiled.

"Well of course you are, you're from Scotland," The man said and chuckled as William came in through the doors.

The porter showed them to their room, which was lovely and told them that dinner would be served at eight. Peggy pulled the heavy velvet curtain back and looked out of the large window. She could just make out the pretty harbour, she turned to William and smiled.

"This hotel is just wonderful!" she said and flopped onto the bouncy bed. William laughed and did the same. After half an hour of just lying there, recovering from the journey, and taking in the beautiful furnishings, William looked at his watch as he yawned.

"Come on hen, we need to change for dinner," he said as he jumped up and threw open his case. Peggy sighed and then reluctantly climbed off of the comfortable bed, if she weren't so hungry, she could have happily stayed there, she was thinking to herself as she walked over to her case, threw it onto the bed and opened it, and as she did she gasped.

"Oh William, look!" she said as she stared into her case. William tutted and walked over to her, looked into her case and he too gasped.

"Oh Peg!" he said with his hand over his mouth when he saw Peggy's clothes, covered in Carrie's ashes and the lid of the urn buried beneath them. Peggy looked at William in bewilderment as she began to shake the clothes and lift them out of the case.

"William, what am I going to do? How can I get it back into the urn!" Peggy said.

"I'll be back in a wee minute," William said as he dashed out of the room. William reappeared with a small hand shovel and smiled.

"Shake your clothes off and then I'll scoop the ashes back into the urn with this," he said and smiled, Peggy smiled, then her smile turned into a chuckle and then very soon they were both howling with laughter, as William scooped the last of the ashes back into the urn. Peggy threw her arms around him.

"Thank you, what would I do without you," she said and kissed him. When he released her, he paused for a moment and then smiled as he shook his head.

"It could only happen to you, my Peg!" He said and again they both howled with laughter.

Once dressed, Peggy carefully placed the urn onto the mantlepiece and then they both went down to the dining room for dinner, Peggy was starving and the smell of cooking food that was wafting through the corridors, just made the hunger worse.

The waiter showed them to their table and gave them each a menu. Peggy smiled as she was reading through and then looked at William.

"What are you having?" she asked over the top of her menu, he smiled and then looked at the window with the rain pouring and the wind howling.

"I'm going to have the steak pie, it's pie kind of weather," he said and licked his lips.

"Ooh! Me too!" Peggy said as her tummy growled again with discontent from the lack of food.

After the delicious dinner, followed by a generous portion of spotted dick and custard, they were both contently full but exhausted.

"Do you want to go to the bar and get a drink?" William asked as Peggy yawned and shook her head.

"No, I want to climb into that comfortable bed and listen for a wee while to the rain and the wind," she said and smiled, the very thought of it made her happy.

"Aye, me too," he said as they both left the table and walked back to their room.

The following morning Peggy woke and smiled, the sun was streaming through a gap in the curtains, and she couldn't wait to see the place that Carrie held so dear in her heart. She leapt out of bed and walked to the window, pulling back the heavy curtains, and she smiled a huge beaming smile when she saw Boscastle in all its splendour! The small quaint village had a small river running through it that ran to the sea, she could hear the waves crashing as she looked at the harbour, the fishermen were preparing their boats to set sail, and people were walking outside, popping in and out of the small assortment of shops that lined the cobbled road.

"William, wake up, you have to see this!" Peggy exclaimed excitedly.

"What?" William replied sleepily.

"Come on, wake up," Peggy shouted. William sat up and stretched, then climbed out of bed and walked to the window. He rubbed his eyes and then looked.

"Wow! I understand why she loved it so, it's beautiful," he said and kissed Peggy on the cheek. "Right, well, I'm getting dressed, I could kill for a cup of tea," he added as he walked to the wardrobe and took out his clothes, looking back at Peggy as he did. "Come on Peg, I'm parched," he called out as he got dressed.

CHAPTER 8

After breakfast they took a slow walk through the tiny village, nestling sweetly within the wild, rugged, granite cliffs that wrapped themselves around protectively. The air was filled with remnants of salt from the ocean and sweet notes from the wildflowers which were in abundance around the banks of the small river. As they walked along, their arms entwined, Peggy stopped, looking upwards towards the top of the cliff, she was staring with her mouth open. William gently pulled at her to nudge her along, but she would not budge, she was fixed firmly on the spot where she was standing.

"Come on Peg, it's nearly lunchtime," William said as he gently tugged at her arm, thinking about filling his rumbling, empty tummy. He turned and looked at her, still staring at the same spot in a trance-like state. "What is it? What are you looking at?" He asked as he used his hand to shade the bright sunshine, he could see nothing or nobody.

"There was a wee lassie, up there on the edge of the cliff, I was afraid that she would fall over the edge," Peggy said and gripped her chest to still her thumping heart.

"I didnee see anyone Peg," William said as he looked again. Peggy turned and looked at him, dumbfoundedly.

"She was waving at me, then she completely vanished," Peggy said vaguely as she was so deep in thought.

"It's because you need food, you are seeing things, come on," William replied and pulled her towards a quaint-looking teashop.

So after five wonderful days of relaxation and enjoying the sea air, the time had come to let Carrie go, Peggy wanted to do it when the place was quiet, free from the hustle and bustle of everyday life, so they waited until dusk and slowly walked towards the harbour. The air was wet with the drizzle from the thick mist that was swirling around them, making it all rather atmospheric, Peggy was thinking to herself as they climbed up onto the large outcrop of rock and walked towards the edge, which shelved them from the angry, crashing waves that were hitting the shore and cliffs below.

Once she had found the perfect spot, she lifted the urn from her handbag, but again felt that there was someone on the cliffs above, she reluctantly looked and exhaled with relief when she realised that there was no one there. Her hands were shaking as she attempted to lift the lid from the urn. This was it, the time that she truly had to say goodbye to her beloved grandmother, she hadn't realised that she would find it so hard. William looked at her and smiled.

"Carrie, Peggy knows that you always wanted to return here to your happy place, and now finally you have, be happy Carrie, be free," William said as he placed his hands over Peggy's and together they released the ashes into the cold, windy Autumn air. As the tears ran down her face, Peggy's attention was yet again drawn to the clifftop, and she smiled when she saw the wee lassie, who was holding hands with Carrie as they both waved, Peggy cried tears of happiness when she realised that the small girl who was waving at her before, was Polly, Carrie's daughter whose life had been cruelly snatched away at such a young age, was now waving at her again while she held onto her mother's hand. Carrie smiled, then waved as they both vanished into the mist.

Peggy and William walked back to the hotel hand in hand and yet she breathed not a word to him, not a single word, that was her moment, besides, he would never believe her, she was thinking to herself as they both climbed the steps to the hotel, preparing themselves for the long train journey home.

The next two years were dull if nothing else, with William working long hours on the farm, and constantly nagging Peggy into having a child of their own. Peggy's days were usually filled with keeping the house, baking, and preparing lotions, teas, and ointments for the local folk, well except for Wednesdays, when Shona would come and pick her up, and together they would travel to different places, visiting stately homes, ruinous castles, and museums. How she looked forward to Wednesdays, how sad she felt when

Shona would pull up outside the cottage to drop her off, and from the moment that she stepped out of the car, she would long for the next six days of loneliness to hurry, so that she could once again, seek new horizons with her best friend.

She closed the car door, waved at Shona, and then walked up the path to the cottage. She opened the door and walked inside, hanging her coat and scarf on the hook in the hallway. She put the kettle on to boil and opened the back door to let some air into the room. She stood at the door, cradling her cup of hot tea, looking over to the fields that surrounded her, sometimes she felt suffocated, she desperately wanted to see new places and meet new people, but William was always working, or down the pub with his Dad. She sighed and walked back into the kitchen to prepare the evening meal.

She was peeling potatoes when the back door opened and William walked in, traipsing mud and muck from the farm with him, Peggy tutted and walked to the pantry to grab the mop, shaking her head as she mopped behind every inch where he was walking.

"I wish you would take your boots off at the door William, it would make my life so much easier," Peggy sighed as she walked back to the pantry with the mop, she almost jumped out of her skin when she walked into him as he loomed at the pantry door, scowling. He grabbed hold of her arm tightly.

"Make your life easier eh, what have you been doing today, oh yeah I remember, you have been swanning around the place with that stupid cow that you call your friend," he sneered. Peggy tried to break loose from his tight grip, but he would not let go.

"William you are hurting me let go!" She shouted as again she tried to free herself. He glared at her, with such a look of disdain, then finally released her and laughed.

"You wouldn't know hard work if it bit you on the arse!" He scoffed as he sat at the kitchen table. "Where's my tea?" he asked and looked at the clock on the wall.

"I'm just doing it now," Peggy replied as she rubbed her arm.

"It's always the same, every bloody Wednesday, I have to wait for my tea because you and your friend have been out galivanting, it's not on Peggy, I will not allow it to continue!" He shouted. Peggy slammed the knife down on the worktop and turned to look at him, she had had enough.

"Two years I have asked if we can find my brother, two years, William! You are never here and when you are, you just moan. I have had enough!" She bellowed and ran out of the kitchen, up the stairs to her bedroom, slamming the door closed behind her and sliding the bolt across. It made her think back to the last row that they had, when again he grabbed her, hurting her. She had gone to the shops the following day and Reg had noticed the bruising on her arm. He told her to wait there, then returned from the hardware shop with a bolt, which she passed to Peggy.

"If you will insist on staying with the nasty bastard, at least protect yourself," Reg said as he passed the paper bag to Peggy. She looked inside and smiled. "The screws and everything you need are in the bag, do you want me to swing by to fit it?" Reg asked and smiled.

William was thumping on the door, hollering as he did.

"Open the door now!" He ordered.

"I told you before, that I will not put up with being treated like this, go away William, I want you to leave!" Peggy cried.

"Sorry Peggy, look, I have just had a bad day that's all, let me in so that we can talk about it," he said quietly.

"Go away!" she repeated and buried her head into her pillow, fearing his reaction.

"LET ME IN NOW!" he roared and thumped the door continuously. "Fine, I'm going down to the pub, I'm sure that Jean will fix me something nice to eat," he said, and she sighed with relief as she heard him walk down the stairs, and out of the door, slamming it behind him. She watched him go from the window and then went down the stairs, into the kitchen and prepared the meal anyway. She went into the lounge, put the radio on and sat listening as she ate her meal alone, once again. Once she had finished and cleared the dishes, she sat in the lounge, wondering what to do, then a memory appeared in her head, it was the morning that the tarot cards were left on the doorstep for her. She had put them away in Carrie's chest and completely forgotten about them. She went up to the bedroom, pulled out the chest and opened it. There on the top was a photograph of Robert, her baby brother, just before he was sent away. She held it close to her heart and then rummaged around looking for the tarot, which she eventually found, right at the very bottom!

She sat with the small occasional table in front of her and shuffled the cards, then she placed them face down on the table, she heard a chuckle and smiled when she saw Carrie standing in front of her shaking her head. One by one she turned the cards face up and looked at them, and the pictures meant absolutely nothing to her. She looked at Carrie in bewilderment, and again Carrie chuckled. She sat down beside Peggy. "You read from here," she said as she pointed to the centre of Peggy's forehead, "Not here," she continued as she pointed to the cards. "Close your eyes, fill your mind with nature, then look," Carrie said and then faded away. Peggy closed her eyes and thought about the meadow of wildflowers, then her thoughts took her to the crashing waves at Boscastle. She slowly opened her eyes and looked back at the cards, still, they made no sense to her, so she closed her eyes again, her thoughts took her to a doctor's surgery, where the doctor pointed to her tummy and shook his head, this told her exactly what she had suspected for the last two years, she was unable to bear children.

Then her thoughts took her to London. She was standing on a bridge, there was a river below. A young man was walking towards her, when two men that were walking behind him, ran and began to beat him, she ran towards them, then the front door slammed, breaking her thoughts as she quickly grabbed the cards and hid them under the sofa cushions, knowing that William would not approve. She jumped up from the sofa, her hands trembling, not knowing what mood he was going to be in especially as he had been drinking. The lounge door flung open, and he fell into the room, reeking of alcohol.

He grinned at Peggy and lunged forward towards her, she quickly moved out of the way as he landed face down on the rug, mumbling as he hit the ground, and there he stayed. Peggy quickly gathered the hidden tarot together and went up to the bedroom, she didn't bother locking the door behind her, she knew that he was in no fit state to climb the stairs. She undressed, climbed into bed, and tried to take herself back to the bridge, as hard as she tried she could not get back there, but she instinctively knew that the young man who was being attacked was Robert she just knew it. After an hour or so of tossing and turning, she eventually drifted off to sleep.

The following morning she woke up with renewed energy, she had to find her brother and if William would not go with her, she would go alone, she thought to herself as she put on her slippers and dressing gown and walked down the stairs, into the kitchen, she didn't bother checking on him, at that moment in time, she really couldn't care less about him. She filled and put the kettle on, and opened the back door, the wind was howling, and the rain was lashing down, she popped her head out of the door, pulled a face of disgust, and then closed the door just as the kettle boiled. William walked out to the kitchen just as she was pouring the steaming tea from the teapot. He sat at the table and put his head in his hands. Peggy chose to ignore him and stared out of the small kitchen window, watching the patterns that the raindrops were making as they danced down the glass.

"Peggy sit down," William said quietly.

"No thanks, I'm all right where I am," she replied not turning to look at him.

"Please Peggy, there is something that I have to tell you," he replied, his voice barely audible. She tutted, turned, and noticed how solemn he looked. She frowned then reluctantly walked to the table, pulled out the chair and sat opposite him.

"Well?" She asked impatiently. He looked up, wearing an expression of great remorse.

"It's about last night," he mumbled. Peggy chuckled and nodded her head.

"You may as well save your breath William I have heard it all before, yes you're sorry, and you'll never behave like that again, how many times do you think that it will be before I send you packing?" Peggy said calmly. He looked up at her and sighed.

"I slept with Jean last night," he mumbled. Peggy sat back in her chair and folded her arms, nodding as she did. He looked at her and she could have sworn that she saw an expression of pride slowing creeping across his face. Peggy said nothing, she just stared at him. "Well?" he asked surprisingly, shocked that she had not flown into a fit of rage, swearing that she would beat the life out of Jean Douglas the next time that she laid eyes on her.

"She is welcome to you, if you could arrange to move your belongings out of my cottage by tomorrow, that would be much appreciated, you see I am going to London in the morning," Peggy said as she stood up and pushed the chair back under the table, poured herself a fresh cup of tea, which she took into the lounge and put the radio on. She desperately wanted to cry, scream, shout, and bellow, but she would not give him the satisfaction of that, instead, she sang along to a tune that was playing on the radio as she looked out of the window.

"What do you mean you are going to London?" William asked as he walked through the lounge door.

"As I said, I am going tomorrow to find my brother, I'm not sure how long it will take," she said and smiled inside herself.

"How can you, you have no money?" William said and smirked.

"Oh don't worry yourself about me, I'll get by," Peggy said, Carrie had left her a substantial amount of money, and Abe had made Peggy promise not to tell William, she was happily thinking to herself as he towered over her.

"I forbid it!" William snapped, making Peggy roar with laughter.

"I will make an appointment with my solicitor as soon as I return William, I am going to begin divorce proceedings," Peggy replied as she stood up and faced him, now nose to nose. He pulled his arm back to strike her and as he did a large vase that was sitting on the windowsill flew up in the air and hit him on the head. He looked at Peggy in horror, then looked at the broken pieces of vase that were at his feet.

"How the hell did you do that?" He asked, his voice trembling, his hand covering his head. Peggy laughed, turned, and left the room, back up to the bedroom where she again bolted the door. She sat on the edge of her bed and put her face in her hands. She heard the clapping of hands and when she looked up, Carrie was walking towards her, she sat down beside Peggy and smiled.

"Well done you!" she said and chuckled.

"I didnee throw the vase," Peggy said anxiously, Carrie nodded.

"I know you didn't, I did!" she said and laughed. "I will not let him hurt you, ever again," Carrie said as her silhouette faded. Then there was a gentle tapping on the door. Peggy sighed, she already knew what was about to happen, he would spend an hour grovelling, she would give in, and all would be well again, until the next time, she was thinking to herself, when the tapping became louder.

"William, will you please just go away!" Peggy shouted.

"Peggy dear, it's me Morag," Peggy heard William's mum say. Peggy jumped up from the bed and opened the door, Morag looked at her and then threw her arms around her. She grabbed her hand and walked her to the bed where they both sat down.

"Andrew has taken William to the hospital, he has a nasty cut on his head," Morag said.

"It wasn't me Morag, he was going to hit me when the vase fell off the windowsill and hit him on the head," Peggy said as she began to panic, Morag chuckled.

"I know dear, sometimes these men just canee control their temper, Andrew is exactly the same, but you know the day that we married them we agreed to love them warts and all," Morag said as she tapped the back of Peggy's hand. Peggy moved her hand away and stood up.

"I never agreed to allow him to hit me or allow him to cheat on me with Jean bloody Douglas," Peggy sneered as she was filled with rage. Morag looked at her wearing an expression of disbelief.

"No dear, you must be mistaken, you know how folk around here like to gossip," she said as she stood.

"He told me himself!" Peggy fumed.

CHAPTER 9

Peggy got dressed and then hastily left the cottage before William returned from the hospital, she wanted to see Shona before she left for London. The walk took her about forty-five minutes, and she was thankful, that the driving rain had abated, and the sun was desperately trying to make his autumnal appearance.

She glanced at the butcher's shop as she walked along the road towards Shona's house, yes he was there, and yes he noticed her, as the biggest smile spread across his face, and he waved frantically at her. Peggy chuckled as she walked up the steps and knocked on the front door.

Peggy could hear someone running and smiled when Shona opened the door, she looked shocked to see Peggy standing there. "What are you doing here? It's Thursday Peg," Shona said breathlessly.

"Aye I know, I wanted to see you before I left," Peggy said smiling. Shona placed her finger to her lips in an attempt to hush Peggy as Wilf, William's brother came running down the stairs, looking ever so flustered as he rushed past Peggy and ran down the steps. Peggy began to laugh as Shona grabbed her by the coat and pulled her inside the house.

"And I thought that we were friends!" Peggy exclaimed as she took off her coat and hung it on the hook.

"What do you mean? We are friends," Shona said anxiously.

"Aye, but friends don't keep things from one another do they?" Peggy said and smiled.

"Oh Peggy, I wanted to tell you, but with the way that you and William are, I didn't think that it was a good idea," Shona said as she walked through to the kitchen, Peggy following her as she did. "Oh my goodness, what happened to your arms?" Shona said as she looked at the bruising on both of Peggy's arms. "It was him wasn't it?" she added and scowled, Peggy nodded.

"Aye and if you take my advice you will steer well clear of the men in that family," Peggy sighed as she looked out of the large window which overlooked the beautiful garden.

"Wilf's not like that, he's a kind soul," Shona said dreamily, Peggy shook her head.

"Sweet William, that's what Carrie used to call him, well, that was before I married him!" Peggy replied as her thoughts dragged her back to Carrie's last day when they were sitting beside the river, as Carrie told her the final chapter of her story.

"Peggy, did you hear me?" Shona said from the open cupboard.

"Sorry, I was miles away, what did you say?" Peggy replied.

"Do you want tea or coffee?" Shona asked.

"Oh, coffee please," Peggy said and smiled. They took their drinks into the lounge and Peggy told Shona what had happened the night before. Shona sat back in the seat and shook her head.

"What an absolute bastard!" She scowled. "Anyway you said that you are going somewhere, are you leaving him?" Shona asked, Peggy shook her head.

"No the cottage belongs to me, if anyone is leaving it will be him!" Peggy said adamantly. "I am going to London, I need to find my wee brother," Peggy continued as she sipped the delicious coffee.

"On your own, you can't be serious, London is no place for a young woman on her own!" Shona said as she frowned.

"I must find him, whether it is on my own or not!" Peggy said as she thought about the vision that she had on the bridge.

"Where are you going to stay?" Shona asked.

"A boarding house, I guess," Peggy replied and shrugged.

"Well you make sure that you write to me every week, I need to know that you are ok," Shona said anxiously. Peggy nodded, smiled, drank the last of her coffee and stood.

"Well I had better get going, I have lots to do before I go," She said as she walked out to the hallway and put on her coat.

"Do you want a lift home?" Shona asked as she walked out of the kitchen after taking the empty cups out, Peggy shook her head.

"No, thanks for the offer, but I still have some errands to run, and I must go and collect my train ticket," Peggy replied as she kissed Shona on the cheek and opened the door, running down the steps onto the pavement. "See you" Peggy called out as she walked towards the row of shops.

"Take care," Shona called back and slowly closed the door. Peggy walked to the butcher shop, she knew that there was gammon in the pantry for supper, but she wanted to see Reg, so she would buy some sausages and have them instead, she thought to herself as she walked through the shop door and the bell rang above her head. She looked up and realised that Reg was no longer there, it was Stan his older brother, she frowned.

"Is everything ok Peggy?" Stan asked noticing the expression on her face, he took her by surprise, and she jumped and then smiled.

"Oh yes, er, sorry Stan, I thought for a minute there that I had forgotten my purse," she replied quickly, blushing as she did.

She walked out with a pound of sausages that she didn't really want, sighed, and made her way to the station. Once her ticket was paid for she began to feel happier, and she quickened her pace to something short of a skip and made her way home. She was so excited, she had a feeling that this time she would find him, all that she needed to do was find that bridge, and be there at the exact time that he would be, she was thinking, she thought about it again then realised that it was never going to be that simple, there must be over one hundred bridges in London, and twenty-four hours in a day, and thousands of men the same age as Robert, would she ever find him? She thought as she heard the sound of a car horn, which made her jump. She stopped in her tracks, turned, and looked. It was Reg in the delivery van. He pulled up beside the pavement and pushed the passenger door open.

"Get in, I'll drop you off," he shouted, Peggy blushed and shook her head. "Ah come on," he said and smiled. "I don't bite," he added.

"Aye but folk will talk, it will be all around the place that you and I are locked in some sort of passionate affair," Peggy said bashfully.

"What do you mean like William and Jean Douglas," he said, Peggy's heart sank like she had been hit by the atomic bomb, less than twenty-four hours and the whole town already knew! "Sorry, that was mean, come on Peggy," he said. Peggy looked all around, as thoughts of William and that trollop together, ran through her head. She shrugged her shoulders and jumped in.

"What have you been up to?" Reg asked as he drove down the quiet road.

"I have just collected my train ticket," she replied and grinned widely.

"Why, where are you going?" Reg asked as he frowned, wearing a look of disappointment.

"I'm going to London tomorrow," Peggy replied still smiling.

"Don't tell me, you are running away to find your fame and fortune," Reg said, trying to play-act as a fortune teller, making Peggy chuckle.

"No silly! I am going to look for my wee brother," she replied. A look of concern crept across Reg's face.

"Not on your own?" He asked anxiously, Peggy frowned and tutted.

"Not you too, yes on my own, believe it or not, I am a lot stronger than folk around here think I am!" Peggy said steadfastly and turned to look at Reg.

"I don't doubt that for one minute, it's just that I'll miss you, Peg, that's all," he said sadly. "What time is your train?" He asked.

"Seven- thirty" she smiled.

"So, he's not joining you then?" Reg said as he pulled up outside the cottage and nodded at William walking up the path.

"No Reg, he's not," Peggy replied as she watched William who was now scowling when he noticed that Peggy was inside the van.

"Will you be ok, going back in there?" Reg asked anxiously. Peggy laughed, a nervous laugh.

"I'll be fine, thank you for the ride," she said as she climbed out of the van. Reg leaned over and grabbed her hand.

"If he so much as lays one finger on you, you tell me, I will gladly throttle him, you hear me," Reg said, his face one of anger.

"Thank you," Peggy replied as she moved her hand and closed the door. She slowly and reluctantly walked up the path towards him, trembling as she did. Reg was still sitting parked, all the while watching.

"What were you doing in that?" William spat as he watched Reg.

"I was walking home, he was delivering around here, so he stopped and offered me a ride," Peggy said as she brushed past him and walked into the hallway.

"I bet he did," William sneered as he followed her inside, slamming the door behind him. Peggy quickly hung up her coat and shot into the kitchen. She placed the bags down on the side and put on her pinny, then filled the kettle and put it on. William started to look in the bags, Peggy was quietly relieved that she had the insight to put her ticket in her skirt pocket.

"Peggy, we need to talk," William said, putting on his sweetest smile, surely he must realise by now that it no longer worked, she had seen the very worst of him, and no veil could ever disguise that, she thought as she poured the boiling water into the teapot. She looked up at him expressionless.

"Peg, come on," he said gently.

"Well, go on then, talk," she replied coldly. He leaned over in an attempt to grab her hand, but she pulled it away and glared at him, she despised who he was now, and she could not wait to put some distance between them.

"Look, I know that I can be a bit of a pig sometimes, but I am always so tired, I work long hours you know," he said trying to justify his actions.

"Not too tired to go to the pub, not too tired to sleep with that trollop, are you," Peggy sneered. "And not too tired to hurt the woman that you married and promised to take care of," she added and walked to the sink, running the water.

"I'm sorry ok, I promise that if you give me another chance, I will prove to you that I can be the man that you fell in love with, I will," he said pleadingly.

"I need time to think William, time on my own," she replied, not looking at him, she was secretly trembling inside, she never could gauge how he was going to react to anything that she said.

"No Peg, no you don't. Why don't we go to London again, see if we can find Robert, the change will do us both good," he said as he now stood behind her.

"We'll see," she said, knowing full well that the following day she would board that train alone. "Why don't you go and get some rest while I cook the supper," she added.

"Aye, I will, my head is killing me," he replied as he walked into the lounge.

She had finished peeling the potatoes and put the sausages under the grill, she walked along the hallway and peered around the lounge door, William was fast asleep on the sofa. She quickly tiptoed up the stairs as quietly as she could and packed her case, which she sneaked back down the stairs and hid it in her workshop in the garden. She had packed the Grimoire and other things from the chest and if she had the chance she would hide that also, she was thinking as she walked back into the kitchen, she sighed with relief, there was still no sign of him waking. She turned the sausages then went up and grabbed the chest, struggling to bring it down the stairs, but she did it and then took it out to the workshop, throwing a blanket over it, to disguise it.

She dished up the food, inhaled deeply, and then walked in to wake him. He was already awake and sitting up. "Where do you want to eat?" she asked and attempted to smile.

"I'll have it in here," he replied. She placed it on a tray and took it to him. "Where's yours?" he asked.

"I'll go and get it now," she said and reluctantly walked out to get her food.

Once the dishes were washed she walked back into the lounge, where William was lying on the sofa.

"I'm going to run a bath, is there anything that I can get you before I go up?" she asked.

"Aye you can pour me a large brandy, it might help the headache," he said and smiled. She smiled a false smile, walked to the sideboard, poured him a very large brandy, and passed it to him.

"Thanks, hen," he said.

After a lovely warm bath, Peggy set to work on her lawless hair, once happy with that, she crept down the stairs, peering through the crack of the lounge door as she passed it, he was getting up off of the sofa. Quickly she walked to the kitchen and put the kettle on. William walked out and stood in the doorway.

"Do you want some tea?" She asked, turned, and looked at him. He shook his head.

"No, I'm heading off to bed," he replied and walked towards the stairs. "Will you be long?" he asked, Peggy nearly choked! After all that, he still expected her to share the same bed as him, well, he could forget it! She thought to herself.

"I'm just going to have a cup of tea and then I'll turn in," she lied. He walked up the stairs. Once she heard the bedroom door close, she took her tea into the lounge and put her feet up on the sofa, she was so tired, but she was worried that she would wake late and miss her train.

She opened her eyes and jumped up off of the sofa, she just knew that she would fall asleep! She thought to herself as she rubbed her tired eyes and looked at the clock. She sighed when she saw that it was five-thirty. She quickly dressed in the outfit that she had hidden in the pantry, and then slowly closed the kitchen door behind her. She grabbed her case from the workshop and began the long walk to the station.

She turned the corner and walked along the roadside carrying her heavy case, she had only been walking a matter of minutes and the case felt as though it was full of bricks already! She saw the lights of a car coming up behind her, so she jumped up on the verge. The vehicle stopped, and much to Peggy's relief, she saw that it was Reg.

"Well don't just stand there, get in," he said as he threw the door open.

"You are a blessing!" she sighed as she climbed into the van and Reg pulled away.

"You didn't think that I would leave you to walk to the station did you," he said and smiled.

"Thank you Reg, you are a good friend," Peggy said as she watched the light creeping up into the sky.

They pulled up outside the station, and Reg jumped out and opened Peggy's door, grabbing her case as he did. "I will carry it inside for you," he said and smiled, so together they walked into the deserted station. The café was just about to open, it was a good job too, Peggy was parched, she had not had the time to have her morning tea before she left. Reg placed her case down on the floor in front of her and sighed.

"Thank you so much Reg," Peggy said smiling.

"You take care of yourself down there, and don't be away too long, you hear," he replied as he blew her a kiss and headed back out to the van.

She struggled with her case into the café and placed it on the floor beside the table. She ordered Tea and a bun and sat at the table, looking out of the window. She was now so nervous, for two reasons, one, was, what if William had woke up and put two and two together, what if he got to the station before her train left and made a huge fuss, and the second reason was, going to London all by herself, she told everyone that she was able to care of herself, but was she?

Her train pulled up at the platform, right on time, she threw her case aboard and then climbed in, the satisfaction of slamming the door closed was second to none, she thought to herself as she entered the compartment, threw her case up on the luggage shelf and sat beside the window. As the whistle blew and the train pulled away she spotted William running down the platform, he was too late, she was on her way and doing it alone!

CHAPTER 10

She had thought long and hard for the largest part of her journey, could she leave him? How could she, she was nowhere near as fiercely independent as Carrie, folk would frown at her, and every woman would see her as a threat, it just wasn't the done thing, but how could she stay with him, not only did he treat her so badly, but he was also a cheating, lying bastard too, she was thinking to herself as she drifted off to sleep. The train ground to a halt with a jerk, waking Peggy from her uncomfortable slumber. She sat up with a jolt and looked out of the window, sighing when she saw that there was still quite a way until they reached London. There was now an older woman sitting opposite her, who was reading a book, every now and then she would peer over the top of the pages, sneaking a look at this young woman, who was travelling alone. Peggy caught her gaze and smiled, the woman reluctantly smiled back.

"Have you travelled far?" The woman asked as she placed her book down on the seat beside her. Peggy yawned,

"Yes I have travelled from Scotland," she replied with a smile. The woman frowned.

"Goodness me, that is rather a long way to travel by one's self! Where are you going?" She asked pryingly. Peggy thought that she was being rather too inquisitive, but she replied anyway.

"I'm going to London," Peggy said and smiled,

"On your own! Is someone meeting you at the station?" She asked, Peggy, raised her eyebrow, what the hell did it have to do with her? She was thinking to herself.

"No," she replied and looked out of the window, hoping that she would take the hint and stop the interrogation, and luckily she did. They had travelled for another hour and Peggy could tell from the changing landscape that they would soon be arriving. She dragged her heavy case down from the luggage shelf, took out her make-up bag and powdered her nose, then took out her lipstick which she was applying with great caution as the train once again ground to an urgent halt sending the lipstick up her cheek. She growled with frustration as she rummaged through her handbag for her hanky, when she noticed that the woman was stifling a laugh, she then leaned over and passed Peggy a clean hanky.

"Thank you," Peggy said as she blushed, not that you could tell, one side of her face was positively scarlet as she dragged the lipstick even further.

"Where are you staying?" The woman asked as Peggy rubbed frantically at her cheek, looking into her compact mirror, she licked the hanky much to the woman's disgust, trying in vain to remove the bright red mess that had spread all over one cheek.

"I'm not sure yet, I need to find a boarding house," Peggy replied.

"Well I guess that it is your lucky day young lady, I happen to own a boarding house, and I have just returned from visiting my ailing sister, so there are plenty of rooms available, you can have your pick of the bunch!" the woman said enthusiastically. "My name is Mrs Warley," she said as she held her hand out to Peggy, Peggy smiled as she shook her hand.

"Peggy," she replied.

"Well come along young Peggy, we have a cab waiting for us," she said and ushered Peggy to the train door.

The cab journey was uneventful and before long, it pulled up outside a large white house with Georgian windows, Peggy was impressed, from the outside it was so much prettier than the last boarding house in London and Mrs Warley seemed so much nicer than the other woman, the dreaded Mrs Bloomer! Peggy was thinking as the cab driver carried the cases up the stone steps, swiftly followed by Mrs Warley, then Peggy. She opened the door and Peggy gasped, it was beautiful, Peggy looked all around at the stunning interior of the building, but then a rush of dread ran through her, how much was this going to cost? She was thinking to herself as Mrs Warley hung up her coat and patiently waited to take Peggy's from her. Peggy looked at her and then realised that she was waiting, so she quickly took off her coat and scarf and passed them to her.

Mrs Warley then walked behind the reception desk and grabbed a handful of keys. "Right then Peggy, let's go and see which one you prefer," she said as she walked towards the sweeping staircase, Peggy was frozen to the spot, unable to take a step. "Come along dear, what on earth is the matter with you?" Mrs Warley asked briskly.

"I, er, I'm not sure that I could afford to stay in a wonderful place like this," Peggy replied awkwardly. Mrs Warley let out a chuckle.

"Nonsense, we can work around your budget, now come along, it's almost time for supper," she replied and hurried up the lush, carpeted stairs. Peggy quickly followed and reached the top just as Mrs Warley excitedly opened the first door for Peggy to see. Again Peggy gasped when she peered inside, the room was light and airy and so big, there was a beautifully dressed bed, a wardrobe, a chest of drawers, and a writing desk, all made from the most beautiful highly polished wood.

"So this room is one of my absolute favourites!" Mrs Warley said proudly.

"Aye, I'll take it!" Peggy replied quickly. Mrs Warley frowned,

"But you haven't seen the others yet?" she said disappointedly,

"I know, I don't need to, this room is wonderful, so it is," Peggy said wearing the biggest smile that her small face would stretch to. Mrs Warley let out a cry of joy and clapped her hands, she was obviously incredibly proud of her house and was overjoyed whenever someone expressed their own adoration.

"You get yourself settled in, I usually serve supper at eight-thirty, if you need anything in the meantime, I shall be in the reception area somewhere," Mrs Warley said as she pulled the door closed behind her.

"Thank you," Peggy shouted and looked around. She threw her case on the bed and smiled, how lucky she was to happen to sit opposite Mrs Warley on the train, she was dreading the thought of going back to Mrs Bloomer's gloomy boarding house!

Peggy had unpacked, written letters to Shona, William, and Reg, changed for supper and made her way down the stairs, the aroma coming from the kitchen was wonderful and Peggy sniffed the air, she was so hungry, all she had eaten that day was the bun in the station café and that was hard!

Mrs Warley appeared from behind the large wooden desk and smiled.

"I must say, you do brush up rather well, "she said and chuckled, Peggy wasn't quite sure how to take that comment, so she just smiled her sweet, innocent, smile.

"Ordinarily I would serve supper in the dining room, but as there is only you, I and Mr Rogers, I will serve it in my private lounge, follow me," Mrs Warley almost sang as she floated through the door marked PRIVATE, Peggy following behind, like a duckling following mother duck.

Her private lounge was equivocally beautiful to the rest of the house, well the parts that Peggy had seen anyway, and she gestured for Peggy to sit at the table, which was covered in a beautiful lace tablecloth, but Peggy noticed that there were only two place settings, she sat down, and Mrs Warley disappeared through a door, very soon returning with two small glasses filled with sherry. She handed one to Peggy and then sat opposite her and smiled.

"I always have a sherry before supper, helps with digestion, don't you agree," she said as she elegantly sipped from the small glass, Peggy shrugged her shoulders.

"I don't know, I have never tried it," she replied and sniffed at the sweet-smelling liquid.

Over the delicious supper Peggy explained why she was in London, Mrs Warley listened intently as she told her the sad story of her life.

"Oh my poor child!" she said on the brink of bursting into tears.

"Where do you intend to begin the search?" Mrs Warley asked as she wiped the rogue tears from her eyes.

"Hammersmith I guess, although I just came up against a brick wall the last time I was here," Peggy sighed.

"There must be a way to trace him," Mrs Warley said as she sat deep in thought, "If you write down his name and the address where he was sent to, I have a good friend who works in the government offices, I will see if he can discover anything," she said as she tapped the back of Peggy's hand.

"Thank you so very much, Mrs Warley, you are too kind," Peggy said gratefully,

"Not at all darling, now please, call me Martha," she replied as she began to collect the empty plates from the table, Peggy jumped up to help, and Martha shook her head.

"My dear, you must be positively exhausted, get yourself off to bed and I will see you bright and early in the morning," Martha said as she walked through the door.

"Ok, thank you Martha and goodnight," Peggy shouted,

"Sleep well dear," Martha shouted as Peggy left the room and walked up the stairs to bed.

ROBERT

He tapped on the door with bated breath, he was shitting himself, but it had to be said, Robert was thinking as he waited for Philpott junior to call him in.

"What?" He heard him shout through the closed door, usual scenario, Robert thought, the lazy bastard couldn't even lift his arse off of the chair to open the door! Reluctantly he opened the door and peered around. Jack Philpott looked up and shook his head.

"Well come in, don't just stand there like a pillock" he bellowed. Robert stepped into the room, closed the door, and looked around, it had to be the first time he had been near the bloke without his two henchmen standing in the room, looking like a pair of disgruntled gorillas. He walked to the desk and looked at Jack, who gestured to the seat opposite, Robert sat down.

"Now what is it? If it's about 'what do you know Joe,' I aint interested, do you hear," he snarled. Robert shook his head.

"No, it aint that," he replied. Jack glared at him,

"Well! What is it, I aint got time to play silly buggers," he said shaking his head,

"I, er, I'm leaving," Robert said trying to sound confident, but failing miserably. Jack threw his head back in laughter.

"I don't think so, me old son," he sneered. Robert looked at him in bewilderment, not knowing what to say next. "And where exactly do you think you are going?" Jack asked. Robert looked at the floor.

"I wanna join up like," he almost whispered, again Jack threw his head back in overexaggerated laughter.

"You, in the army, don't make me laugh," he said as he wiped tears away from his eyes. "If you aint no good for anything else, you're always good for a laugh Bob, now go on fuck off, I have got important stuff to think about," he said and gestured to the door. Robert sighed and stood up, turned, and walked towards the door.

"Oi! Don't forget that you're doorman tonight," Jack shouted.

"Yeah, how could I fucking forget," Robert mumbled as he opened the door.

"What did you just say?" Jack shouted.

"I said, yeah, I know," Robert replied as he closed the door and walked out of the building. He walked up the road in the direction of the bookies, mumbling to himself as he did. He desperately wanted out of this game, but he could see no way out. Why did the squire send him to be look-out all those years ago? Why did he hand him over to Old Philpott, why did his Mum send him away when he was so little, all these and many other thoughts had run through his mind for so many years. He jumped as he walked into the path of an unsuspecting woman, who jumped also. "Sorry love," Robert mumbled, not even looking at her as he walked towards the bookmakers.

He walked in, pushing his way through the smelly punters and the smoke-filled shop until he walked through to the back office.

"All right, Bob?" Bernie said, fag hanging out of his mouth as he checked the racing form in the newspaper.

"No!" Robert replied as he poured himself a cup of stewed tea from the pot, he pulled out a grubby chair, sweeping it with his hand and slumped down.

"Blimey, what's up with ya now?" Bernie asked and jiggled his empty cup at Robert. Robert sighed, took the cup, and poured Bernie a cup, which now looked like thick soup rather than tea, he handed it to him, then slumped back in his chair. "Well?" Bernie asked again.

"I told him that I wanted to join up and he laughed," Robert said, Bernie, chuckled.

"I told ya, didn't I, you aint got a chance in hell of leaving the firm boy, you just gotta get that into your fik skull aint ya," Bernie said as he lit another fag from the dog end that he had just finished.

"I will, I will get out if it's the last thing that I do," Robert said and slammed his cup on the table and stormed out of the room.

He walked down the street towards his digs, he walked up the steps and unlocked his door, he looked all around, he had the distinct impression that he was being followed, there didn't appear to be anyone there, so he walked into his room and threw himself on his bed. He looked around the room, I mean it was all right, it wasn't half bad. There was everything that he needed, there was a wardrobe for his clothes, a writing desk, which served no purpose, he had never done a day of school in his life, and there on his bedside table was a small photograph of him, his Mum and his beloved Peggy, most days it was that what kept him going, one day he would get out for good, he would join the army, make some money, then he would find them his Mum and Peggy. Never a day went by that he hadn't thought about that moment when they all became reunited with one another. He wondered what they both looked like now, mum must be getting on a bit now, he often thought, how grateful he was that Peggy had slipped that photo into his pocket before he was dragged away, if it weren't for that he would have surely forgotten about both of them. That photograph had kept his memory alive every single day!

He climbed off of the bed and walked to the window, pulling the curtain back just enough to see out. There was a bloke standing on the corner, now he was one of two things, he was either the old bill, watching him because of the fight between him and 'what do you know Joe,' or it was one of Philpott's men, and silently he prayed that it was the old bill, he could run from them, but if Philpott had given his henchmen the nod, he was a gonna for sure, he thought as he dropped the curtain back and walked to the sink to wash his face.

Suited and booted he walked down to Cyril's café for his usual before he had to start his shift at the Black Cat. He opened the door of Cyril's café to be greeted by the stench of stale fat and 'Ageing Ada' behind the counter, who batted her eyelashes at him like a lovesick schoolgirl.

"Hello Bob love, your usual is it?" she asked as he approached the grubby counter.

"Yeah go on then, might as well, the pipes could do with a bit of a clear out," Robert said and laughed as he sat at his usual table.

"Bloody cheek!" Ada said as she slammed his cup of tea onto the table in front of him. "You're early today aint ya?" Ageing Ada said and looked into his big brown eyes.

"Ada how many times, leave the boy alone," Cyril said as he walked out from the back of the café.

"I can't elp meself can I, the boys so bloody handsome," she said and winked as she walked back to the counter.

Cyril walked over to the table and sat on the chair opposite Robert.

"Ere what time's the game tonight?" he asked quietly.

"Midnight Cyril, you know that" Robert replied and smiled at Ada who had brought his food, well it kind of represented food, to the table.

"Yeah, but am I guaranteed a spot?" Cyril asked anxiously.

"I dunno, you'll have to ask the guvnor won't ya?" Robert said as he sawed at the rubbery egg.

"I had better do son, if not I am in the right shit," Cyril said as he stood, tapped Robert on the shoulder and walked to the back of the café shaking his head forlornly as he did.

He finished as much as his stomach could handle, then left the café to make his way to the Black Cat nightclub, where for the first part of the evening, he was on the door, and then at midnight he was a doorman for the private game, which he despised, a room full of gangsters, all paranoid that the others were cheating, all of them wearing weapons for fear of one turning on the other, and most of the time none of them would win because Philpott had rigged the game. Robert felt sorry for old Cyril, who always fancied himself as a bit of a player, the others all took advantage of that, the bastards! Robert thought to himself as he walked through the back entrance of the club. He turned and noticed the bloke that was watching his digs earlier, he smiled at him and then saluted!

CHAPTER 11

Peggy was so nervous, she hadn't seen William for nearly six months and now he was coming to London to see her. Martha had been just brilliant, she and Peggy moved another single bed into Peggy's room to make it a twin, Martha's idea! Martha had given Peggy odd jobs around the place when she wasn't out searching for Robert, to pay for her board and lodgings, that way she did not have to spend a penny of Carrie's inheritance.

Martha was a wonderful person, and Peggy knew only too well that she wanted Peggy to stay, to quell her loneliness, her husband had been killed in action during the war, and since that day she had dedicated her life to making her guests as happy as she could.

Every evening they would sit down discussing where Peggy had been in her search and whom she had spoken to, Martha all the while taking notes, they would rule people and places out, Martha had powerful contacts, but even they could not locate Robert.

"Peggy darling, your cab is here," Martha called up the stairs to Peggy.

"Coming," she replied as she took one final look in the mirror before she ran down the stairs.

"Jolly good luck," Martha said as she kissed Peggy on the cheek.

She was waiting on the platform, an incredibly sweet guard allowed her to go through the gate. She inhaled deeply as the train from Edinburgh pulled up alongside the platform. She watched as the hordes of people disembarked, she tiptoed so that she could see over the top of traveller's heads, but she still couldn't see him. The platform soon cleared, leaving Peggy and a guard the only people remaining. She looked up and down, sighed, and then walked towards the gate.

"Peggy!" she heard, it was him, she recognised his voice immediately. She turned and watched as he ran towards her and as he got to where she was standing he dropped his case and lifted her up, swinging her around, holding her close. "I have missed you so much Peg," he whispered in her ear and then kissed her.

Peggy told William all about her search, about Martha, how she had looked after her, about some of the miserable places that she had to visit and all about the close calls she had when she was walking the dark London Streets alone. When they walked in Martha couldn't have been more welcoming, despite the fact that she knew all about William, the evenings when she and Peggy had sat in front of the fire and told each other of their lives, yet still, she welcomed him with open arms, and she did it for Peggy.

They went up to the room and William instantly noticed that there were twin beds and not a double, he looked at the beds and then at Peggy. "She has no double beds,"

Peggy lied, knowing that Martha would back her up. "Anyway, how was Christmas?" Peggy asked as she sat on the edge of her bed, William sat down beside her.

"It was awful, Mum and Dad fought the whole time, while Wilf and Shona sat together all loved up," he sighed.

"They are still going strong then?" Peggy said in amazement, William nodded.

"Aye they are getting wed in a few months, I take it that you will come back for the wedding?" he said with just a hint of sarcasm in his voice. Peggy smiled and nodded.

"Of course, I wouldn't miss it for the world," she said and grinned, William was now wearing an expression of great angst.

"What's wrong? I thought that you would be happy about that," Peggy said, fearing that something was very wrong.

"Peg," he began, Peggy was nodding frantically in anticipation of what was coming next. "I have something to tell you," he sighed, not making eye contact, instead looking at the floor. Peggy's heart sunk, he was going to tell her that he wanted a divorce, that he and the trollop were madly in love. "Peggy," he said trying to gain her attention.

"What is it William?" she asked anxiously.

"It's Jean, she's pregnant," he said ashamedly. Peggy stood and walked to the window, at that very moment she could not possibly look at him, her legs were trembling, her heart was racing, and she desperately wanted to scream at him, to hit him, but she mustered every ounce of self-control and instead she sighed. She turned and looked at his pathetic persona, full of self-pity, she shook her head in disgust. "Peggy, please, just say something, anything," he begged.

"I hope that you will be very happy together," she said quietly and again turned to watch the heavy traffic from the window.

"What do you mean? I don't want a divorce," he replied anxiously.

"Well I do," Peggy said still watching from the window. William jumped up and walked to stand behind her, he placed his hands on her shoulders, which she shrugged, to move him away.

"Do not touch me, how dare you come here, knowing how hard it is for me, trying every waking moment to find my brother, and you come here and land this on me, you selfish bastard!"

"Peggy please,"

"That is the only reason that you came here isn't it? How many times William, how many times did it take to make the trollop pregnant? Have you slept with her in my cottage? In my bed? WELL HAVE YOU?" Peggy turned and shouted in his face. He grabbed her at the top of her arms.

"Peggy calm down," He said through gritted teeth.

"Let go of me or I will scream!" She seethed, he loosened his grip, and she walked back to her bed. "I want you to leave, leave London, and leave my cottage," she whispered as tears sprung into her eyes.

"I am not going anywhere, I have to prove to you that I have changed, I don't want to be with Jean, I love you, Peggy, please you have to believe me," he said as he sobbed.

"I will ask Martha to move you to another room, I cannot bear to look at you," Peggy said as she wiped the tears away and left the room.

Peggy spoke to Martha and explained what had happened, she wasted no time at all preparing a separate room for William and once he had moved his things into the other room, they sat in the dining room waiting for supper to be served.

Martha came out of the kitchen and laid another place setting at Peggy and William's table, Peggy looked at her and frowned.

"Why I hope there are no objections to joining you both on this wonderful spring evening," she said and winked at Peggy, she smiled, then looked at William, who was looking very gaunt and almost grey in colour.

"Have you been feeding yourself properly?" Peggy asked when she noticed how much weight he had lost.

"Sometimes," he mumbled, as Peggy shook her head.

"Why didn't you eat at your mum's if you couldn't be bothered to cook for yourself?" Peggy asked as Martha sat at the table and smiled. William was about to answer, then looked at Martha and decided against it, so he stayed silent throughout the meal. After they had eaten Peggy got up and cleared the table, then began to clear the other diner's tables, it was how she paid for her keep, so she left William in the trusted hands of Martha.

They retired to Martha's private lounge, once the tables had been laid for breakfast, a ritual that they did every evening since Peggy's arrival, there was a small fire lit, and the air was surprisingly mild for early March, Peggy was thinking as she loosened the neck of her sweater. Peggy and Martha were in deep discussion about the search for Robert, William just sat and listened.

"Have you gone back to where we went before?" William asked, Peggy, nodded.

"Yes, not too long ago," she replied.

"Did you go back to the shop?" He asked.

"Shop, what shop?" Peggy asked.

"You know, the newsagents, where that funny man was talking about gee gee's," William said and looked at Martha who was now frowning.

"I'm sorry, he was talking about gee gee's. What on earth is that?" She asked and hiccupped from the overindulgence of sherry. Peggy burst out laughing.

"Aye I remember now, he was talking about betting on horses," Peggy said as she laughed.

"Oh, I see, how odd," Martha replied as she walked over to the drinks cabinet and poured herself another sherry.

"I had completely forgotten about that shop," Peggy said as she thought back to that day.

"Well, I could do with some air, do you fancy a walk, maybe walk that way and see if it is still there?" William asked, praying that Peggy would say yes, he desperately wanted her all to himself. Peggy looked at the clock, it was nine-thirty, then she looked at William's face, he was wearing his sweetest smile.

"Aye go on then, not for too long mind, I have breakfast to serve in the morning," Peggy said as she stood up.

ROBERT

The club was pretty full, and Robert felt as though he needed eyes in the back of his head, not that anyone in there would play up, not if they had heard about Jack Philpott's reputation anyway, Robert was thinking.

"Do you want a pint Bob?" he heard a familiar voice say.

"No cause I'm not eighteen yet am I ?" Robert said and smiled. Frosty rubbed the top of Robert's head, while his girl Rita nudged him in the ribs.

"Don't do that Mick, you'll embarrass the poor lad," she scorned and flattened Robert's hair. With that, Jack

Philpott approached them and nodded at Robert, meaning that he wanted him to follow, which Robert did. They walked out to the back office, where Jack sat in the chair behind the desk.

"Shut the door and sit down," Jack ordered, which Robert did. "I want you to stick old Cyril tonight," Jack said as he lit a cigar, blowing the smoke into Robert's face, he had always relished in belittling Robert, even when they were both so young, mind you Old Man Philpott used to pay Jack to beat Robert up, just for entertainment, Robert was thinking to himself as he wafted the smoke from his face.

"No not me, why can't you get Frosty to do it?" Robert asked, he couldn't hurt old Cyril, in any case, Robert owed the man for hiding him from the old bill after the fight with 'what do you know Joe,' he thought. Jack slammed his hand on the desk, making the desk jump into the air and things on top fall to the floor. He got up from the chair and walked around the desk, grabbing Robert by the cuff of his shirt.

"No, I won't fucking get Frosty to do it, you are going to do it, RIGHT!" Jack snarled, Robert nodded his head frantically, Jack's grip was getting tighter by the second. Jack released him and returned to his seat.

"The game will be rigged, Cyril will be quid's in, he borrowed a ton to play. When he collects his winnings and leaves, you will be waiting around the corner from the café, stick him in the back, take the cash and bring it back here, do you hear me?" Jack said as he studied the blade of the knife he was now holding. Robert nodded, and then Jack

136

passed him the sharp-edged knife. "Do not lose this, wipe it, then hide it in your sock," Jack continued, again Robert nodded.

"Right, fuck off now," Jack said and gestured to the door, Robert walked back out into the club not knowing what to do. He hadn't signed himself up for this, his involvement was never his choice, he couldn't stab Cyril, he couldn't stab anyone, he was thinking when Frosty and Rita reappeared.

"What did the boss man want?" Frosty asked and gestured to Philpott's office. Robert shook his head.

"Oh, he just wanted to give me the heads up about the game tonight," Robert sighed as he watched Philpott parade around the club as though he was the most important bloke in the world.

"Which poor bastard is it tonight?" Frosty asked. Robert looked at him suspiciously, why all the questions, had Philpott put him up to it, trying to sniff him out, seeing if he would squeal, Robert was thinking, if that were the case it would be a real shame, Mick Frost had been Robert's closest ally, he took him under his wing, and taught him everything about the game.

"I dunno, he just said to keep a close eye on a few of them," Robert mumbled, now distracted as he watched as Philpott bullied a pretty young lady into joining him for a drink, Robert could clearly see that she was not interested in Philpott, she was looking at Robert, but by his reputation alone she would dare not say no.

Later that evening Robert gulped when he watched old Cyril walk toward him. He winked at Robert and then walked to the bar, wearing an unusual cheeky grin, usually, Cyril would wear an expression of anguish. Philpott called them all to the private room at the back of the club. Now Robert had the biggest decision of his life to make. Did he stay and undertake what was ordered of him? Or did he cut his losses, take his chances, and run, he was thinking as he watched from the door, as the game began to unfold.

Cyril was winning every other hand and was becoming really cocky, which was irritating Philpott, everyone in the room could tell. "Fetch me a drink will ya," Cyril said and held his empty glass in front of Phillpotts face. He pushed the glass down to the table and then gestured to Robert, who walked over to the table.

"Get him what he wants will ya," Philpott sneered. Robert nodded took the glass and left the room. This was his golden opportunity to get out. He walked out to the staff room, placed the glass on the worktop, quietly opened the fire exit door and slipped out. He walked around the corner, avoiding the front entrance of the club and walked in the opposite direction, trying to not act suspiciously. He continued to walk hastily for a few minutes, making his way towards Hammersmith bridge, he needed to get to the other side of the river, he was thinking, when he heard footsteps, slowly he turned and saw two men walking behind him, one of them he recognised from watching his digs, he quickened his pace, trying to get where there were more people, if there was a hit out on him, they wouldn't be so stupid to do it in front of witnesses, he turned again, and they had both quickened their pace. Then all of a sudden, a woman who was walking on the other side of the bridge screamed out. "WATCH OUT!" Robert turned as one of the men lunged towards him with a knife, quickly Robert bent down and grabbed Philpott's knife from his sock, waving it around as he stood. The other man was now behind him, pulling Robert's arms tight behind his back forcing him to drop the knife. The other man went to lunge at him again, and then it happened. The man holding the knife was somehow suspended in the air and then thrown across the bridge to the other side. The young woman screamed out again as she ran over to Robert and the man holding him. A man who was walking with the woman then blew a whistle and shone a torch into the eyes of the attacker, who dropped Robert and ran. The young woman grabbed Robert's hand and began to run, back in the direction that she had come, the man with her followed behind, checking every few seconds to ensure that no one else was following. They ran along the road, turning various corners until they came to a terrace of Georgian houses. They stopped, all breathless from the constant running, Robert was bent double trying to catch his breath, as too was the man.

He looked up at the young man and woman and smiled.

"I don't know who you are, and I don't know how to thank you. You have just saved my life," he said sincerely. He looked at the young woman as tears ran down her cheeks. "Don't cry love, look I'm alright," Robert said and winked.

"I have no idea where I am gonna go now, but I'm still alive and kicking, thanks to you two," he said cheekily.

"You are coming with us," The woman said and held out her hand. Robert placed his hand in hers and felt a sense of familiarity as she led him up the stone steps to the impressive house.

"What, you live here?" Robert asked, I mean they didn't look short of a bob or two, but they didn't look like the gentry folk that owned these types of houses, Robert was thinking as the woman opened the door and gestured for him to go inside.

Chapter 12

"Oh my, what on earth is going on?" Martha cried as Peggy and William entered with the young man. Peggy gave Martha a knowing nod. "Quickly, take him through to the lounge," Martha said and led them through the door marked PRIVATE.

Peggy gestured to the sofa, and Robert reluctantly sat down, it was the poshest place that he had ever been in, well he had been in posh places before, but was never allowed to sit down, he was thinking, now it was just him and the young woman.

"Is your name Robert Wells?" Peggy asked gently. Robert looked at her suspiciously.

"Who wants to know?" he asked, all the time thinking that they must be the old bill.

"My name is Peggy, I travelled to London six months ago from Scotland to find my wee brother, Robert Wells," Peggy said tearfully, knowing full well that he was indeed her Robert.

"What? Eh? You mean, you're my sister Peggy," Robert said, clearly shaken and his voice breaking with emotion. Peggy who was now sobbing nodded her head as she took the seat beside him.

"You're my Peggy," he sobbed as he gently touched her face. She threw her arms around him and held onto him for the longest time, how she had longed for this moment, every second of every day, for fifteen long years she had waited. The emotional reunion was broken up by Martha and William walking through with a tray full of sandwiches, cakes, and a pot of coffee. Robert moved back wiping the tears away as he did. Martha placed the tray down on the highly polished coffee table and smiled.

"Peggy, I will retire now and leave you good people in peace. Robert it has been an absolute pleasure to meet you and I simply cannot wait to become better acquainted with you, " she said and smiled, then passed a key to Peggy. "It is the room beside yours dear," she said and left the room.

"Thank you, Martha!" Peggy shouted out, hoping that she heard her.

William poured the coffee and passed them around, while Peggy dished out the cake, Robert seemed to be overwhelmed.

"So, who are you?" Robert asked William as he sat in the armchair.

"Oh, how rude of me, sorry, Robert, this is William, my husband," Peggy beamed. Robert held out his hand and shook William's hand, smiling as he did.

"And where's mum?" Robert asked as he took a sip of the hot coffee, burning his tongue as he did. An immense wave of sadness swept over her as she now realised that she had to tell him, about her mum, and about Carrie.

"I am really sorry Robert, but she died nine years ago," Peggy said sadly. Robert looked at the floor and nodded.

"So what happened to you when she died? Robert asked, there were so many questions that he wanted to ask, so many things that he needed to know.

"I was sent to live with our Grandmother Carrie," Peggy replied and looked at William, who gave her a reassuring smile. Robert looked up and looked at Peggy.

"Who's side is she on?" he asked.

"She is our father's mother," Peggy said and smiled as she thought about Carrie.

"I take it that you left her at home then," Robert said and laughed. Peggy solemnly shook her head.

"She died two years ago, nearly three," Peggy replied.

"So, it's just you and me then kid," Robert said and winked.

"There is so much that I have to tell you Robert, and tomorrow, I can't wait to begin," Peggy said as William yawned. Peggy looked at the clock it was two in the morning. "So now, I'll show you to your room, get yourself a good rest and tomorrow, we can spend the day catching up ok," Peggy said as she took his empty cup from him. William took the tray out to the kitchen and washed the dishes, while Peggy showed Robert where his room was.

She climbed into bed and yawned, she had to be up at six! She felt compelled to look toward the window and smiled when she saw her. Carrie was wearing her biggest smile.

"I knew that you would do it, Peggy I cannot tell you how proud you have made us all," Carrie said before she faded into the curtains. Peggy closed her eyes and drifted off to sleep.

She stepped out of the kitchen into the dining room and jumped when she saw Robert standing at the window, peering out of the side of the curtain.

"I never put you down as a curtain twitcher," Peggy said and chuckled.

"Nah, you see that bloke over there on the corner?" Robert said and pointed. Peggy nodded. "He is part of the firm that I work for, I reckon that Philpott has sent him to stick me," Robert said nervously as still, he watched Frosty walking back and forth desperately searching for him. Peggy was now completely confused and had to sit at a table to clear her thoughts.

"So what is a firm?" Peggy asked naively. Robert chuckled.

"I forget that we come from very different backgrounds," Robert said through the laughter, all the while, watching Frosty's every move. "Do you know anything about the London firms?" He asked, Peggy, shook her head.

"Do you mean like Selfridges and department stores like that?" she asked, now Robert roared with laughter as he shook his head. "The squire sold me to a notorious London gangster, he runs illegal bookmakers everywhere on the West side of the river, it is a way of cleaning dirty money see," Robert said, trying to explain, but confusing Peggy all the more. "I was his lookout, five years old, I must have been the youngest gang member in the world!" Robert said and shook his head.

"What is dirty money?" Peggy asked thinking to herself that they had maybe dropped it in a puddle or something, but she didn't want to say it for fear of making a fool of herself.

"It's money that has been earned illegally, it's a way of pushing it back through the system, without the old bill getting a whiff of it," he continued. Peggy smiled and nodded, she was still none the wiser, but the more he spoke about it, the more confused she became.

"So, you're a gangster?" Peggy asked apprehensively. Robert, who was still intently observing from the window, shook his head.

"I just did as I was told Peg, do you mind if I call you Peg?" He asked.

"Of course, I don't silly!" Peggy said and laughed.

"Yeah well, I just did as I was told, but I wanted out see, and when I told the guvnor, he told me to stick an old boy, I couldn't do it, so I ran, and he put a hit out on me, and you saved me," Robert said. Peggy frowned and nodded, she sort of got the gist of what he was saying.

"'Ere, what's she up to?" Robert asked as he pulled the curtain back more. Peggy walked to the window and watched as Martha approached Frosty, standing with her hands on her hips, Peggy shrugged, then shook her head. Martha said her piece, Frosty swiftly walked away and she returned to the house.

"I told him to go away, that he has no business here," Martha said as she walked into the dining room.

"Shit!" Robert said under his breath and shook his head.

"Peggy would you be a dear and put the toast on for me," she said and smiled.

"Of course Martha," Peggy replied and walked to the kitchen.

"Robert please," Martha said as she sat down at a table and gestured for Robert to join her, which reluctantly he did. "I have a very close friend, who is Chief inspector in Scotland Yard. When Peggy arrived, I made some enquiries, I was told that the force was watching a notorious gang and believed that you had been used for child labour from a very young age, which I now know is correct. That gentleman, whom I have just spoken to is an undercover police officer, and he was checking in, seeking assurance that you are safe, you see, today they are to begin the raids," Martha said as Robert looked at her wide-eyed. "I assured the officer that you would travel to Scotland for a few weeks, let the dust settle so to speak, then you can return here if you please and board with me," Martha said and smiled.

Robert looked at Martha suspiciously. "You're secret service aint ya?" he said and grinned a cheeky grin, Martha smiled, and then winked as she got up and left the table to join Peggy in the kitchen.

William walked in and sat at the table with Robert, who smiled as he sat down. "I hope you don't mind Bill, you don't mind if I call you Bill do you? William chuckled and shook his head. "Yeah, where was I? Oh, that's it, apparently, I am coming to Scotland for a few weeks, *to let the dust settle,*" Robert said imitating Martha's voice, making William roar with laughter.

"That's great Bob, you don't mind if I call you Bob, do you?" William said and Robert creased up with laughter.

"I like it, me and you are gonna get on, I can see it," Robert said as he laughed.

"Peggy, could I have a few moments of your time, I need to speak to you in private?" Martha asked. Peggy looked around the busy kitchen.

"What about the breakfasts?" she asked.

"Lucy and Hilda can manage, can't you?" Martha replied and looked at the two women, Lucy smiled and nodded, and Hilda on the other hand huffed and continued to grill the bacon. Peggy followed Martha through to the private lounge.

"Please sit down dear," Martha asked, Peggy, gulped nervously, she had never seen Martha behave like this before, but she sat down, nevertheless. " I have a slight confession to make," Martha began as Peggy frowned, "I may have been a little erroneous," Martha continued hesitantly. Peggy didn't understand, so she shook her head.

"I am part of an organisation, my late husband was too," she began and smiled, Peggy returned the smile and Martha exhaled nervously.

"We, or should I say I, work in connection with Scotland yard, and yesterday I received a call which concerned Robert. The gang that has been using Robert for child labour are today being raided. That gentleman outside is an undercover policeman, I have assured him that Robert will return to Scotland with your good self and William, once the dust settles Robert can return and board with me," Martha said and smiled. Peggy's face lit up.

"Or maybe, he will choose to stay with me," Peggy said her voice full of hope and happiness.

"Indeed, maybe he will," Martha said and tapped Peggy's knee, she was thrilled to see Peggy so happy, she had grown so fond of her.

Later that day William had gone to the station to book three tickets for the following day, while Peggy and Robert sat in the lounge, Peggy told Robert how she had cared for their ailing mother, then after she died, how her life with Carrie panned out, she told him about Carrie's life, her magical ability, and the sacrifices that she had made. Robert shook his head and then looked at Peggy. She wasn't sure if he believed her, so she said that she would show him the grimoire and the chest on their return to Scotland.

"It's funny Peg, but I always knew that this day would come, it was like I have already seen it," Robert said and smiled.

"Me too!" Peggy said excitedly.

After dinner, the four of them retired to lounge as always. William and Robert sat at the table and played cards while Peggy and Martha sat on the comfortable sofas in front of the fire and chatted.

"I will miss you so, my dearest Peggy," Martha said sadly. It was at that moment that Peggy realised that she was going back and what she was going back to! She would miss Martha and in a strange kind of way, she would miss London too, it had become her home for the last six months, and Martha had been so kind, but if nothing else, she knew that she would leave with incredibly fond memories.

How was she going to hold her head up high back home, knowing that behind her back, folk would be laughing at her, knowing full well that William had impregnated Jean bloody Douglas, knowing full well that Peggy could not have children of her own, how would she be able to face people, she was thinking as tears formed in her eyes. Martha could see, she tapped Peggy's knee and then looked at William, and then Robert.

"I say, shall we get out and catch a breath of fresh air Peggy, just you and I?" Martha asked, Peggy quickly wiped the tears away and nodded gratefully.

They walked along the road towards the park and once they reached it, they sat on a bench that overlooked the river.

"It worries you going back, doesn't it?" Martha said, Peggy nodded.

"I have had the most wonderful time here, Martha I really have and that is all down to you, but I must go back, it is my home," Peggy sighed.

"Well of course you do my dear, you must return and hold your head high, for you have done nothing wrong. William on the other hand should be the one, who hangs his head in shame. You are one of the most wonderful human beings that I have had the pleasure to meet Peggy and you deserve nothing better than the best!" Martha said and smiled as she wiped her tears away. "And of course, you will return happy in the knowledge that you now have Robert in your life, which I am sure will make all the difference concerning William's behaviour," Martha said and placed her finger aside her nose, making Peggy chuckle.

"Will you come and visit?" Peggy asked. Martha nodded frantically.

"Why of course I should love to!" She exclaimed, making Peggy smile.

"I mean the cottage is not as grand as your beautiful house, but it is cosy and it's clean," Peggy said and smiled.

"Peggy my darling, if it is yours I am sure that it is simply wonderful, now come along, there is a spring chill in the air, and I have a bottle of sherry frantically calling for me!" Martha said as she pulled Peggy to her feet, and they returned to the house.

Early the following morning, with tired eyes and a heavy heart, Peggy turned and looked at her room for the last time, she wiped the tears away, inhaled deeply and then walked down the sweeping staircase, to be met by Martha waiting for her.

"The boys are already in the cab, come now young lady, you do not want to miss your train," Martha said as she shooed Peggy out of the door. Peggy opened the door, and as the driver threw her case into the trunk, she turned and looked at Martha, "Thank you, Martha, from the bottom of my heart thank you," Peggy said in the most heartfelt way.

"Get off with you!" Martha said as she wiped the tears that were running freely down her cheeks. She walked back inside, closed the heavy door, and sobbed.

Robert was incredibly excited, he had never ventured out of London and everybody that was travelling on the same train was fully aware of that. Every few seconds he would shout "Cor" or "Look at that!" as he watched the landscape changing, Peggy spent most of the journey laughing at him, and William too.

"I need the lav," Robert stood and said loudly, all the other passengers tutted or shook their heads.

"It's just at the end of the carriage," William said and pointed to the left.

"Nice one Bill" Robert replied as he opened the compartment door and whistled as he headed towards the toilet. William leaned into Peggy's ear.

"Where is he going to sleep?" He whispered. It hadn't even crossed Peggy's mind, she was just so happy to be taking him home. She shrugged her shoulders.

"You will have to move in with me, no funny business though, I have not forgiven you, William," She whispered and frowned. William hung his head and nodded as Robert returned from the toilet.

It was dark when the cab pulled up outside the cottage, so Robert couldn't really see it in all its beautiful glory. They walked inside, William turned on the lights and lit the fires, while Peggy filled the kettle and put it on to boil. She showed Robert to his room after William had quickly cleared his belongings out. He looked around the room and smiled.

"What a lovely home you have Peg," he said and smiled.

"Thank you, the bed is really comfy, it used to be mine when I cared for Carrie," she said and pointed to the bed. Robert ran to the bed and took a running jump at the bed, which he overshot and landed with a thud on the floor on the other side. Peggy squealed with delight as she thought back to when they were both small and would have competitions to see who could jump the highest on their beds, being scolded by their mum for making so much noise, oh it was so good to have him back in her life she was thinking to herself, as he picked himself up and brushed himself off.

CHAPTER 13

Completely exhausted from the travelling and the events of the past few days, Peggy, William, and Robert retired to bed with a hot cup of cocoa each. Peggy took her nightclothes into the bathroom to change, she certainly did not want William getting the wrong idea, and once she had changed she slipped in under the crisp, clean sheets. William was already in bed at that point, and he smiled as she pulled the blankets up and sipped her hot drink.

"What a day that was yesterday, eh Peg," William said, deep in thought.

"Aye, I'm just so grateful that we finally found him!" she replied and smiled.

"No, there is no we about it, that was all down to your own persistence and perseverance," William said.

"I cannot take all the credit, if you hadn't suggested that walk, we would never have been on that bridge, oh, I have been meaning to ask you, where did the whistle and torch come from?" Peggy asked. William chuckled.

"I always have them in my pocket on the farm, you know when it gets dark, or one of the sheep is misbehaving. When I got dressed in the morning I put them in my trouser pocket, probably out of habit!" William said. Peggy yawned and placed her cup on her bedside table, snuggling beneath the warm blankets.

"Night," she said sleepily as she soon drifted off to sleep.

The following morning, the bright sunshine woke Peggy as it streamed through the curtains, she sat up, stretched, yawned, and climbed out of bed, leaving William fast asleep and snoring! She was in the kitchen, waiting for the kettle to boil, while she waited at the door, enjoying the fresh air, it felt so good to be back, inhaling the beautiful, clean Scottish air, she was thinking, when Robert walked out into the kitchen and was watching her, she gestured for him to join her.

"Do this," she said and inhaled deeply, he looked at her as if she were stark raving mad, but did as she asked, nevertheless. He took in a deep breath, held it for a few seconds then exhaled, smiling as he did.

"Feels good doesn't it," she said, Robert nodded and then followed her into the kitchen.

She poured the water into the pot, "Do you want some porridge?" she asked. Robert looked at her in bewilderment, then screwed his nose up.

"What is it?" he asked.

"What? You have never had porridge! You don't know what you are missing young man," Peggy said as she poured the oats into the saucepan and added the milk.

"How come you talk so posh, was mum posh?" Robert asked as he sipped the tea that Peggy had poured him. Peggy chuckled.

"It's since she's been staying with Martha, the poshness must have rubbed off on her," William said as he walked through the kitchen, kissed Peggy on the cheek and poured himself a cup of tea. Peggy howled with laughter when she realised that William was right, her use of language had improved so much!

She handed two big bowls of steaming porridge to them both. William smiled, he loved the way that Peggy cooked porridge, she always made it just right, while Robert sniffed it, looking rather confused. William opened the jar of strawberry jam, placed his spoon into the jar and pulled out a large spoonful, which he placed in the middle of his porridge, as Robert watched intently. Robert, then took a small spoonful, not quite sure if he liked it, then dished a large spoonful of jam into the centre of the bowl and stirred it around, tasting it again, this time he smiled and tucked in.

"That there is a proper Scotsman's breakfast Bob, it will certainly put hairs on your chest," William said as he scooped the last of the porridge from the bowl and looked at Robert.

"I don't think that I need any more Bill, what do you reckon?" Robert asked as he opened his shirt to reveal his incredibly hairy chest.

"Put it away will you, my flowers will start to wilt," Peggy said and laughed as she nudged him. Robert laughed, and so too did William.

"What are we up to today then?" William asked and looked at Peggy.

"I need to pop to town and fetch some groceries, the pantry is empty, so I thought that we could walk in and show Robert around," Peggy said and looked at Robert who nodded in agreement, then William.

"We can't," he said and frowned.

"Why ever not?" Peggy asked.

"We can't walk,"

"Of course, we can, we always do," Peggy replied. William stood up, put his empty bowl in the sink, grabbed hold of Peggy's hand and walked her into the lounge, walking her up to the window, he pulled the curtain back and gestured for her to look.

"What?" she asked as she looked at him wearing a blank expression.

"Today, we will drive to town," he replied and pointed to the car that was parked outside of the cottage. Peggy frowned.

"I don't know what you are getting at," she sighed.

"The car, it's ours," William announced proudly. Peggy was still frowning. "I passed my test while you were away, and mum and dad brought us the car," he said and grinned.

"Really! Oh William that's wonderful!" Peggy said and hugged him. William looked at Robert, who was standing behind Peggy, tiptoeing so that he could see over the top of her head.

"You can teach me!" Robert said cheekily and winked.

"Aye, that I can Bob, that I can," William said.

Later that morning they all climbed into the car and drove to town, Peggy was holding on for dear life, all the while thinking that William definitely needed to practice more often! William parked the car, well it kind of resembled being parked, and then the three of them walked to the high street. They went into the greengrocers, where Peggy introduced Robert to Angus, they chatted for a few minutes and then left. Standing out on the pavement, came the moment that Peggy was dreading, she needed to go to the butchers, but she did not wish to face Reg, she had written to him so many times and had received not one single reply, then she saw Shona's car park up outside her house.

"William, you take Robert to the butchers, I just want to see Shona," Peggy said and handed William the shopping list, then ran across the road towards Shona calling out her name as she did.

"Peggy!" Shona shrieked with delight as she watched Peggy run towards her and into her open arms. They hugged and then Shona stood back and looked at Peggy.

"You are looking well, London life certainly suits you," she said and grinned.

"Aye, I'm glad to be home though, I hear that you and Wilf are getting hitched," Peggy said and smiled.

"Yes, I want you to be Matron of honour," Shona replied as Peggy squealed and they jumped up and down.

"I would love to," Peggy said happily.

"Oh hello, who is that?" Shona asked as William and Robert walked towards them. Peggy laughed.

"That's my wee brother Robert," Peggy announced delightedly.

"Get away, what that handsome chap there is your brother," Shona said as she gazed at Robert, making Peggy roar with laughter.

"Shona this is my brother Robert," Peggy said and stood aside. Robert walked to Shona and kissed her on the cheek.

"Hello love, pleased to meet ya," he said cheekily, Shona was left standing with her mouth gaped open.

They left Shona and walked to the bakers, William and Robert waited outside, the shop was so small. Mrs McCutchen was placing Peggy's order into a box when she suddenly blushed and cleared her throat, Peggy turned and was faced with Jean. She glared coldly at her.

"Back then," she sneered into Peggy's ear, and Peggy nodded.

"It appears so," she replied and faced the counter once more.

"I must say, you should really buy some new bed linen, I was covered in scratches, oh no sorry I forgot, that was what William did in the throes of passion!" she said and laughed loudly. Peggy turned, now filled with rage, and put her face into Jeans, not wanting to bring attention to either of them.

"I will not stoop to your level, I will not hit a woman with child, but, YOU will not be pregnant forever Jean Douglas, and my god once you have had that child, if I were you I would get as far away from here as possible, I cannot be held responsible for what I might do to you, do you hear me," Peggy said through clenched teeth.

"You can keep William, he is a nasty piece of work, I quite like the look of him though," She sneered and pointed to Robert who was now chatting to Reg and Stan outside.

"You stay the fuck away from him, do you hear, because if you don't I will finish you, baby or no baby," Peggy said quietly.

"She is no longer pregnant Peggy, I heard that it was Gin and a hot bath," Mrs McCutchen said and grinned at Jean. Peggy nodded and smiled, then turned.

"May your God help you, Jean Douglas," Peggy sneered, as she grabbed her box from the counter and walked towards the door. Jean grabbed her arm.

"It wasn't the gin and bath that did, it was that animal out there, he shouldn't be allowed near women," Jean sneered. Peggy held her head high and continued to the door.

"No more than you deserve Jean Douglas" Peggy heard Mrs McCutchen say, and she smiled to herself as she joined the group of men outside of the bakers.

"Hello Peggy, you are looking well!" Stan said and smiled.

"Thank you, Stan, how have you been?" Peggy asked awkwardly, trying her hardest not to make eye contact with Reg.

"Not bad hen, can't complain, all the better for seeing you though," he said and nudged Robert, who laughed. Jean walked out of the bakers and barged into William scowling at him as she did, then she turned and looked at Robert.

"Well aren't you a sight for sore eyes," she said provocatively. Robert raised his eyebrows, and looked at Peggy, judging from her expression there was no love lost there.

"Shame I can't say the same about you then innit," Robert replied, making all of them laugh, as Jean scurried along the pavement with her head hung low.

Back at the cottage, Peggy was preparing the pie filling, while William took Robert out for a driving lesson, she was green with envy, how dare William muscle in on her time with him, she wanted to spend as much time as was physically possible getting to know him, they had so much to catch up on, she thought as she sang along to the radio. Unforgettable began to play, it was her and William's song and it took her back to their first dance together at the hall. That night ended in disaster because of Jean Douglas too, she thought. What did she mean when she said that it was William's fault, that there was no baby? Had he forced her to have an abortion? Or had he hit her? Peggy was thinking as she placed the pot of meat and vegetables onto the hob and turned it on. She drink the remainder of her tea, placed the lid on the pot, and then walked back to the table to collect her cup, knocking it over as she did, spilling all of the remaining tea leaves into the saucer.

"Butterfingers!" she muttered to herself as she walked to the sink. She turned on the tap and placed her cup into the soapy water. Then something on the saucer caught her eye. The tea leaves had formed together in the shape of a boxing glove. She swilled the remnants of tea around, and they made the form of a person bending over. Peggy shook her head and rinsed the saucer under the running tap before placing it in the sink. She couldn't get that thought out of her mind, she knew it, she knew what it meant, she just needed to hear it from him, she knew better than anyone, what a foul temper he had, she needed to pick her moment, she was thinking, when they walked through the back door, chatting, and laughing.

"How did he do?" Peggy asked and smiled, Robert was positively buzzing with happiness.

"Really well, the boy is a natural," William said and kissed Peggy on the cheek. She wished that he would stop, she didn't want him anywhere near her, especially now, he was only doing it because he knew that she wouldn't want to cause a scene in front of Robert, she was thinking.

"Hmm, what's that smell?" Robert asked as he sniffed the steam coming from the bubbling pot on the hob.

"It's the pie filling," Peggy replied and smiled, then there was a knock on the door. Peggy wiped her hands on her pinny and walked to the front door. She stood back and smiled. It was Mrs Tanner and her daughter wee Heather.

"Hello," Peggy said and smiled.

"I hope that you don't mind Peggy, Mrs McCutchen told me that you were back, and I really need some of that tea that you make, my problem has got so much worse since you've been gone," she said awkwardly.

"Aye, of course, come on in and I'll fetch you some," Peggy said, opening the door wide, letting them walk past her. She took them through to the kitchen.

"Sit yourselves down, I won't be a wee minute," Peggy said and pointed to the table. William put his head around the door.

"I'm just going to take Bob to the pub to meet my dad and Wilf," he said and smiled, Peggy scowled, there he was again, taking over, anyone would think that he didn't want her to spend any time with Robert, she thought to herself as she walked to the workshop, swearing to herself as she did.

She walked back into the kitchen and smiled, even though she didn't feel like smiling. "Would you like some tea?"

Peggy asked as she passed the bottle of dandelion tea to Mrs Tanner and then filled the kettle.

"As long as it's no trouble," Mrs Tanner replied and smiled. Peggy walked out to the pantry and grabbed the biscuit tin, luckily she had brought some shortbread from the bakers earlier, she placed a few fingers onto a plate and put it on the table, she looked at wee Heather and smiled.

"Help yourself," Peggy said to the small shy girl, who beamed a large smile.

"Dinee tell her that for God's sake, she will polish the lot off!" Mrs Tanner said and laughed. Heather reached over and grabbed two fingers of shortbread. "What do you say, young lady, where are your manners?" Mrs Tanner scolded.

"Thank you," Heather whispered, and Peggy smiled.

Peggy placed the dinners on the table in the dining room and scowled at William, then she sat beside Robert, who had already begun to tuck into his meal.

"Oh my God Peg, this pie is delicious. You should come to London and open a pie and mash shop, you would make a killing," Robert said with a mouth full of food, making Peggy laugh. She spent the remainder of the evening ignoring William, just chatting to Robert about his life in London.

"Blimey, there was that sort from the bakers in the pub earlier, she aint half got a problem with Bill," Robert said as he thought back to earlier.

"Yes it appears so, why is that William?" Peggy asked smugly and looked at him. He scowled at Peggy, then sighed.

"You know damned well why Peg, it's because you beat her to it," He said and laughed. Peggy shook her head and growled, then looked at Robert who was watching William intently, it was almost as if he was weighing him up, Peggy thought to herself.

"So did we live around here, you know when we were kids?" Robert asked, Peggy, smiled and shook her head.

"No we lived in the highlands," she replied.

"How come our Gran lived here, but our folks lived up there then?"

"Our dad took a job on a farm way up in the far north, he wanted to get away from here," Peggy replied.

"Was he in a bit of bother then?" Robert asked, Peggy, chuckled and shook her head.

"No, but as I told you before, trouble followed Carrie, he didn't want us to grow up like he had to," Peggy replied sadly, her thoughts turning to Carrie. "The farm next door belonged to our mum's parents back then," Peggy continued.

"Are they still there now?" He asked.

"No, after our mum Tilly moved away, they missed her too much, so they moved to the highlands to be closer,"

"Where are they now then?" Robert asked. Peggy sighed and shrugged her shoulders.

"I don't know, after I was sent here, I never saw them again," Peggy replied sadly.

"Were they around when mum died?" Robert asked. Peggy shook her head.

"No, they used to visit, but then they stopped, not long after you were sent away,"

"So you had to deal with it all by yourself then," Robert asked sadly. Peggy smiled a sad smile.

"Aye, but at least she had me, eh," She said.

"I'm sorry that I wasn't there to help," Robert said as tears formed in his eyes. Peggy moved closer and put her arm around his shoulder.

"I'm sorry that you weren't there full stop, I tried to stop her from sending you away, I begged and begged, I truly did," Peggy said as the tears ran down her cheeks. Robert threw his arms around her and hugged her. When he leaned back, he wiped the tears away and laughed.

"We're a right pair you and me, aint we?" he said, and Peggy laughed and nodded.

CHAPTER 14

For the next few weeks, Peggy took every opportunity to spend as much time as she possibly could with Robert, they got on so well, and despite growing up in completely different circumstances, they were very similar in many ways.

Martha had called and told Peggy that it was now safe for Robert to return to London, and as much as Peggy desperately wanted to keep that information to herself, she just couldn't, she had to tell him, she was thinking to herself as she washed the breakfast dishes, gazing out of the window, the cottage garden looked beautiful, with the early spring flowers in bloom. The daffodils were standing majestically, reflecting the rays of the sun, which gave the appearance of illumination, almost as though the sunshine was coming from within the centre of each flower.

"Any tea in the pot Peg?" Robert asked as he had finally managed to drag himself out of his bed and join her in the kitchen. He kissed Peggy on the cheek, and she looked at the kitchen clock, shaking her head and tutting.

"I don't know how you can stay in bed for so long, doesn't the sunlight make you want to leap out of bed?" Peggy asked brightly. Robert laughed and shook his head.

"No!" he replied exaggeratedly,

"You don't know what you are missing, there is nothing better than waking early, standing outside listening to the symphony of the dawn chorus, taking in the fresh crisp morning air, and feeling the new-born rays of the rising sun," she replied dreamily.

"Have you been reading that poetry book again?" Robert asked and laughed as he filled the newly rinsed-out teapot with the boiling water from the kettle.

"Well, I might have done," Peggy said and laughed.

"Ah, my Peg, you're such a romantic at heart aint ya," Robert said as he smiled such an endearing smile.

"I spoke to Martha last night," she said as the smile left her face.

"Everything alright?" He asked,

"Aye, she says that you are all right to return now, I mean there's no saying that you must, I would be more than happy for you to stay here with me," Peggy said beseechingly. Robert looked up, frowned, and then touched her cheek.

"You know that I have loved every minute of being here, getting to know you, but my life is there Peg, I have to go back," he said sadly. Peggy attempted to smile and nodded knowingly.

"Aye, I know, I can live in hope though, can't I?" She sighed.

"Of course, you can, anyway, you have to promise that you will come to the smoke, and I can show you around the city properly," Robert said, his eyes lit up at the very thought of returning to his home town, Scotland was beautiful, and Peggy well, she was just the most wonderful person that he had ever met, but he missed London, and couldn't wait to get back there, he was thinking.

"Ooh, I'd like that very much! You will stay for the party though, won't you?" Peggy asked anxiously.

"When is it?"

"This Friday, please say that you will, I just know that Jean Douglas will make an appearance and I could do with the backup," Peggy said, then she could have thumped herself, what had she just said? She thought as she winced. Robert nodded.

"Yeah, course I will, but what is the issue with you and that bird?" Robert asked, Peggy had the feeling that he already knew, but she dared not say anything, just in case he didn't.

"She has always had a fancy for William, she hates me because he picked me over her," She replied quickly. Robert looked at her suspiciously.

"I'll get the train on Sunday then, gives me a day to get over it," he said and winked.

"Over what?" Peggy asked dumbfoundedly, Robert laughed and placed his cup and saucer on the worktop.

"What are we up to today then?" He asked, rapidly changing the subject.

"Shona will be here at eleven, she is going to drive us to Nessie," Peggy said excitedly.

"Eh?"

"Loch Ness," Peggy replied and laughed.

They spent the entire afternoon around the Loch, it was the most beautiful spring day, and the three of them had such fun. They were sitting on the shoreline of the Loch, when Peggy looked at her wristwatch and gasped, making both Shona and Robert look at her anxiously.

"What's wrong?" Shona asked.

"We must go, I have to cook the tea," Peggy said as she began to panic, the last thing that she wanted to do in Robert's last days there, was to upset William and cause a scene.

"Peg, it's only half three," Shona said and frowned.

"Aye, but I can't be late putting it out," Peggy said, her heart now racing, Robert picked up on her anxiety and looked at Shona, frowning.

"Why can't you?" He asked, still frowning.

"William likes his tea as soon as he gets in from work, he works hard you know," Peggy snorted, trying her hardest to portray a woman defending her husband, yet all the while, she would happily leave him there to rot! She was thinking.

"So we can grab some fish and chips on the way home, my treat," Shona said and smiled as she nudged Peggy with her elbow. "What do you say?" she continued, Peggy smiled and nodded.

Robert ran out to the car, with the newspaper-wrapped dinner, for fear of it getting cold and Shona drove like a maniac back to the cottage, no sooner had Shona pulled up outside the cottage, than Robert jumped out of the car and ran to put the food into the oven, as Peggy climbed out, Shona grabbed her arm.

"He won't cause a scene, he is scared of Robert, Wilf told me," she whispered. Peggy smiled and exhaled, Shona must have been reading her thoughts, she was thinking as walked up the path to the cottage with their arms linked.

How wrong she was! They walked in and the atmosphere could be sliced with a knife. Robert was leaning up against the kitchen sink, scowling at William who was sitting at the table, reading the farmer's almanack. "I have put the oven on Peg," Robert said, not taking his eyes off of William, she smiled and then looked at William as she tied her pinny around her waist.

"Have you had a good day?" Peggy asked him as she filled the kettle, he completely ignored her.

"William, I said..."

"I know what you said," he mumbled, not averting his eyes away from the small magazine.

"Well?" Peggy asked again nervously and then looked at Shona, who shook her head in disbelief, he was most definitely playing with fire, she was thinking to herself as William continued to ignore Peggy. That was it, Robert had seen enough. He calmly walked to the table and sent his fist thumping down, knocking the magazine out of William's hand.

"My sister is asking you a question," Robert sneered in Williams's face, which had now turned a deep scarlet colour. William got to his feet and turned to Peggy.

"Yes, I have had a great day," He growled through gritted teeth, turned, and left the kitchen, walking towards the lounge. Robert looked at Peggy, then moved to follow him, she grabbed his arm.

"Please Robert, leave it, for me," She begged, it was clear to see that Robert was absolutely seething, and Peggy did not want trouble. Robert inhaled deeply and nodded.

"I'll leave it, Peg, for now, for you, but let me tell you this…" He was saying when William walked out of the lounge and up the stairs. "I need some air, call me when the grub is ready," Robert said and walked out of the back door, slamming it behind him.

Peggy looked at Shona wide-eyed as she slid into the chair and held her head in her hands. Shona sat opposite her and moved her hands away. "So much for my theory," Shona said and then mouthed sorry as the telephone in the hallway began to ring, making Peggy jump. She ran to it and answered it.

"Peggy darling it's Martha,"

"Oh hello Martha," Peggy replied awkwardly.

"I say is everything alright? You sound rather anxious," Martha said, Peggy nodded, not realising that Martha could not see through the telephone. "Peggy, Peggy," Martha said concernedly.

"Yes, yes sorry Martha, I think that there is something wrong with the line," Peggy lied.

"Oh, I'll make it quick then, is Robert there? I did ring a little earlier, William said that he would tell him to call me back," Martha said.

"Hang on, I'll go and grab him," Peggy replied as she placed the receiver onto the table and called out to Robert, who came in and grabbed the phone, smiling at Peggy.

While Robert was speaking to Martha, Shona laid the table while Peggy warmed the plates. As she closed the oven door, William walked through the kitchen towards the back door, then he opened it.

"Where are you going, tea is ready?" Peggy asked meekly.

"To the pub, I'll have mine later," he growled as he slammed the back door closed. Peggy looked at Shona, and exhaled with relief, she was happy that he had gone to the pub at least they could eat their meal in peace, she was thinking as Robert, who had finished the call with Martha walked back into the kitchen.

"Where's he gone?" Robert asked.

"Pub," Shona replied.

"Come on let's eat, I'm starving," Peggy said as she took the hot plates from the oven and carried them through to the dining room.

"Peggy, we need to talk about this," Robert said with a mouth full of fish. Peggy shook her head.

"Can we at least eat first, please," she asked, he smiled and nodded, Shona then very cleverly turned the conversation around by discussing her wedding plans.

After the meal Shona helped to clear the dishes and then left, she was supposed to be helping her Mum prepare the buffet food for the engagement party! Which left just Peggy and Robert in the lounge, in front of the fire.

"So Peg, what is his problem, does he wallop you?" Robert asked angrily. Peggy shook her head as she looked at the rug, unable to make eye contact with him.

"No, he is just set in his ways that's all," Peggy lied, she hated the fact that she felt the need to lie to her brother, but if he knew the truth, he would kill him, and she didn't want that.

"If he ever so much as lays a single finger on you, tell me and I'll rip him apart with me bare hands," Robert seethed, Peggy nodded and smiled nervously, she could now see a huge similarity between him and Carrie at that moment, which made her smile.

"You are so like her," Peggy said,

"Like who?" Robert replied,

"Carrie, she had a temper," Peggy laughed,

"I won't have him hurting you Peggy, no woman deserves that, especially not you," he said and smiled.

The next few days were really fraught in the cottage, Robert would not speak to William, and William would not speak to Peggy! Then the evening of Shona and Wilf's engagement party arrived, which filled Peggy with even more dread, she knew William only too well, and when he had a drink he thought that he was a great warrior, he claimed to be the reincarnation of Robert the Bruce, but Peggy knew only too well, that he could not fight his way out of a paper bag, well unless he was fighting against a woman!

William went to his parents straight from work, so Peggy and Robert made their way to the farm at seven, the evening was warm, so they decided to walk. The sky had the most beautiful colours running through it, all pinks and lilacs, Peggy was looking up, not watching where she was going and fell down into a ditch. Robert started to panic as Peggy yelped out in pain, he grabbed hold of her and pulled her to her feet, but she could not put weight on her foot, her ankle was now doubled in size, and Robert was becoming hysterical, not knowing what to do! A van was driving along the road, so hastily Robert ran into the road, waving his arms around frantically, the van ground to a halt and Peggy winced when she saw that it was Reg.

"What's happened? Are you alright Peg?" He asked as he walked over to where she was sitting.

"She went down a ditch, over on her ankle, I think that she has done some damage, look at the size of it," Robert said as he paced back and forth. Reg bent down to inspect Peggy's ankle and winced when he saw it.

"I think we'd better get you to the infirmary Peggy, it looks like it could be broken," Reg said as Robert now stood beside him. They lifted her up and helped her get into the van, Robert sat in the back, amongst the empty delivery boxes.

It was busy in the infirmary, Reg sat beside Peggy, and Robert paced back and forth until finally she was taken for an x-ray. As the porter wheeled her away, she called out to Reg. "Will you go to the party and tell William what has happened, he will be wondering where we are?" She asked anxiously.

"Of course, I will, then I'll come back to take you both home," he called back as he raced towards the exit.

A young nurse spotted Robert and could see that he was on the brink of hysteria, he had never cared for anyone in his life until now, and here she was in the hospital, unable to walk, he felt so helpless. The nurse walked over to him and tapped him on the shoulder. "Come with me, I think that you could do with a cup of sweet, strong tea," she said sweetly as she led him by the arm to the staff cafeteria, where she ordered him his tea.

"She's in the best possible place, you know," The nurse said as they walked back to the waiting room, Robert had insisted.

"But what if she dies?" He muttered, making the nurse laugh.

"She's not going to die, at worst she has fractured a bone and will be immobilised for six weeks," the nurse said, still laughing, Robert sighed when he saw Peggy in the wheelchair, back in the waiting room. He bent down and kissed her cheek.

"Well?" he asked.

"It's a bad sprain, that's all, the doctor has strapped me up, and says that I must rest it for two weeks," she said and smiled. Reg came running back through the doors, he smiled at Peggy.

"Not broken then?" he said breathlessly, Peggy shook her head and laughed.

"No, just a bad sprain that's all," she said and smiled. "Did you manage to see William?" She asked, which brought an immediate frown to Reg's face.

"Aye, I saw him all right," he sneered, Robert looked at Reg, in anticipation of what was coming next.

"Did he not come back with you?" Peggy asked disappointedly. Reg shook his head.

"Come on then, let's get you home and rested," he said and raised his eyebrows at Robert, who then knew that there was most definitely something that Reg was not telling Peggy. They helped her into the van and as Robert walked to the back doors he looked at Reg.

"Well?" He asked, Reg shook his head.

"He was all over mean Jean, I told him about Peggy and they both laughed and said that at least she wouldn't spoil their fun," Reg growled angrily.

"Before you take Peg home, can we stop off at the party?" Robert asked, Reg nodded and drove towards the farm. Peggy looked at Reg when he stopped.

"What are we doing here? She asked.

"Oh, I dropped my delivery sheet for tomorrow, it must have happened when I was telling him about you, Robert has just gone in to grab it for me," Reg lied and turned the van around so that they were facing the lane and not the farmhouse.

Robert ran inside and sure enough, there he was all over Jean like a rash. Shona spotted Robert and ran towards him, grabbing his arm.

"You won't cause any trouble will you?" she asked anxiously, Robert looked at her briefly, pulled his arm away and walked to William.

"A word, outside," Robert leaned in and said. William laughed as he pushed Jean off of his lap.

"Ok then big boy," William slurred and swayed as he followed Robert outside. As they walked out, Robert grabbed William by the throat and threw him up against the wall.

"You fucking disgust me! I am taking Peg to London with me on Sunday, you don't deserve her, you aint nothing but a piece of shit," Robert screamed into William's face.

William threw himself forward in a vain attempt to strike Robert, but Robert pulled his fist back and with one punch sent William to the ground, unconscious. Robert quickly ran to the van and jumped inside, as Reg sped off.

They carried Peggy into the cottage, Robert made her comfortable on the sofa and attempted to light the fire, to no avail! Reg made some tea and then helped Robert to light the fire as they sat around Peggy.

"I have a confession to make," Robert said coyly. Peggy looked at him suspiciously and then chuckled.

"You hit him, didn't you?" she said, Robert nodded.

"Sorry, it's just that, well he don't deserve you, Peg, I know that he knocks you about and when I saw him all over that old sort, I lost it. I told him that you are coming with me to London," Robert said.

"I can't, Robert," Peggy sighed.

"Why can't you? The rest will do you good, if you stay here you'll have no chance to heal, you be too busy running around after that spoiled wee bastard!" Reg said. Then he bent down beside Peggy. "And that way, I can come to London and visit you," he whispered. Peggy looked into his big brown, genuine eyes.

"Why did you never write back?" she asked.

"Because I don't know how to read or write," he whispered back.

CHAPTER 15

Before he left the cottage, Reg had gone to the linen
cupboard in the hallway upstairs and grabbed sheets and
blankets for Peggy, making her as comfortable as he could
on the sofa, he bid Peggy and Robert a goodnight and left.
Robert decided to sleep in the armchair so that he could
keep watch in case William returned.

The following morning after a restless night, Peggy opened
her eyes, Robert was not in the armchair and his blanket
and pillow had gone. She swung her legs around, then
putting her good foot down, attempted to get up. The pain
coursed through her leg, forcing her to fall backwards onto
the sofa. She was not relishing being incapacitated, she was
the one who did the caring, and she hated having to put on
people, she became so frustrated in her thoughts that she
pushed herself up once again, swallowing the pain and
limped out into the kitchen.

She laughed out loud when she saw him, her wee Robert,
standing at the sink, wearing her lilac polka dot pinny,

washing the dishes. "The colour suits you," she laughed as he turned and looked at her frowning as he did,

"Oi you, what are you doing, you have been told to rest!" Robert said as he dried his hands on the towel and walked toward her.

"I can rest out here, I don't want to sit in there all by myself," she sulked as she awkwardly sat on the chair, pulling another out to elevate her still incredibly swollen ankle.

"Alright, have it your way," Robert said and smiled as he poured her a cup of tea from the pot.

"I must say, you make a very good nurse maid," she said chuckling.

"Right, what do you want me to pack for you?" Robert then asked, Peggy frowned.

"Eh?" she asked.

"For London,"

"Oh, if I had a stick I could use it to help me climb the stairs, you'll never pack it properly Robert, and then all my clothes will be creased and unwearable," Peggy said as she looked around the kitchen, then she remembered.

"Robert would you be a love and go to the dining room, I am pretty sure that Carrie's old walking stick is in the corner?" Peggy asked, Robert, saluted and did as she asked, returning a few seconds later with said walking stick. He handed it to Peggy and laughed as he watched her struggling to get up off of the chair.

"Do you want a hand?" he asked as he laughed.

"No, I can bloody well do it myself!" she scorned as she attempted it once again, this time she managed it. "There see!" she said and smiled, as she did the telephone rang.

"I'll get it," Robert said and ran to the hallway. "Hello,"

"Put Peggy on," William growled.

"I don't think that she wants to talk to you," Robert said and looked at Peggy, who was shaking her head. The bastard, she knew that his facade would not last, how dare he make her look like a complete fool once again, she was thinking, then she realised that she had to speak to him, she had to tell him to collect his belongings. She looked at Robert and began to nod frantically. "Wait, you still there?" Robert growled down the silent phone.

"Aye"

"She does want a word," he said as he handed the receiver to Peggy.

"William," she said as she trembled from head to toe.

"Aye, when is he going?" he asked.

"Tomorrow,"

"Good! I'll be back then," he said firmly.

"No, you don't understand," Peggy said as she inhaled deeply, ready for the reaction. "I want you to come back today to collect your belongings before I go," She said nervously.

"WHAT?" he roared, Peggy moved the receiver away from her ear, and Robert then grabbed it from her.

"She wants you to get your stuff out of her cottage, and she wants you to do it today, do I make myself clear?" Robert said forcibly.

"I'll send Wilf for it, put her back on," William ordered, Robert laughed and shook his head.

"I don't think so mate, she aint got anything else to say," Robert said and replaced the receiver back down, rubbed his hands together and looked at Peggy smiling.

"Right, pudding, let's get you upstairs, you pack your bits and I'll throw his into his case," He said as he helped her towards the staircase. She looked up at the narrow stairs which filled her with dread at the thought of having to climb them, she thought back to Martha's beautiful winding staircase and thought about how much easier that would be. She made her first attempt, but it was far too painful. She leaned on her stick and cried out in frustration.

"Peg, why don't you sit on your bum and push yourself up backwards with your good leg?" Robert suggested and then gave her a demonstration. She smiled and then before she knew it she was at the top, using the post to pull her to her feet. She nodded and smiled at Robert then made her way to the bedroom. She threw her case onto the bed and began filling it with clothes when a macabre thought crept into her mind. What if, in her absence, William broke into the cottage? Or even worse, what if he and Jean moved in?

"I can't go to London," she said still lost in her thoughts. Robert closed the case and looked at her.

"What do you mean? Of course, you can go," Robert said and shook his head.

"I can't Robert, what if he moves her in here?" Peggy said despairingly.

"I can tell you most definitely, that under no circumstance will that ever happen!" Peggy heard Carrie's voice, she turned to look in the direction of the voice so too did Robert.

"How do I stop it?" Peggy asked Carrie, who was standing beside the window. Robert looked at Peggy and then at the window.

"I have had a word, Abe will return tomorrow and keep watch until you return," Carrie replied and then faded away. Robert looked at Peggy once again and then back to the window in disbelief.

"Who the heck was that? And who the hell is Abe?" he asked as he looked back and forth to Peggy, then to the window, Peggy roared with laughter.

"You mean, you could see her?" she asked. Robert's eyes glazed as he nodded slowly, recollecting that moment once again.

"And hear her," he replied, still dazed.

"That was Carrie," Peggy replied.

"What? You mean, our grandmother Carrie, dead Carrie?" he asked fearfully, which made Peggy laugh all the more.

"Aye," she laughed.

"So who is this Abe then?" He asked.

"He's our grandfather," Peggy said and smiled, a warm fond smile, how she had grown to love that man, despite all of his faults.

"Is he dead?"

"No, he is still very much alive," Peggy said as her eyes lit up at the thought of seeing Abe again. It had been nearly three years since she had seen any of them, and she missed them all so much!

Wilf arrived at the exact same time as both Reg and Shona. Robert grabbed the case and almost threw it at Wilf who was waiting at the door. "Hey, don't take it out on him, he is nothing like William!" Shona shouted defensively as she walked up the path.

"Sorry mate, no hard feelings eh," Robert said and held his hand out to shake. Wilf stared coldly at him, ignoring the gesture, picked up the case and without a word walked back down the path. "Well you can't say that I didn't try," Robert said as he moved to allow Shona to squeeze past him.

"Yes, yes you did," she sighed as she headed for the lounge.

"How is she?" Reg asked as he now stood at the door.

"Come on in, you can help me make the tea," Robert said and held the door wide open. Reg walked into the kitchen and Robert followed him in, as Reg filled the kettle. "She's using a walking stick to get about," Robert said and smiled, Reg chuckled.

"I bet she hates that," he laughed, Robert nodded as Shona walked into the kitchen.

"Making quite a habit of being here aren't you Reg?" Shona said and raised her eyebrow in a disapproving manner.

"Aye, not that it's any of your business Shona," he said as he walked past her and into the lounge to speak to Peggy, he had waited all morning, he was desperate to see her.

"How's the wounded soldier doing?" He asked. Peggy looked up at him and smiled the widest smile.

"All the better for seeing you young Reg," she beamed, meanwhile in the kitchen things had taken a turn.

"Oi, what's your problem, I thought that you were supposed to be Peg's best mate?" Robert asked as he frowned.

"I am Peggy's best friend, but how are she and William ever going to make up, when Reg is always sniffing around?" Shona replied. Robert burst out laughing.

"That's a fucking joke! Pretty sure that William was all over that Jean at YOUR party last night, I never heard you say anything to her, the bloke is a fucking wanker, and he doesn't deserve Peggy, he is better suited to that old toby!" Robert roared.

"Look, I'm sure that you mean well, but you have only just met her, you don't know her as I do, you will swan off back to your seedy London life and leave her here, high and dry, she needs William," Shona replied.

"My seedy London life, you aint got a clue love, now it's obvious that you have been put up to this, I have seen it too many times before, so I suggest that you sling your fucking hook, do you hear me," Robert shouted, so loudly that Reg appeared at the kitchen door.

"Everything alright Bob?" he asked. Robert nodded his head.

"Yeah, Shona was just leaving, weren't you love," Robert sneered. She barged past both of them and almost flew out of the front door, slamming it behind her.

"What on earth was all that about?" Peggy asked as she hobbled into the kitchen.

"Bob asked her to leave, she was being rude about him and me," Reg said and winked at Robert, Peggy shook her head.

"I knew that would happen when she hooked up with him, they are all the same," She sighed.

Reg finished his tea and was about to take his cup to the sink when Peggy shouted and gestured to him to give her his cup, which reluctantly he did, whilst wearing the most puzzled expression. She swirled the dregs of tea around then turned the cup onto the saucer, studying the remnants as she did. Reg looked at Robert in bewilderment as Robert laughed.

"Look at that Reg, love is coming to you, look at that massive love heart," Peggy said and showed him it.

"Oh aye," he said, smiled at Peggy then frowned at Robert, making Robert laugh all the more. "Well, I had better be off, I've still got a few deliveries to make," Reg sighed. He kissed Peggy on the cheek.

"I'll be here at seven o clock sharp, make sure that you give me your telephone number in London," he said as he walked to the door.

Peggy managed to cook them a fry-up that evening, and she was just about to dish it up when the back door opened, and Abe walked in. Peggy screamed and desperately wanted to jump at him, but her ankle just would not allow her to!

"Peggy!" he said once he had finished hugging her, he leaned back and looked at her. "I can't leave you alone for five minutes can I?" he said and laughed. Robert ran out to the kitchen on hearing Peggy scream and smiled as he saw how happy she was at seeing Abe. He looked at Abe and shook his head, then looked again. Abe released Peggy from yet another bear hug and looked at Robert and gasped.

"Oh, my, goodness, you are the spitting image of your father," he said in disbelief. Robert smiled and nodded.

"And you have held your age really well," Robert replied as Abe opened his arms for a hug. Robert wasn't too sure about this, men weren't supposed to hug men, but reluctantly he did and was happy that he did, it felt right, it felt like family, Robert was thinking as he smiled.

Luckily Peggy had cooked enough to go around the three of them and after what seemed forever of talking, telling Robert stories, and catching up, Peggy looked at the clock and yawned, Robert grabbed her bedding and made her comfortable on the sofa, and almost immediately she was sound asleep.

"Well, that's awkward," Abe said as he walked to the sideboard and poured himself a brandy. "Would you like one?" he asked as he waved the bottle in the air.

"No ta, I'm not eighteen yet, and besides, I need to keep a clear head, in case that husband of hers shows up," Robert whispered. "And what's awkward?" He added.

"Oh, where am I sleeping, do you have any idea?" Abe asked as he sipped the brandy and smiled.

"Peg said that you could have her room, the bedding is clean," Robert replied, Abe, nodded.

"So tell me about William," Abe said as he swirled the brandy around the glass in deep thought.

"Blimey, where do I start, should I tell you that he knocks her about, sorry he hits her," Robert corrected himself for fear that Abe who was very well-spoken, would not understand him. Abe chuckled.

"I understood the first time, I was married to Carrie, you know," he said and laughed. "Anyway, please continue," Abe added, desperate to discover how the past couple of years had been for Peggy.

"He was having it off with some old sort from the town, Jean her name is, got her in the pudding club, then Bill apparently walloped her, and she lost the kid, but the other night, there was a party, that's when Peg hurt her ankle, Reg the butcher went there to tell him about Peg and that Jean was all over him, so on the way back we stopped, I went in, took him outside and slapped him," Robert said, brimming with satisfaction at the very thought of it. Abe was sort of frowning and smiling at the same time, which confused Robert, he really wasn't quite sure how to read him.

"Thank you, Robert," Abe said and smiled,

"The pleasure was all mine," He replied and grinned. "Anyway Abe, how is it that you look so young?" Robert asked, Abe, chuckled.

"She hasn't told you then," Abe sighed. Robert looked at him bewilderedly.

"Eh?"

"Has she spoken about Carrie and myself?" Abe asked.

"Well, she told me that you were both magical and that you were madly in love, but because of your magic, you couldn't stay together, something along those lines anyway," he replied. Abe nodded.

"It runs far deeper than that, and I can tell you this Robert I am not proud of the way that I treated Carrie, I took her for granted and she certainly did not deserve that. I am part of an organisation called the Guardians of Albion, and because of that, I will not age until I have served my purpose," Abe said hoping that Robert would understand.

"I've never even heard of them, are they a London firm?" he asked, Abe, laughed loudly, causing Peggy to stir.

"No Robert, we are based in the South West, and we are not a firm, well not as such," he laughed.

Robert did not really have a clue what he was talking about, and he made that quite apparent, Abe looked at him and could see so much of both Carrie and his son Albert in him, which he found so endearing.

"Listen, Robert, because of my work, I will stay here until Peggy is due to return, but I must leave before she gets back, I am taking a great risk in being here now. I would love nothing more than to get to know you properly, but for your own safety, that is not possible, what I will say, however, is that I am so happy that Peggy has found you, and now I can continue with my work, safe in the knowledge that you will take care of her for me," Abe said sadly.

Robert nodded, he kind of understood, and if he were to be completely honest, he didn't know this bloke from Adam, so it really made no odds to him, he was thinking.

"Of course, I'll look after her, she's the only thing that I've got," Robert said, looked at Peggy was still sound asleep and smiled, the most endearing smile!

CHAPTER 16

The following morning Peggy, Robert and Abe were waiting for Reg in the lounge, they heard the horn beeping, Peggy sighed and looked at Abe, "You won't be here when I get back will you?" She said knowingly, Abe smiled a sad smile and shook his head, Peggy placed her arms around his shoulders and held him for the longest time, not wanting to ever let go, she had been incredibly fortunate to have had this time with him, and she knew that this would be the last time that she ever saw him. He touched her cheek as his eyes filled with tears.

"Go on, you don't want to miss your train," he said and helped her to the door, Reg was now waiting at the door, and he took over from Abe, taking her arm and helping her to the van. Abe looked at Robert endearingly.

"Thank you, Robert, it has been an absolute pleasure," Abe said as he held out his hand.

" Nah, bugger that!" Robert replied as he placed his arms around Abe and held him tightly.

"Have a safe journey, and take good care of Peggy," Abe called out as Robert ran out to the van. He watched the van drive up the road, then saw a car parked at the end, he stepped out and walked to the end of the path, he could clearly see that it was William sitting in the car, and Abe's first reaction was to run to the car and give him a bloody good hiding, as he ran, William spotted him, started the engine, and drove away, leaving Abe standing in the middle of the road shaking his fists in anger.

Peggy also recognised the car and as they passed it William glared at her, she turned and looked at Reg in horror.

"Peg, it's fine," he said, smiled and tapped her on the knee, but as he drove towards the station, he could see that William was now on their tail, "Robert," Reg called out to the back of the van.

"Yeah,"

"It appears that we have company," Reg said and looked again. Peggy looked in the wing mirror.

"Oh No! this is all we need," she cried as Reg pulled up outside the station.

"You wait here, Robert and I will get the cases out and then I'll come back for you, oh, Peg, it might be a good idea to lock the door," Reg said and gestured to the silver button on the door, she pushed it down and huffed. Reg climbed out, walked to the back, and opened the doors for Robert, who climbed out and immediately looked at William, who was now parked opposite. He wasted no time at all in running towards the car, William being the coward that he was, drove away hastily. Robert laughed, then walked back to the van.

They waited on the platform, they only had a matter of minutes until their train was due. Peggy gulped as she saw it coming along the tracks towards them, and she looked at Reg. "You will come to visit, won't you?" She asked anxiously.

"Of course, I will, next weekend," he replied and smiled as Peggy handed him the note with Martha's telephone number on it. He kissed her on the cheek, shook Roberts's hand and then waved at them as the train continued on its journey to London.

"Oh my darling Peggy, you poor thing!" Martha declared as she watched Peggy struggle to climb the stone steps.

"I'm fine Martha," Peggy said breathlessly as she reached the top step, using a stick made walking so much more hard work, she was thinking as Martha took her arm and walked her into the house. Peggy smiled when she was taken into the lounge, Martha had moved a chaise longue in there so that Peggy could comfortably convalesce.

"Sit yourself down, I'll fetch the tray," Martha said as she fussed around Peggy like an old mother hen. Peggy sat on the chaise longue and looked at the table that Martha had placed beside, it was piled high with books that Martha knew Peggy would enjoy, she was such a kind, thoughtful lady, Peggy thought as Martha returned with a tray followed by Robert who was carrying another tray, loaded with cakes and scones.

"Robert, I hope that you don't think me presumptuous, but I have a friend who has the contract to construct new offices in the finance sector of the city, your name came up in conversation and he said that he would like to employ you," Martha said coyly as they had their tea. Robert grinned and looked at Peggy.

"Really, that's brilliant Martha, doing what?" he then asked, making Martha chuckle.

"He would like to train you in all aspects of building works, with the aspiration that you will become one of his site managers, in due course," she replied and smiled.

"Brill! When do I start then?"

"Tomorrow morning, he will pick you up at six thirty sharp," Martha replied.

"Nice one! But I aint got the gear for it," he replied and frowned.

"I have put suitable clothing and footwear in your room," Martha said. Robert jumped up, threw his arms around her, and kissed her on the cheek, making her howl with laughter.

So Robert was happy with his new job, Peggy was enjoying being spoiled rotten by Martha, and Martha, well Martha was just happy to have them there, they were the family that she could never have, being part of the secret service made it impossible, but now she had had the fortune of a chance meeting on a train and a new chapter in her life had begun.

Peggy woke and looked at the window, something that she did every morning, the sun was shining, and the birds were in full song, and then she remembered, Reg was travelling down today. The butterflies were somersaulting inside her empty tummy, as the excitement of seeing Reg in completely different circumstances and surroundings built deep within. She hobbled to the door, five days of rest and her ankle was well and truly on the mend, she could now walk unaided, which pleased her greatly, she slowly walked down the stairs and into the dining room for breakfast.

"Your ability to walk unaided has improved so much Peggy," Martha smiled as she placed a tea tray on the table.

"I know, hopefully, I will be able to help around here next week, you know, I must pay my keep," Peggy said smiling as she poured them both a cup of tea from the pot.

"Nonsense, I love having your company, and I would not dream of accepting payment of any kind for it!" Martha said and frowned. "Peggy, you have a certain glint in your eye, it would have nothing to do with a certain gentleman coming to visit, would it?" Martha said and laughed as Peggy blushed profusely, saying not a word.

All day long Peggy sat thinking about Reg, and how she wished that she had never married William, she should have taken Abe's advice and finished with him. How she wished that Reg had told her how he felt, long before, then she certainly would never have married William. She was sitting in front of the mirror at the dressing table, painstakingly removing the rollers from her hair, when there was a knock on the door, she looked at the time on her wrist watch and her heart jumped into her mouth.

"Yes," she called out, the door opened, and Robert walked in.

"Looking beautiful girl," he said as he kissed her on the cheek.

"Thank you,"

"I thought that I would let you know that I'm off to the station now to grab Reg,"

"Are you walking?" Peggy asked, Robert, laughed.

"Martha has ordered a cab," he said as he shot out of the door, she could hear his heavy feet running down the stairs.

Peggy was waiting in the lounge with Martha when the cab drew up outside, as soon as Peggy heard the engine cut, and the doors slam, her legs began to tremble. Martha was watching her, she walked over to the drinks cabinet and poured Peggy a sherry, passing it to her. "Drink it quickly, it does wonders for the nerves," Martha said hastily when she heard the front door close, Peggy drank the contents in one gulp, then burped really loudly, placing her hand over her mouth as she blushed, Martha roared with laughter. They seemed to be taking forever to come into the lounge, and Peggy checked the time, for what seemed like the fifteenth time, then the door knob turned, and Robert walked in alone. Peggy's face turned ashen, she had played this scenario out over one hundred times in her thoughts throughout the day and now all of her hopes and dreams had been dashed. Both Peggy and Martha looked at Robert, impatiently waiting for an explanation.

"I'm sorry Peg, he weren't on the train, he must have changed his mind," Robert said sadly. Peggy sighed, she was just about to have a rant about how she didn't like him that much when the door opened and Reg walked in, looking at Robert.

"Sorry Bob, I just couldn't do it, I have been waiting for this moment all week," he said as he walked straight to where Peggy was sitting, she awkwardly stood up, and he pulled her into his arms and kissed her passionately, she was lost in the moment, swirling through the fluffy clouds, until he released her, and she remembered where she was and who was also present. Robert wolf whistled as Martha cheered and clapped, Peggy, blushed and then laughed.

Peggy and Reg had been out for a short walk to the park on Saturday afternoon, and Peggy's ankle began to swell on their return, Reg sat her on the chaise longue and handed her a drink, he sat beside her and placed his arm around her shoulder.

"I wish that we could be like this always," Reg sighed. Peggy smiled and looked at him.

"Me too,"

"Maybe we could, what if we left Scotland, and moved here, we could be together always," he said excitedly. Peggy was deep in thought, he had a point, if they moved to

London, she could file for divorce, nobody there would know and more to the point, nobody there would care! Back home, they would be frowned upon, even though it was William who had been unfaithful and violent, she was thinking. She looked at Reg, he seemed so genuine, so caring, and he had the most beautiful eyes.

"Well we could do that, but wouldn't you miss home, you know and Stan?" Peggy asked. She had nothing to lose and no one to stay for, it would be far easier for her, Reg smiled.

"If I'm with you Peg, I need nothing else," he said and kissed her, just as the door opened and Robert walked through.

"Oi, oi, what's going on here then?" Robert said cheekily and laughed, making Peggy and Reg laugh.

"Where have you been?" Peggy asked as she looked at the many bags that he had placed on the floor.

"Up west, me and a few of the lads from work are going out tonight, " he said full of self-confidence. He never ceased to amaze Peggy, for years, he was forced to be part of a nasty gang network, who, when he wanted out, had put a hit out on him, yet it didn't faze him, in fact, it gave him more confidence, more reason to succeed.

"Very nice, where are you going?" Reg asked.

"Hammersmith Palais do you two want to come?" he asked as he danced across the floor like Fred Astaire, Peggy laughed.

"I would love nothing more, but unfortunately, my ankle will not allow it," She said and dropped her lip, making both Reg and Robert laugh.

"Oh poor Peg, never mind there's always next week," Robert said and messed up Peggy's hair.

"Robert!" Peggy growled as Reg laughed, her hair was now doubled in size.

"It reminds me of that windy day back home when you came into the butchers, do you remember Peg?" Reg said as he laughed.

"Yes, I remember Reg!" Peggy scowled.

"Enough of this idle chit-chat, I have a night out to prepare for," Robert said trying his hardest to replicate a posh accent, Peggy shook her head.

Robert was ready and rearing to go by six thirty, he wasn't meeting his workmates until seven, so he paced back and forth in the lounge, watching the clock every few minutes.

"Anyone would think that you may be a tad excited Robert," Martha said and laughed as she walked to the radiogram and turned it on, trying her hardest to tune into her favourite radio show, eventually she did, and she smiled and swayed when she heard one of her favourite songs being played, 'til the end of time' she sang. Robert ran over to her grabbed her hand, held her back and spun her around the room as she squealed with delight, well that was until she became so dizzy that she felt quite nauseous.

"Put me down!" She shouted and tapped his shoulder, he released her and helped her back into her chair, all the while laughing, he then looked at the clock.

"Time to go, have a lovely evening," he said as he danced out of the room. Peggy and Reg were still laughing as Martha sat in the chair nursing her giddy head.

"Such a loveable rogue isn't he," Martha said as she drank the remainder of the sherry in her glass and frowned at its now emptiness. Reg jumped up and poured her a refill, she graced him with a grateful smile.

Robert and his friends had been into a couple of pubs, had a few pints, then walked to the Palais, he had never been before, he had heard that it was always a great night, but had never ventured out of the usual haunts, it was too dangerous back then. He walked into the Hammersmith Palais and was immediately impressed, not only was the venue amazing, the women, there were so many of them, he was thinking as he looked around at them all.

They had been in the club for around forty-five minutes, when Robert decided to go for a wander, the lads from work were alright, but they were all quite a bit older than him and all they wanted to talk about was work! He ordered a drink and walked around, then he spotted her on the dance floor, she was the girl in the Black Cat club, who was being hounded by Philpott. He straightened his tie, put down his drink and then confidently marched onto the dance floor, he tapped the shoulder of her dance partner, who frowned and then walked away sulkily. She instantly recognised him as he took her hand and danced all around the floor with her.

"Are you a professional?" she shouted into his ear above the band. Robert laughed, he said nothing, just continued to dance. After a few minutes, he was worried that someone else might try to muscle in.

"Can I buy you a drink?" He asked. She nodded and they left the dance floor and walked to the bar. "What are you having?" Robert asked, she blushed.

"Just a lemonade please," she replied bashfully.

"I'll have two lemonades please mate," he shouted to the barman. She looked at Robert, her big blue eyes glistening in the light.

"You didn't have to do that for me, it's just that, I'm only seventeen," she whispered into his ear.

"Me too," he whispered back, and she laughed.

After a few more dances, Robert's feet were killing him. "Do you fancy a walk?" he asked. She nodded, so they walked to the cloakroom, collected their coats, and walked outside. "How are you getting home?" He asked as he slipped his coat around her shoulders. She only had a thin coat, and the air was damp and chilly.

"I only live around the corner," she replied and smiled as she snuggled into the warmth and the strong scent of his aftershave on his coat.

"Let's have a walk around the park and then I'll walk you home if you'd like?" He suggested, she nodded frantically, she had never met anyone quite like him before.

They sat on a bench looking out at the river and told each other all about themselves. Her name was Maggie, she was training to become a seamstress, and Robert thought that she was absolutely smashing!

When they reached her house she took his coat from around her shoulders and handed it to him.

"I have had a wonderful evening Bob, thank you," she said and smiled.

"So have I Mags, can I see you again?" he asked.

"Yes please," she said, he leaned in and kissed her gently.

"What about tomorrow, we could go out for dinner?" He asked, she nodded.

"I'd like that,"

"I'll pick you up at seven then," he called out as he skipped down the pavement, whistling as he did. He was floating on air, she was the most beautiful thing that he has ever seen, and she liked him! He had never been so happy!

He spent around an hour telling Peggy, Reg, and Martha all about this wonderful young woman, Peggy could clearly see that he was totally and utterly smitten.

"How wonderful! Robert darling you must invite her for supper, before Peggy returns to Scotland," Martha slurred after she finished what must have been her tenth glass of sherry.

"I will Martha thanks," Robert beamed, Peggy watched him, she felt warm inside seeing how happy he was, it was about time, she thought, he had seen enough suffering in his young life, and now it was his turn to for once find happiness, she was thinking, she looked at Reg and yawned.

"Would you like me to help you up the stairs?" he asked, noticing how tired Peggy looked, she smiled and nodded, so they said their goodnights and she hobbled up the staircase, while Reg stood behind her in case she lost her footing. They reached her room and Peggy leaned against the door.

"You know Reg, maybe leaving Scotland and coming here is something that we should both think about," she said, Reg did a small dance.

"Really Peg, you really mean that?" He asked his eyes alight with excitement.

"Aye Reg, I really mean it," she said and so he lovingly kissed her goodnight.

CHAPTER 17

She laid in bed for hours, thinking about Reg, and William, what should she do? Should she follow her heart and leave William, or should she stand by her vows and stay with him? These thoughts were constantly swirling around her head until eventually, she drifted off to sleep.

She could see blue flashing lights, she could see a smashed-up car in a ditch, and she could see an ambulance arriving.

"Peggy, breakfast is being served," she heard as she sat bolt upright, the images in her dream, still apparent. "Peggy, are you alright?" Martha called out.

"Yes I'm fine, sorry Martha I didn't get much sleep, I'll be down in a few minutes," Peggy replied sleepily, as she climbed out of bed and hobbled to the dressing table, her hair was a complete mess and she had to face Reg like that, if that didn't put him off nothing would she thought to herself as she ran the brush through her hair, making it twenty times worse. She slammed the brush onto the dressing table, growled as she got dressed, and then walked down for breakfast. Reg was sitting at the table waiting for her, waving his hands in the air, he was hardly going to go unnoticed, she thought, there was only one other table, with two guests on, she chuckled as she approached the table and kissed him on the cheek.

"I was beginning to think that you had changed your mind," Reg said, now feeling much calmer that she was there.

"You silly bugger, of course, I haven't," Peggy replied and smiled, Reg grabbed her hand and kissed it.

"When should we do it then?" he asked as Lucy placed their breakfasts in front of them, looking at them curiously.

"Shh," Peggy said and looked at Lucy in a 'don't say anything in front of her, she is like The news of the world' kind of way. Reg laughed. "We can go out for a walk after breakfast, what time is your train?" Peggy asked.

"It leaves at half past two," Reg replied solemnly, he desperately wanted to stay, to never go back. Peggy checked the time on her watch.

"Ok, well it's half past eight, so we should get a couple of hours out before your train," she said and smiled, which soon turned to a frown as she noticed Reg's expression.

"What's wrong, don't you want to go out?" She asked, Reg shook his head.

"It's not that, I don't want to go back," he sighed, looking down at his now empty plate.

"Hey, it's not forever, sure I'll be back on Friday," Peggy said as she grabbed his hand.

"Aye I know, but I won't be able to come near you, will I? You know what folk are like back home," he sulked, Peggy chuckled.

"Look, I promise that we will get things moving as quickly as possible, I will have to put the cottage up for sale, and tie up all the loose ends, and we have to find somewhere to live here," Peggy leaned over the table and said quietly, even so, Martha overheard. She smiled at them both and pulled out a chair at their table and sat down.

"I know that one shouldn't eavesdrop, but I caught the last snippet of your conversation," she said barely above a whisper, Peggy raised her eyebrow and Reg nodded. "You could both live here with Robert and me," she added, Reg seemed overjoyed at the suggestion, Peggy was unsure, she loved Martha and would love nothing more than to be close to Robert, but she was happy in her own company, she was too familiar with spending time alone and sometimes she became, well a little overwhelmed, she was thinking, then she looked at Martha and smiled. "Why don't you sleep on it? It is always an option anyway," Martha said, stood and cleared the plates away from the table. Reg then left to get packed, Peggy drank the last of her tea, and she looked into the now empty cup, it was almost as if the tea leaves were asking to be seen. She swirled them around, then turned the cup over onto the saucer. She lifted the cup and looked. There was what looked like a nasty storm cloud, and a bolt of lightning. She shuddered, then placed the cup onto the saucer and took it out to the kitchen.

Peggy and Reg spent a couple of hours walking, Peggy showing him the sights and chatting about the future, as much as she would love to just stay put, she knew that she had to return, she had to tie up the loose ends of the mess that she had left behind, but there was something else, something nagging away at her sub-conscience, something that she couldn't quite put her finger on.

That evening, Peggy sat miserably thinking about seeing Reg off on the train, how sad he looked, how empty she now felt, she was lucky, she was sitting comfortably in Martha's lounge, poor Reg had to endure hours of travelling before he could get home and comfortable. She thought about their last embrace, how he held her like he never wanted to let go, William had never held her like that, she knew that she had to leave, Reg was the man for her there were no two ways about it, she had finally made up her mind, which for a fleeting moment put a smile onto her miserable face. The door opened and Martha popped her head around, she had just returned from visiting a friend, as she always did on a Sunday.

"Peggy darling there is a phone call for you," Martha said, Peggy got up and followed Martha to the office.

"Hello," Peggy said as she lifted the receiver from the desk.

"Peggy is that you?"

"Aye, Shona, what's wrong?" Peggy asked as she heard the distress in her voice.

"There has been an accident, a terrible accident," Shona cried.

"What, what has happened?" Peggy asked as she began to panic,

"William and Wilf had gone to pick up their mum and dad from church, there was a bad storm, the car hit a tree and ended up in a ditch,"

"Oh No! Are they alright?" Peggy asked.

"William is in a critical condition in the big Infirmary, he's asking for you Peggy," Shona said. Peggy leaned back against the wall and slid down it.

"What about the others?" Peggy asked.

"They all died," Shona wailed, "Please Peggy won't you come back, I feel so alone," she sobbed.

"Aye, I'll be back on the earliest train tomorrow, I promise," Peggy said, Shona ended the call. Peggy sat shell-shocked on the floor, with the phone receiver still in her hands. How could this be happening? Why has this happened? She was thinking as the tears formed in her eyes. The front door opened, and Robert walked in whistling, when he saw Peggy, he ran to her.

"Eh, what's happened, Peg? Did you fall?" He asked anxiously as he picked her up and took the receiver from her, she was dazed, and she slowly shook her head, as Martha walked out, and jumped back when she saw Peggy.

"Was it the phone call darling? Peggy you must tell us," Martha asked as Robert looked at her bewilderedly. Peggy was still staring into mid-air, saying nothing. "I think that we ought to get her into the lounge," Martha added and nodded at Robert, who held her hand and walked her through the door marked private. Martha followed and was frantically rooting through the drinks cabinet, "Ah, here it is, I knew that it was here somewhere," she said as she poured a double measure of brandy into a glass and took it to Peggy, "Drink this, it's good for shock," Martha said pushing the brandy into Peggy's hand.

Peggy's trembling hand took it from Martha, and she drank the entire measure in one gulp, shuddering deeply as she did.

"It's William, there has been an accident, and he is in a critical condition," Peggy murmured.

"What kind of accident Peg?" Robert asked concernedly.

"His car, he was collecting his mum and dad from church, there was a storm, and the car hit a tree," Peggy trailed off.

"Oh, how awful! Are his parents alright?" Martha gasped, her hand over her mouth, Peggy shook her head.

"No, they and William's wee brother Wilf are dead," Peggy replied, she was still reeling from the shock.

"Shit!" Robert fumed as he watched Peggy, knowing that she would now return dutifully because she was so kind and so thoughtful, always putting others' happiness before her own.

The following morning, the cab collected Peggy at half past five to take her to the station, Robert was most insistent that he accompanied her, but she would not have it, he had a job to go to, and a new girl to woo, she wanted to do it by herself, she had to!

The train journey seemed to fly by, probably because she was dazed throughout, she had not slept a wink the night before, thinking about William's parents, Wilf, Shona, and William. She walked out of the station with a heavy case and a heavy heart, straight into the arms of an incredibly distraught Shona. They held each other for what seemed an eternity, then as they separated they walked to Shona's car.

"Do you want to go home, or to the Infirmary?" Shona asked.

"Infirmary," Peggy replied and in no time at all Shona had parked the car, in the car park. They walked to the main doors, Peggy's legs were trembling, her heart was pounding, and she was so scared. The last time that she had seen William, they were not even on speaking terms and now here he was, his life dangling by a thread, and she did not know how she felt, was she there because of duty? Was she there because she still loved him? Or was she there through guilt? All these thoughts and others were swimming around in her head as she walked towards the room where he was. She gulped as she walked to the nurse's desk. The nurse on duty instantly recognised Shona and smiled.

"You must be Peggy," The nurse said and stood up, "Come this way," she added and walked towards a door. She opened it and stood to the side beckoning Peggy to walk through. She gasped when she saw him, lying there, attached to different machines, his swollen eyes closed, his head covered by a bandage. Peggy looked at the nurse in bewilderment.

"He slipped into a coma this morning, but before that, he was constantly saying your name," the nurse said gently. Peggy sat on the chair that was beside the bed and took hold of Williams' limp hand, she thought about the times when she first met him, when he would whistle and she would know that he was there before she saw him, how he would tease her because she was shy and awkward and how he wooed her with his charm and his big brown eyes.

"If you talk to him, there is a chance that it could bring him out of the coma," The nurse said as she left the room.

"Why, William, why did it turn out like this," Peggy sobbed as she looked at him.

"We could have been so happy, we should have been so happy, I wish that we could turn back the clocks and start all over again," she cried, the tears falling rapidly down her cheeks. She felt a hand on her shoulder, she turned and saw Carrie standing behind her.

"My dear Peggy, how my heart aches for you," Carrie sighed despairingly as she held onto Peggy's hand. "You my darling are at that point in your life where there is a decision to make, and how your life plays out, all depends on that decision, choose wisely my darling, and listen to your inner self," Carrie said and vanished.

Shona walked into the room, carrying two cups of coffee, well they loosely resembled coffee, they were wet and warm and at that moment in time, Peggy couldn't care less.

"It's nearly eight, we have to leave at eight," Shona said as she listened to the loud tick of the clock on the wall. Peggy nodded. "Peggy, can I stay with you tonight, my parents are in Morocco?" Shona asked. Peggy turned and smiled.

"Of course, you can," she said, then looked through William's locker to see if there was anything that she needed to bring back with her in the morning. At eight o'clock on the dot, a different nurse opened the door.

"Come now ladies it's time to leave," she said sternly, Shona looked at Peggy and screwed up her face, forcing Peggy to chuckle, as they stood. Peggy kissed William on the head and they both left the room, Peggy walked to the nurses' desk.

"You will telephone if there is any change won't you?" She asked. The stern-looking nurse looked at Peggy and frowned.

"Yes!" she huffed.

"Thank you, you are too kind," Peggy said and walked away shaking her head, she turned to Shona, "Unbelievable!" she snorted as they walked to the exit.

All week Peggy's days were spent at the Infirmary, there was no change in William's condition, but the doctor said that he was now at least stable and no longer critical. She had to leave at two, which was the patients resting time, and then return at five, which she did diligently every day. She would walk around the city, wandering in and out of the shops, if the weather were kind, she would take a book into the park and sit and read. Shona had been great, dealing with her own sorrowful grief for Wilf, taking her every morning, and then collecting her at eight, it would seem strange this evening, Shona was going home as her parents had returned, which meant that for the first time in years, Peggy would be truly alone.

Peggy walked out of the doors and saw Shona in her usual parking spot, she waved and ran to the car. As they pulled up outside the cottage, Peggy noticed that someone was sitting on the doorstep. "Do you want me to come in with you?" Shona asked as she too saw the figure, Peggy smiled and shook her head.

"No, I'll be fine, thanks Shona," Peggy said as she climbed out of the car.

"I'll see you on Monday," Shona shouted as Peggy closed the car door and rushed across the road.

"What on earth are you doing here?" She asked as she saw who it was, patiently waiting for her.

"The guvnor gave me the day off, I told him what had happened, and he said that I should be here with you," Robert said as he threw his arms around her. She was silently relieved, she missed him so much, and she was so happy to see him.

She made them both supper and they sat in the lounge eating and catching up.

"Was Abe here when you got back?" Robert asked, Peggy, shook her head.

"No he had already left," she replied sadly, she wished he had been there.

"But how did he know that you were coming back early?" Robert asked curiously.

"He's magical, duh!" Peggy said and chuckled.

"Oh yeah Duh!" Robert replied and laughed as he tapped his head with his fist. "See, empty it is," he said, and Peggy roared with laughter.

There was a tap on the back door, Peggy looked at Robert fearfully, nobody knocked on the back door. Robert jumped up from his seat and ran to the kitchen, she heard him talking, then she heard the reply, it was the moment that she had been dreading, she had been meaning to speak to him she just hadn't had the chance. Robert put his head around the door, Peggy looked at him and nodded as she got up from the comfy sofa and followed him into the kitchen, Reg looked awful, Peggy instantly felt the sting of tears as she looked at him and he looked back at her.

"Right well, I'll leave you two in peace, I have to unpack," Robert said and hastily left the kitchen.

"Would you like some tea?" Peggy asked as she walked to the kettle.

"No, you got anything stronger?" He asked, Peggy, smiled a sad smile and gestured for him to follow her into the lounge.

 She poured them both a brandy, they both needed it, then sat beside him on the sofa.

"I'm sorry Reg, I should have come to see you, but I have been at the infirmary every day," Peggy said as she nervously exhaled. Reg nodded,

"It kind of puts things on hold doesn't it?" Reg said sadly, not looking at Peggy, just staring into his glass of brandy.

"Aye it does, I'm so sorry Reg," Peggy said as she placed her hand on his, he pulled it away, and then looked deep into her eyes.

"I think that its best that we stop all this now, we can't carry on while he is in the Infirmary, that would be terrible," Reg said his voice breaking with emotion. Peggy nodded, as the tears ran freely down her cheeks. "I want you to know one thing though Peggy," he added as he held her face in his hands, Peggy nodded.

"I will never love anyone, the way that I love you and you will always be in here,   (he held his hand over his heart) until the day that I die," Reg said, he jumped up as he wept aloud and ran to the door, slamming it behind him. Peggy fell to the floor and sobbed, she sobbed as her heart shattered into a thousand pieces. She did not make that decision Reg had made it for her, to make it easier for her!

Chapter 18

Saturday brought a welcomed change to the week, she had two days of not having to travel to the hospital, she had told the staff that if there were any significant changes to call her, so she was going to enjoy having two days at the cottage catching up on all the jobs that she needed to do.

She hung the freshly washed sheets on the washing line, enjoying the warmth of the sun's rays, she would definitely have a coffee in the garden once she had finished all of her chores she was thinking to herself. Robert had gone into town to pick up the groceries, he had his first pay packet so he said he would treat them both to a nice piece of steak each, which Peggy was excited about but slightly worried, she had never cooked steak before. She placed the washing basket in the pantry and then began looking through Carrie's old recipe books, praying that there was a steak dish in one!

She had worked it out in her mind, when she eventually stopped sobbing and pulled herself together, she had given herself a good telling off, then decided that she must stay busy, if she were to do nothing, her thoughts would be filled with what if's and how much she missed him, no she needed to put Reg out of her mind, for many reasons. So her afternoon had been planned to do some baking, once

Robert returned with the groceries, prepare them both a lovely meal and have a bath and a well-needed shampoo.

She had finished dusting the lounge when she heard a van pull up outside, she knew that it was Reg's van without looking. She pulled the curtain back slightly and watched as Reg and Robert chatted for a few minutes, and then Robert climbed out of the van, Reg looked directly at Peggy, who quickly released the curtain and moved away from the window. It took all of her strength not to run after him, to tell him to stay, to tell him how much she loved him, but instead, she furiously rubbed the dust from the sideboard as she fought the compulsion to cry. "Pull yourself together woman!" she told herself as she heard Robert carry the boxes through to the kitchen.

"Did you remember the eggs?" Peggy asked as she helped to unpack.

"Yes Peg, look," Robert sighed as he held up a dozen eggs, then pretended to drop them.

"NO!" Peggy screamed out as Robert laughed and pointed at her,

"Martha's right you know, you are a rogue," Peggy scowled.

"Yeah but a loveable one eh!" He said and gently nudged her with his arm. "Listen, what time are you cooking the food?" He asked. Peggy looked at the clock, and knowing that she had baking to do, began calculating in her head. Robert was waiting, looking up at the ceiling, whistling. Peggy scowled.

"It should be on the table for er, seven, is that ok with you?" She asked.

"Anytime is all right with me Peg, it's just that I said that I would meet Reg, I have a few things that I have to talk to him about," Robert replied. Peggy's curiosity was now pricked.

"Such as?" she asked inquisitively.

"Ah never you mind, nosey," he replied as he pinched her nose, she slapped his hand away.

"Cheeky bugger!" she mumbled as she began to take all her baking ingredients out of the pantry.

"See you before seven," Robert shouted as he closed the back door, Peggy tutted, then walked to open it, the weather was beautiful, and it was so nice to let the fresh air flow inside.

She had her bath, styled her hair and was in the kitchen cooking the steaks when she heard the front door close, she smiled, it was good to know that he was there, that she had someone whom she could rely on, it felt incredibly comforting.

He walked out to the kitchen and sniffed the air. "That smells beautiful! I am Hank!" Robert said and grinned. Peggy frowned.

"Hank?"

"Hank Marvin, starving," Robert said and chuckled as he went up the stairs to wash his hands and face before the food was served.

She was pleased with the way that she had cooked the steaks, they were lovely, and Robert clearly enjoyed them, he finished Peggy's off too and was now sitting on the sofa rubbing his full, overfed tummy. Peggy sat in the armchair and watched him endearingly, feeling incredibly grateful that she had found him and had him in her life.

"What are you looking at? Have I got sauce on me chin or sumink?" Robert asked as he rubbed his chin frantically, making Peggy chuckle,

"No, I was just quietly thanking the universe for leading me to you, and how you have made such a difference in my life," she sighed.

"Aww, thanks, you aint too bad yourself, me old skin and blister," he replied and winked, Peggy looked at him in bewilderment.

"Sister!" they both said in unison and laughed.

"So what did you have to speak to Reg about?" Peggy asked coyly. Robert sighed and shook his head.

"He asked me if I could get him a start on the site for a bit, I think he just needs to get away," Robert said awkwardly, he didn't want her to think that he was taking sides, but he liked Reg, and he could see that it was killing him. Peggy smiled a sad smile and nodded.

"Aye, did you get him a start then?" she asked. Robert nodded.

"Yeah, he's coming back with me next week," he replied.

"How long are you staying?" Peggy asked, she thought that he had only come for the weekend.

"I'm going back a week Sunday, well that's if it's all right with you,"

"Of course it is, Robert you will always be welcome here, this is your home as much as it is mine,"

"Cheers Peg," Robert said and lifted his tea cup in the air.

"Cheers, now tell me all about Mags?"

"She is the sweetest, funniest, prettiest thing, , she is really shy, but when she gets going, she is really funny," Robert said now all gooey-eyed.

"You'll have to bring her up here so that I can meet her,"

"Well, I had hoped that you would be able to get down to London for the party," Robert said as he nibbled his fingernails.

"Party, what party?"

"Me and Mags are having a joint eighteenth birthday party, Martha knows the bloke that runs the hall down the road, so we are getting it on the cheap,"

"When, when is it?" Peggy asked.

"It's on the twenty-second," he replied.

"What, that's next week!" Peggy shrieked. Robert laughed.

"No silly, of August!" he said still laughing. Peggy held her heart and exhaled.

"Yes Robert, I will most definitely be coming!" she said and smiled.

So two months flew by, Peggy was making her bed when the telephone rang, and she quickly ran down the stairs to answer it.

"Hello"

"Peggy! How's things, darling?" Martha asked, Peggy, smiled at hearing her voice.

"Good Martha, really good,"

"Wonderful, a little dickie bird tells me that you are expecting William home tomorrow," Peggy nodded.

"Aye, he's back up on his feet now and can't wait to get home,"

"How is he coping with the loss of his family?"

"He has good days and bad days, but he still doesn't have his memory back fully, lots of things are still really vague,"

"Oh dear, will he be accompanying you to the party darling?"

"Aye if that's all right Martha,"

"Of course it is, I cannot wait to see you, it has been an age!"

"Me too, well I'll see you on Thursday then," Peggy said and smiled.

She walked back to the bedroom and stood staring at the bed, she didn't know what to do. Should they go back to sharing a bed, or should she give him the spare room? He didn't really remember much of his life, except for the major events, he remembered Carrie, their wedding, and after that, it all became a bit of a blur, well that's what he told Peggy anyway, she, however, had a sneaking suspicion that his memory was fine, that this was his way of righting some terrible wrongs, and Peggy being Peggy was always ready to give someone a second chance. Double it was then!

She was waiting for Shona to pick her up and thought about the day that he finally woke from his coma. She was arranging the flowers that she had brought in, standing in front of the window, when he called out her name. at first, she thought that she was hearing things, but then he said it again, she slowly turned and walked to the bed, he had his eyes wide open, she looked at him, tears forming in her eyes as he smiled, the biggest smile. She ran out of the room screaming for the nurse. The nurse followed Peggy back to the room and was shocked to see that he was now trying to sit himself up. She scolded him, telling him to wait for the doctor as she ran out of the room, towards the doctor's office, and every day since that day he had strived to get himself up and mobile as best he could, which posed quite a problem, as part of his knee was missing, so he would never be able to work long hours on the farm again, but nevertheless, he endeavoured and persisted and now he was ready to come home.

The horn of Shona's car broke her thoughts, she inhaled deeply and walked out of the door.

ROBERT

"Are you going out again?" Martha asked disappointedly as Robert came into the lounge, reeking of aftershave, straightening his tie in the mirror.

"Yes Martha, Mags and I are going to the Palais," Robert said and smiled his sweetest smile at her. Reg then walked in, again reeking of aftershave.

"On a Wednesday?"

"Yes, Martha on a Wednesday!" Robert replied and rolled his eyes at Reg.

"I suppose that you are joining them?" She said disapprovingly, Reg smiled and nodded.

"Double date innit, Mags is bringing her best mate along," Robert said and nudged an incredibly nervous-looking Reg. Then they both kissed Martha on the cheek and walked out.

"I am so glad that I invited you both to stay to keep me company!" she sighed and looked into her empty sherry glass. She got up and walked to the drinks cabinet, pouring herself another and switching on the wireless, she walked back to the sofa.

"It's just you and I again tonight I'm afraid," she said and raised her glass as though she were expressing good wishes to somebody in the room.

Robert was striding along, Reg was having trouble keeping up with him. "Come on Reg, what's up with ya?" Robert asked as he turned to see him trailing behind.

"It's all right for you, you're a regular 'Jack the lad' and I'm just a Scottish lad who has led a sheltered life," Reg sulked and quickened his pace. Robert put his arm around his shoulder.

"You'll be fine mate, honest, Alice is a smashing girl," he said and nudged him, Reg managed a small smile as they walked around the corner and saw the two ladies waiting for them.

They had a wonderful evening, dancing and laughing, Reg and Alice really hit it off, and once they had said their goodnights they walked back to Martha's. "Did you ask her about Saturday?" Robert asked as Reg told him how much he liked Alice, Reg nodded.

"Aye, she said that she'd love to!" Reg exclaimed happily.

"Nice one Reg," Robert said and winked, then he remembered that he had to tell him about Peggy and William. "Reg, there's er something that I've got to tell you," Robert said awkwardly. Reg looked at him still wearing the biggest smile.

"What's that then?"

"It's about the party, you do realise that Peg will be there," Robert said, Reg nodded and then sighed. "And Bill will be with her," he reluctantly added. Reg scowled. "Look, I've promised her that we would all make an effort, he has lost most of his memory and hopefully half of his personality as well," Robert said and laughed, making Reg laugh too.

They walked into the house, still laughing, and joking as they walked to the door of the lounge, Robert stopped dead in his tracks, he heard music and he heard Martha singing, he gestured to Reg to be quiet as he gently opened the door and peered in, he stifled a laugh as he beckoned Reg to take a look. Martha was dancing around the lounge, she was dancing however as if she were dancing with a partner, her arm outstretched, her back straight and incredibly light on her feet. Robert pretended to cough loudly, he didn't want to embarrass her, and then he and Reg walked into the room. She looked at them both but did not stop, still, she continued to dance with her imaginary partner, as they both looked at one another, neither knowing what to do or to say.

PEGGY

She took William's empty plate and put it on top of hers. "Would you like a cup of tea?" she asked and smiled. He grabbed her hand and smiled, a most beautiful, genuine smile.

"Aye please,"

"Peggy love?" He said gently.

"Yes,"

"Thank you," he sighed. She tapped him on the shoulder and put the dishes into the sink and ran the hot tap. She was singing away to herself as she washed the dishes, waiting for the kettle to boil, when she felt hands go around her waist, he nestled his face into her neck.

"Just like old times eh," he whispered gently. She slowly turned and smiled.

"You remember then?" she asked.

"How could I ever forget you, always dancing, singing and smiling, whatever life threw at you, you would always have that beautiful cheerfulness about you," he replied. She smiled, and then he kissed her, and it was exactly the same as the first time that he had kissed her, her legs trembled as her heart fluttered, and she hoped and prayed that she had her William back, the William that she fell in love with, many moons ago.

The morning of the journey to London had arrived and Peggy was filled with dread, she was so anxious that she almost phoned Robert and told him that she couldn't do it, then she listened to her inner self, her voice of reason, that told her to stop being ridiculous, she must do this for Robert, and that they would welcome William with open arms, despite everything.

The cab dropped them both at the station and slowly they walked to the station café. William insisted on ordering the tea he wanted to show Peggy that he could do it, that she could rely on him. They were drinking their tea and chatting when their train was being called on the tannoy. They both drank up and wandered out to the platform where they boarded the express to London, which had just pulled up alongside the platform.

Luckily, the train was quiet, and they had the entire compartment to themselves. It seemed to be taking forever when William pulled out a deck of cards from his pocket and waved them at Peggy. "William you are a genius!" Peggy exclaimed, relieved that there was something to kill the boredom.

A while later, and ten games of rummy, a woman walked into the compartment, she placed her bag into the luggage shelf, then threw herself into the seat beside Peggy, shoving into her as she did. William shook his head and tutted, looking at all the other empty seats that remained in the carriage. She began to cough and splutter, not covering her mouth, and it all being directed at Peggy, who screwed up her nose in utter disgust. William looked at Peggy and tapped the seat beside him, she smiled and quickly moved so that she was now opposite the ghastly woman.

"Not long now," William said quietly as the woman again coughed and spluttered all over the carriage.

"I'm sorry, did you say something?" the woman shouted. William sighed and looked at Peggy.

"I was talking to my wife," he replied.

"I'm sorry, I didn't quite catch that?" she shouted again.

"I SAID THAT I WAS TALKING TO MY WIFE!" he bellowed hoping that she would leave them both alone.

"Yes, of course, it is rather bright, pull down the blind if you wish," she replied and began rooting through her oversized handbag. Peggy looked at William and was trying her hardest not to laugh, William was also stifling a laugh, then the woman stood up and reached to the luggage shelf, and as she did she broke wind, incredibly loudly. That was it, Peggy could no longer control herself and burst out into a fit of laughter, forcing William to do the same.

"I say, what's the joke?" The woman asked as she returned to her seat, breaking wind once again as she did.

"We're nearly there, shall we grab our bags and wait by the door?" Peggy suggested as she laughed, she could not stand the smell any longer. William nodded, stood, and began to pass the cases to Peggy, then they left the compartment, walked to the door, and opened the window, both of them gasping for fresh air!

Chapter 19

Robert was eagerly waiting for them on the platform, Peggy noticed him as soon as the train slowed to a halt, she was waving frantically at him as her tummy was turning somersaults due to the excitement and anxiety. William stepped down from the train and Peggy handed him the suitcases, then she too stepped down, Robert then saw them both and ran over to them, Peggy threw her arms around him, she hadn't seen him for two long months, and she had missed him terribly. Once she eventually released her brother, he turned and looked at William, Peggy could sense his concern as he smiled a nervous smile. Robert smiled, the biggest beaming smile and threw his arms around William, Peggy clearly noticed when William sighed with relief and then a genuine smile crept across his face.

"Good to see you, Bill, how are you feeling mate?" Robert asked as he lifted Peggy's incredibly heavy suitcase, as William lifted his.

"Much better thanks Bob, the knee is still giving me jip though," he replied as he began to walk in the direction of the exit.

"Oi, hold up, I'm still waiting for Joyce," Robert called after him, William turned and frowned at Peggy, who shrugged her shoulders, and then they looked at one another in bewilderment as the woman whom they had shared their compartment with was calling out and waving at Robert.

"That's Joyce?" They both asked in unison,

"Yeah, why have you met her?" Robert replied, Peggy and William, nodded their heads,

"Aye, she was in our compartment, who is she?" Peggy replied.

"Martha's sister," Robert replied as he walked over to Joyce and greeted her. William and Peggy then reluctantly walked over to join them, Robert made the introductions, and then they all walked out of the station, Peggy was expecting to see a cab waiting for them, but to her disappointment, there wasn't one, she looked at Robert and frowned.

"How are we getting to Martha's?" she asked and looked at the empty taxi rank.

"Follow me," Robert replied cheerfully as he then began to whistle, walking towards the car park. Robert stopped beside a black car and much to Peggy's surprise he opened it, then walked to the boot and opened that.

"Wait, who's driving?" Peggy asked anxiously, she was now always worried to travel in a car after William's accident, they both chose to walk everywhere, even though William still struggled to walk long distances.

"I am!" Robert replied boastfully, Peggy frowned. "I passed my test three weeks ago Peg," he added and smiled.

"Oh Robert, that's wonderful!" Peggy exclaimed and threw her arms around him in a congratulatory manner. "Why didn't you tell me?" She then asked.

"I wanted to surprise you, didn't I" he replied and chuckled.

After arriving at Martha's and unpacking, Peggy and William went down to join the others for dinner. Martha had surpassed herself, she had laid a large table beautifully, for all of them to dine together. Peggy was sitting between William and Martha and opposite Robert and Mags, Reg was nowhere to be seen, even though there was an empty place setting, Joyce was seated at the end of the table (probably because of her flatulence!).

They had a wonderful evening, dining, chatting, and catching up, Peggy was beside herself with relief as they all went above and beyond to make William feel welcome and included. Peggy and Mags hit it off immediately, which made Robert the happiest man on the planet! He was quietly worried about the two of them meeting, they were of course the most important people in his life, and it mattered greatly that they had a good relationship with one another.

That night Peggy and William climbed into bed, both equally exhausted from the long journey and the company, neither of which, were they familiar with. William took a hold of Peggy's hand and kissed it. "Thank you," he sighed and smiled, Peggy frowned,

"For what?" She asked,

"For giving me a second chance, Peg, I know that I treated you badly, I am so ashamed of that," he said as tears filled his eyes.

"Have you got your memory back?" Peggy asked in the most genuine manner but knowing full well that he had never lost his memory, William sighed and looked down.

"The truth is…"

"You never truly lost it," Peggy finished the sentence for him. He looked up, completely bemused,

"What? You knew all along?" He asked, Peggy, smiled and nodded.

"And yet, you still entertained me, why?" He asked.

"Because my darling, despite everything that had happened between you and me, I believe that everyone is entitled to a second chance, you included," she replied as she smiled. He held her hand to his face.

"Thank you," he sighed,

"Just remember this William, there is only ever one second chance, after that, a brick wall comes down and it is over," she said with a solemn look on her face, remembering how at the blink of an eye he could make her feel so worthless and unloved. William nodded and smiled.

"I won't let you down, I promise," he said, then there was a tap on the door.

"Yes," Peggy called out,

"Is it all right to come in?" Robert called through the door.

"Aye of course," Peggy replied, the door opened, and an extremely happy Robert walked into the room and sat on the edge of their bed.

"So what did you think of Mags then?" He asked apprehensively.

"I think that she is absolutely lovely, don't you agree Bill?" Peggy sighed as both William and Robert looked at her in bewilderment. "What? Did I say something wrong?" She asked.

"You called him Bill!" Robert replied, William was frantically nodding his head, wearing a smile that stretched from ear to ear.

"Aye, I know," Peggy said, wondering what all the fuss was about.

"You never call me Bill, you always call me William," William said astounded.

"I know, sorry don't you like it? It's just that it feels nice, familiar, even endearing when I call you Bill," Peggy said and held onto his hand.

"Peg, I love it that you want to call me Bill," he said and chuckled.

"Well, while we're on the subject, could you please call me Bob and not Robert?" Robert asked. Peggy burst out laughing.

"Yes, of course, what a strange conversation!" she said as she roared with laughter, and then there was another tap on the door. Peggy looked at Bill and Bob and frowned.

"Yes," she called out.

"Wonderful, you are still awake, can I come in?" Martha asked in a loud whisper, causing the three of them to chuckle.

"Come on in" Peggy replied, as the door opened and Martha walked in and sat beside Bob on the bed, Peggy looked at Bill and chuckled.

"Sorry for the intrusion, it's just that I have missed you so and I don't feel as though we have had the chance to have a decent conversation since you arrived," Martha said and smiled, her breath reeked of sherry.

"I know, it's fine, we can catch up now," Peggy said and smiled at Martha, how she had grown to love her, she was the kindest, most thoughtful woman, Peggy was thinking to herself.

"You came in just in time," Bob said and winked at Bill, Martha, and Peggy both frowned.

"For what?" Martha asked, her curiosity now pricked.

"For our introduction" Bob replied and pointed to Bill,

"What? But I already know who you are," Martha replied, Peggy chuckled, she now knew what was about to happen.

"Martha, this is Bill, Bill this is Martha," Bob said and laughed, Martha looked at all three of them like they were all escaped lunatics.

"Martha I am Bob, pleased to meet you," He said and grabbed her hand, shaking it frantically.

"Would one of you mind explaining, just what on earth is going on here?" Martha shouted.

"They would like you to call them Bill and Bob," Peggy explained as she laughed.

"Oh, right, I see," Martha said vaguely, still feeling rather confused by the matter.

"Yes, anyway, never mind that! I wanted to apologise for my sister Joyce, and her you know, little problem," Martha said awkwardly, Bob and Bill both laughed.

"Oh, you mean…" Bob blew a raspberry, making Martha blush with embarrassment. Peggy was bordering on hysterical at that point when she thought back to the dinner and Joyce's constant flatulence!

"She has a medical condition, you know," Martha continued still scarlet in colour.

"Yeah, and don't we know it!" Bob said waving his hand over his nose and laughing.

"Bob! Don't be mean!" Peggy scorned even though she was fighting the compulsion to burst out laughing.

"Anyway, moving on, Peggy isn't Mags the most wonderful little creature?" Martha said her eyes wide with excitement, Peggy was nodding frantically in agreement.

"Yes, she is lovely," Peggy sighed, "But now if you don't mind, I am absolutely shattered, Bill and I have been awake since four-thirty this morning," Peggy said as she yawned.

"Oh gosh! Yes, of course, come, Robert, let's leave these good people to rest," Martha said as she pulled at Bob's jacket, he would not budge, she looked at him in dismay.

"Who were you talking to?" Bob asked, again causing Peggy and Bill to snigger under their breath.

"Sorry! Come now, Bob," Martha let out an exaggerated sigh, he smiled and walked to the door, blowing Peggy a kiss as he did.

Saturday morning was completely chaotic, Peggy was glad that both she and Bill had the chance to rest on Friday after the long journey from Scotland. Bill had gone to the hall with Bob, to put up the decorations, and Peggy was helping Martha, Lucy, and Hilda to prepare the buffet and it was complete and utter pandemonium. Once all the food had been prepared, Jack, Hilda's husband was transporting it down to the hall in his van, he was a delivery driver for the local grocery shop. Once all the food had gone, Peggy sat at one of the tables in the dining room, kicked off her shoes and stretched out her feet, she had been standing for so long, and she had dancing to do that evening, she was thinking when she looked out of the window and saw Bob's car pull up outside.

The front door closed, and she could hear them laughing and joking. "Where's Peg Martha?" Bob called out to the back office.

"Kitchen or dining room," Martha replied as she held her hand over the receiver of the phone. They made their way to the dining room, Bob first, followed by Bill, then Reg, Peggy's heart almost jumped into her mouth as the three of them laughed and joked with one another. Bill walked over to Peggy and kissed her on the cheek, Bob sat at the table, then so too did Reg.

"Hello Peggy, how are you?" He asked, not making eye contact with her.

"I'm very well thank you Reg, how are you?" She asked awkwardly.

"Good thanks," he replied quietly.

"Peggy, you are wanted," Martha called out. Saved by the bell, Peggy was thinking to herself as she slipped her feet back into her shoes and stood up.

"No peace for the wicked eh!" She said and quickly left the room now filled with relief. She walked to the office to be met by Mags and another pretty girl.

"We are heading up west to do some shopping for tonight, we wondered if you fancied tagging along?" Mags asked as she sweetly smiled.

"Aye, I'd love to, just give me a wee minute to get changed," Peggy replied.

"Oh Peggy, this is Alice," Mags said.

"Hello Alice, I'll be back in a wee second," Peggy called out as she trotted up the stairs to her room.

She was rushing around looking for a suitable outfit to wear when Bill came into the room. "Where are you going?" He asked as Peggy took yet another dress out of the wardrobe and held it up against her while she looked in the mirror.

"I'm going up west with Mags and her friend, outfit shopping for tonight," Peggy said as she smiled and nodded, yes the blue one would do just fine, she thought as she stripped off her clothes and began to change.

"Do you mean that lassie in the reception?" Bill asked as he sat on the bed, reading the newspaper.

"Aye," Peggy replied as she refreshed her make-up while sitting at the dressing table.

"That's Reg's new girl," Bill said and discreetly looked over the top of the newspaper to gauge Peggy's reaction.

"He's a lucky fella, she is very pretty," Peggy said and smiled, all the while inside she was green with envy, but that was just Peggy being selfish, her inner self needed to have a word, she was thinking as she stood up and did a twirl.

"How do I look?" Peggy asked. Bill put the paper down and stood up, he walked to Peggy and wrapped his arms around her waist.

"More beautiful than yesterday, and I didn't think that that was possible," he replied and kissed her.

"You smooth talker you," Peggy said as they broke from the embrace, and she touched the end of his nose. "What are you going to do this afternoon?" she asked as she tied her scarf around her neck.

"Bob and Reg asked me to give them a hand," he replied as he again continued to read the newspaper.

"Well, stay out of trouble, I'll see you later," Peggy said and kissed his cheek, leaving a shocking red lipstick stain on his face.

They had been to at least fifty different dress shops, and all of them had the same style of dresses in, Peggy was completely fed up with shopping, she had found her dress in the first shop that they had entered but Alice could not make up her mind. Mags could see that Peggy was losing the will to live, and if she were to be honest, so was she.

"Alice, why don't we go and grab a coffee, then you can think about all the outfits that you've seen, and maybe, just maybe, you might even make up your bloody mind about one!" Mags said and looked at Peggy rolling her eyes as she did.

"Oh, all right!" Alice huffed as she placed the hanger back onto the rail and they left the shop.

"I know, let's go to Covent Garden, the markets on today, you might see something you like after coffee," Mags suggested. Now this excited Peggy, she had never been to Covent Garden, but she had always wanted to, she just never seemed to find the time.

Peggy was in complete and utter awe of the place as they entered, the atmosphere was amazing, almost electric she was thinking as she smiled, watching the street performers. They walked to the café, Mags ordered the coffee and they sat at a table where they could see all around, listening to the string quartet, that was busking.

"I really liked the green dress," Mags said as she blew on her hot cup of delicious coffee. Alice screwed her face up.

"But Reg really liked the blue dress that I wore on Wednesday," Alice sulked. Peggy tried her hardest not to react, Alice was a lovely girl and Reg deserved to be happy.

"You know Reg, don't you Peg, what do you reckon he would like?" Mags asked this sent Peggy's mind reeling, how much did they know, were they aware that Peggy and Reg had had a brief encounter? She was thinking to herself.

"Peg?" Mags said waiting for a reply.

"Oh, sorry I was miles away," Peggy replied and blushed, she looked at Alice and smiled.

"Alice you could wear an old sack and look beautiful, I'm sure that anything you choose, Reg will absolutely love," Peggy replied honestly.

"Oh Peggy, you are so lovely," Alice said and wore the biggest smile, Mags looked at Peggy and touched her hand.

"I feel so blessed, not only have I met the best man in the entire universe, but he has the best sister in the universe!" Mags said endearingly.

"Oh, you girls!" Peggy said and blushed.

Peggy was ready and she looked into the mirror and did one last twirl, Bill had gone down to have drinks with the others while Peggy finished off getting ready, she walked to her case and took out Bob's gift and the gift that she had brought for Mags, placing them inside the gift bags, then joined the others in the lounge.

"Martha, you look stunning!" Peggy gasped as she watched Martha handing out drinks from a tray, and how glamorous she looked.

"Oh, Peggy darling, that dress is absolutely divine!" Martha shouted, causing everyone in the room to look in her direction, she blushed and smiled. Bill walked over to her.

"Wow! I am the luckiest man alive," he whispered into her ear, she kissed him on the cheek, then blushed again as she noticed that Reg was watching.

"You don't scrub up too bad, me old skin and blister," Bob said as he kissed her on the cheek.

"Well, look at you, all lardy dah!" Peggy said and pointed to Bob's new tailored suit.

"Do you like it? Mags made it for me, cor we didn't half have some fun at the fitting!" Bob said, Bill, burst out laughing as Peggy scowled.

"That is something that you should keep between you both," Peggy said sternly, not liking the thought of sharing intimacies with anyone.

"Sorry Peg," Bob said and blushed, hoping that he hadn't offended her. She sensed this, smiled, and then kissed him on the cheek.

"You make me feel very proud," Peggy said and nudged him.

"And since the day that you found me, you have turned my life around Peg, and I can't thank you enough," he replied tearily.

CHAPTER 20

Bob gasped as he unwrapped the gift from Peggy and Bill. It was a gold pocket watch that belonged to their Dad Albert, given to him as a gift on his wedding day.

"Oh Peg, it's beautiful! What does that say?" He asked as he looked at the engraving on the back.

"It says To Albert, Love from Mum and Dad x" Peggy read out loud.

"What, so Carrie and Abe gave it to him?" Bob said wide-eyed and in complete awe of the timepiece.

"Aye, on his wedding day to Mum, Abe knew a man, who was really good at metalwork, he made it, Cedric I think his name was," Peggy said as she thought back to Carrie's recollections.

"Well he is bloody skilled I'll give him that! Look at that detail," Bob said as he showed it to Martha who was standing beside him, she smiled,

"It's an exquisite piece," she replied as Bob placed the watch in the top pocket of his jacket, looking well pleased as he did.

"The cars are here," Martha called out loudly above the chit-chat. Everyone put their glasses onto the empty tray and began to gather in the reception. Martha led them all out to two limousines that were waiting. A man dressed smartly in a black tailored suit opened the back doors and directed them inside. Peggy was in the first car with Bob and Bill, Martha was in the car behind with Reg and Joyce, and as they drove to the hall Peggy was looking around at the posh interior of the car.

"This must have cost a fortune!" Peggy whispered to Bill and Bob, and they both nodded, as the car pulled up outside of the hall, Bob smiled when he saw Mags and Alice waiting outside for their arrival.

Inside the boys had done a wonderful job of decorating the hall, and Peggy was smiling widely as she and Bill walked to the bar. "What should I get Bob?" Bill asked, Peggy, shrugged her shoulders.

"I don't know, what is it that you drink?" She asked.

"I drink bitter,"

"Get him one of them, I'll have a port and lemon," Peggy said and smiled,

"Port and Lemon, how very upmarket," Bill said trying to sound posh but failing miserably, making Peggy chuckle. "Whatever happened to my shandy swilling Peggy eh?" Bill said as he waited to be served.

"She's all grown up now," she replied and nudged him, they took the drinks to Bob, and Bill handed him his pint. Bob looked at it, then at Bill.

"What is it?" he asked.

"It's a pint," Bill replied.

"Well, I know that duh! A pint of what?" Bob asked and laughed, shaking his head in disbelief.

"Bitter," Bill replied as he licked the foam from his top lip after he took a drink. Bob apprehensively took a sip, while the others waited in anticipation.

"That's not bad, nice one Bill," he said. "Cheers everyone!" he shouted as he raised his glass.

"What would you like to drink Mags?" Peggy asked as she passed her the gift bag.

"Oh thank you, Peggy, you shouldn't have, er I don't know what to have. What are you drinking?" Mags asked as she unwrapped the gift and gasped when she looked at the pretty bracelet. "Oh My! It's gorgeous!" Mags said as she trembled, taking it out of the box.

"It was our Mum's, our grandmother and grandfather gave it to her on her wedding day, they gave our Dad a pocket watch, the one that we gave to Bob," Peggy said happily. Mags threw her arms around Peggy.

"Thank you so much, it means a lot!" Mags said as she tried to put the bracelet on, Peggy helped her with the clasp.

"Fiddley wee things aren't they," Peggy said and smiled, Mags nodded.

"What did you say that you were drinking?

"Oh, I didn't, this is port and lemon, would you like to try it?" Peggy asked and passed her glass to Mags, she took a sip and smiled.

"Ooh, that's lovely," she said.

"Would you like one?"

"Please," Mags replied as Peggy walked to the bar.

The evening was in full swing, and they were all having such a wonderful time, dancing chatting and drinking. Peggy and Bill left the dance floor and sat at the table where Martha was in conversation with a man. They took their seats and Peggy could not help but stare, Bill nudged her. "Peg, it's rude to stare," he whispered.

"Aye I know, but who is he?" she whispered back.

"That's Mags's Dad," Bill replied quietly.

"Oh, where's her mum?"

"Dead,"

"Oh, dear,"

"Peggy darling have you been introduced?" Martha said rather loudly, as she drank yet another sherry.

"No, we haven't," Peggy said and laid on her best smile.

"This is Cyril, Margaret's father," Martha slurred. Peggy leaned over and held out her hand to Cyril.

"It's lovely to meet you," Peggy said as Bill then shook his hand. Bill and Cyril then struck up a conversation, Martha sighed as she looked at her empty glass.

"Peggy, would you accompany me to the bar?" Martha asked as she stood, wobbling slightly as she did.

"Of course," Peggy replied as she held Martha's arm to steady her. "Martha, why are the chauffeurs still here?" Peggy asked as she watched them, it was almost as if they were keeping guard.

"Because they have to drive us back," Martha replied and hiccupped.

Outside, at the back of the hall, there was a pretty garden and Bob had been granted permission to set off a small number of fireworks, so he, Bill, and Reg were setting them up.

"Don't you think that we ought to test one?" Reg asked, Bob, nodded.

"You got matches, Bill?" He asked, Bill, shook his head.

"I'll go to the bar and grab some," he said as he ran back inside the hall. Bob and Reg had set the fireworks up and Bob was checking the perimeter fence to make sure that they weren't too close, and as he did a gloved hand came out from behind him and around his mouth, pulling him to the ground. Bill had returned with the matches and looked at Reg.

"Where's Bob?" he asked, Reg looked and saw that Bob was being dragged towards the back gate. They both ran towards Bob, Reg grabbed hold of his feet, while Bill punched the man that was dragging Bob, straight in the mouth, shocking himself as he did, then they heard screaming and crying, Bill looked to see that all the guests were now running out to the garden.

"Let him go!" Bill shouted as the large old man wiped the blood from his lip, Bob had managed to break free and was now standing between Bill and Reg.

"What do you want Philpott?" Bob growled, as three henchmen climbed the fence and were now standing beside Philpott.

"I want you Bob, who said that you could just up and leave, you were sold to me many years ago, meaning that you belong to me, until the day you die," Philpott growled into Bob's face, Reg lunged at him, so one of the men grabbed Reg by the face squeezing so hard, that Reg's teeth cut deeply into the inside of his cheek.

"Get away from them!" Peggy screamed as she ran towards them, stopping in her tracks when she saw the man claiming to be Philpott.

"Oh if it aint wee Peggy," he sneered mimicking Peggy's Scottish accent.

"What are you doing here? Go away and leave us all alone, we want nothing to do with you," Peggy said her voice trembling with fear as too were her legs.

"Well that's not very nice is it?" he sneered as he grabbed Bob by the throat, choking him as he did. Peggy screamed out as too did all the women that were gathered behind.

"GET DOWN" they all heard a voice shout. Bob managed to break free from Philpott and threw himself on the ground, Reg did the same and Bill pulled Peggy down as Philpott and his men were distracted by the voice that had shouted. Then there was gunfire. Peggy hid her face in

Bill's jacket until the shots stopped. She looked up and saw the four men, lying on the ground. Peggy looked around, desperate to see if Bob and Reg were ok and much to her relief they were. Martha came rushing over, with somebody dressed in all black.

"Come now," Martha said to Bob, Peggy, Bill, and Reg, as they climbed to their feet.

"What the bloody hell?" Bob said and shook his head.

"We had a tip-off that this was planned, I told Martha, which is why these guys are here," The woman dressed in all black said in an Irish accent, pointing at the chauffeurs, who were now wielding guns. Peggy shook her head in disbelief.

"So you knew that Old Philpott was going to do me in?" Bob asked, the woman nodded.

"Wait a minute, why did you call him Philpott?" Peggy asked Bob.

"Cause that's his name Peg," Bob said and tutted, Peggy shook her head.

"No, it isn't!" She said adamantly.

"I think I should know Peg, he's the bloke that the squire sold me to," Bob bellowed.

"That man is NOT called Philpott, that man is called GEORGE!" Peggy shouted, and the woman in black was nodding.

"She's right Robert, that man is called George Wells, he was your uncle, and my cousin," she said. She looked at

Peggy and held out her hand to shake. "My name is Rowan, my mother was Carrie's sister," she said as Peggy shook her hand.

"So, you are Florence's daughter," Peggy said, Rowan smiled and nodded.

"Would someone mind telling me what the bleedin hell is going on here!" Bob shouted.

"I suggest that we take this inside, the police are on their way," Martha said as she pointed to the hall, the gathered crowd then made their way back to the hall.

"So, let me get this straight, that bloke who I have always known as Philpott is actually my uncle George," Bob said as he tried to make sense of everything, Peggy and Rowan nodded.

"But how did you know Peg, it must have been years since you last saw him?" Bob asked, Peggy nodded.

"Aye, but Carrie used to cut out newspaper clippings of him, she kept them and showed them to me," Peggy replied.

"Were they about his dodgy dealings?" He asked, Peggy, nodded. "And you are Carrie's niece, yes," Bob asked Rowan, who nodded.

"Yes, I was taken from my mother when I was young and sent to boarding school, I studied hard and became friends with a young man who was in the secret service, I too then joined. One day I was looking through some case notes on a horse doping ring and saw him, I instantly recognised him from a family photo that my mother had given me. I have been friends with Martha for a while now, so I called her and asked her to give me a hand, which she kindly did, we have been watching you both for a few years now," Rowan said. Peggy looked at Bob wide-eyed and they both turned to look at Martha.

"I would have told you both, eventually," Martha said, suddenly now incredibly sober.

"You're a dark horse, Martha!" Bob chuckled as he put his arm around her and hugged her.

They returned to Martha's after the party had suddenly drawn to a close and were sitting in Martha's lounge.

"You will be relieved to know that there will be no repercussions from this, the case is now well and truly closed," Rowan said and smiled.

"Thank goodness for that!" Peggy sighed. Rowan stood up and smiled.

"Well, that's me done, I must return to Ireland, it was really nice to finally meet you both," she said as she held her hand out to Bob, who shook it, then Peggy, she shook her hand but wouldn't let go. "Would you walk with me to the door, there is something I wish to speak to you about in private," Rowan said in Peggy's ear. Peggy nodded and followed her into the reception. Rowan looked all around, to make sure that no ears were listening.

"Peggy, I have a huge favour to ask," she whispered, Peggy nodded.

"I have a daughter, because of my work, I had to give her to my best friend to raise, it is far too dangerous for her to stay with me, she lives in Cornwall, and her name is Willow. Would you check in on her from time to time, and then write to me at this address?" Rowan asked and passed Peggy a piece of paper, with two addresses on it, one in Cornwall and one in London.

"Of course, it's the least that I can do," Peggy replied. Rowan kissed her on the cheek.

"It was lovely to meet you, Peggy, take good care of yourself," she said as she walked out of the door and that would be the one and only time that they would ever meet.

"Tell me, Bob, were you aware that they were doping horses?" Martha asked as she poured them all a large glass of brandy each. Bob took a gulp of his and nearly choked.

"Oh, Gawd! What the bloody hell is that?" He asked as he choked and screwed his face in disgust, causing Peggy and Bill to roar with laughter. "I sort of knew, I knew that they were fixing races, I just didn't know how," Bob replied after he had recovered. Martha nodded.

That night as they readied for bed Peggy was sitting at her dressing table brushing her hair when she caught Bill's eye in the reflection of the mirror. "Thank you, Bill," she sighed and smiled. He walked up and stood behind her, kissing her neck.

"What for beautiful?"

"For helping Bob when that bastard grabbed hold of him, if it weren't for you and Reg, they would have taken him," Peggy replied.

"I don't know what came over me Peg, you know me, usually I can't fight my way out of a paper bag," he said and chuckled, Peggy, chuckled too. "How do you think that he knew who you were?" Bill asked.

"I think that we have been on his radar for a while, he knew that I would look for Bob," she replied.

"But why did he buy Bob? That's what I don't understand,"

"Because on my mum and dad's wedding day, George turned up and began to cause trouble, then he stabbed Florence, my dad lost it and he and the locals beat the living daylights out of him, but he always said that he would get his revenge,"

"So, George killed Rowan's mum, is that right?"

"Aye is it any wonder that she wanted him dead," Peggy replied and scowled.

"Nasty, vile bastard he was," she continued.

She opened her eyes, the room was still dark, but she could make out a figure kneeling beside her. She rubbed her eyes and smiled, it was Carrie. She took Peggy's hand in hers and held it to her cheek.

"From the bottom of my heart thank you, both of you," she said and then faded into the darkness. Peggy pushed herself up and turned to see Bill sitting up and smiling.

"Did you just see her?" she asked dozily, still not yet properly awake. Bill was nodding frantically.

"There is something that I have to tell you," he said, Peggy nodded, "When I was in the coma, Carrie came to me, she showed me the error of my ways, she showed me exactly what a nasty bastard I was and that you didn't deserve to be treated the way that I treated you. She made me promise to take care of you, Bob and Bob's kids and I promised that I would, she said that she would be watching me," he chuckled.

"You'd better believe it," Peggy said and chuckled.

They missed breakfast, they had both slept in, so once they were awake and dressed Bill suggested that they go out and grab an early lunch which Peggy was more than happy with. Just as they walked to the door they heard Bob.

"Oi! Where do you two think you are going?" He shouted. Peggy looked at Bill and rolled her eyes.

"We are going out for lunch,"

"Nah you can't, I have already got the day planned, we have to meet Mags, Reg and Alice up west," he said gesturing them back inside.

"Why?" Peggy sighed.

"Well, cause it's a celebration innit," Bob said and grinned widely.

"Forgive me if I'm mistaken, but you had your celebration last night did you not?" Peggy replied.

"This is a different celebration though,"

"What Bob? What is it?" Peggy asked frustratedly.

"I asked Mags to marry me…. And she said yes!" He screamed out and danced, grabbing hold of Peggy, and dancing her around the reception foyer as she creased with laughter.

They met the others up west and went for lunch in a lovely restaurant. It seemed strange sitting around a table with Reg, watching how attentive he was to Alice, Peggy thought that it might upset her, but to her astonishment, it really didn't. She was happy that Reg had found someone as lovely as Alice, how he had slipped into London life so comfortably, then she turned and looked at Bill, who was speaking to Bob and Reg, how they all laughed at his jokes, and how they had all made the effort to forgive him and welcome him back into the gang, she was thinking.

"Well come on then, you lovely lot, I promised Martha that we would be back early, so that she can join in with the celebrations," Bob said as he, Reg and Bill went to pay for the lunch.

When they walked through towards the lounge, Bob stopped and listened, he could hear Martha talking, it wasn't to Joyce, she had caught the train home early that morning. Bob pointed to the door and looked at them all. "Ere you don't think that she's on the funny stuff again do ya?" He asked Reg and laughed. Reg whispered to the others what had happened on Wednesday night, and they all stifled a laugh as Bob opened the door. They all stood with their mouths gaped open as Martha danced around the lounge with Cyril, Mags's dad!

CHAPTER 21

It was a tearful farewell at the train station, Peggy was fully aware that it would be another two months until she saw Robert again, they had arranged that the London lot would travel to Scotland for bonfire night, at least she had that to look forward to she thought as she wiped the falling tears from her face as she waved from the departing train's window.

They both rested for a few days following their return, they were both exhausted! On Thursday, Peggy was getting ready, she was expecting Shona who was picking her up to take her shopping. Bill called up the stairs to her.

"Peg, Shona is here, she wants to know if she has enough time for a cup of tea,"

"Yes of course she does," Peggy replied as she applied her lipstick, satisfied with her reflection she nodded to herself in the mirror and then walked down the stairs to join them. Shona threw her arms around Peggy and held her tightly.

"Oh, I've missed you!" she sighed.

"We've only been away for a few days," Peggy replied and sat at the table, Shona sat opposite her as Bill served them tea.

"Aye I know, but this place isn't the same without you, and I was worried that you might decide to stay there," Shona replied. Peggy tutted and shook her head.

"Stay there, no way, I like London, to visit, but live there! Not on your nelly!" Peggy exclaimed, making Shona and Bill laugh.

"What are you going to do with yourself while I'm out?" Peggy asked Bill.

"I'm going to pop to the farm and see the lads," he replied as he looked over the top of the newspaper that he was reading.

"Oh shit, that reminds me," Shona said and put her hand over her mouth. Peggy looked at her and frowned. "The solicitors called about your parent's estate, they asked if I would ask you to call them as a matter of urgency," Shona continued. Bill smiled, folded his newspaper, and walked out to the hallway to the telephone, closing the kitchen door behind him.

"I wonder what is so urgent?" Peggy said as she sipped her tea.

"I don't know, but that snooty receptionist, was more snooty than usual," Shona replied as she drank the rest of her tea. She pushed her cup away, and Peggy could not resist. She swilled the tea leaves around and placed the overturned cup on the saucer, then sat intensely examining the leaves.

"Oh, Shona, I see a ship, you are going to travel overseas," Peggy said still looking at the pictures that were forming from the leaves. "And there you will find true love," Peggy added and smiled as she looked up. Shona reached over and grabbed the saucer.

"What is it that you are looking at? I can't see anything but old nasty tea leaves," she said and frowned.

"Look, there's the boat, there is a heart and there is an ankh, an Egyptian symbol of truth," Peggy said smiling to herself. Shona nodded and attempted a smile, Peggy knew that she didn't believe her, and she couldn't wait for the day when she could say, see I told you so! She was thinking. Bill walked out and slammed his hand on the table angrily, making Peggy and Shona jump.

"What? What on earth is the matter?" Peggy asked frantically, worried that he might return to his bad old ways.

"My Dad was in so much debt, that even after the farm is sold, he will still owe £20,000!" Bill fumed. Peggy looked at Shona and raised an eyebrow.

"Does that mean that the debt goes to us?" Peggy asked nervously. Bill sighed and shook his head.

"Thankfully no, but I was hoping for a small amount of money, so that we could set up our own business, you know as I can't work on the farm anymore," He sighed. Peggy walked over to him and held him.

"Don't worry, we'll sort something out," she whispered in his ear. He kissed her and then smiled.

"Aye, well I guess I'll head over to the farm now and see if the boys can cheer me up," he said.

"Do you want us to drop you off on the way?" Shona asked. Bill smiled and shook his head.

"No thanks Shona, the walk will do me good, besides, I need to exercise this damned knee of mine," he said as he put on his flat cap and walked out of the back door.

So after a long afternoon of city shopping, Peggy walked into the cottage feeling exhausted, to what sounded like a farmyard in her kitchen. She removed her scarf and coat, hanging them on the hook and slowly opened the kitchen door, she jumped back as a duckling waddled towards her, and she quickly closed the door.

"Bill, why is there a duck in the kitchen?" Peggy called out.

"Och, Peg come and look at them," he replied, she slowly opened the door once more and stepped into the pandemonium. There were four of them waddling around and making a terrible mess all over Peggy's clean kitchen floor. "Aren't they adorable?" Bill said as a yellow duckling waddled to him and was gently nibbling his fingers.

"Aye they are Bill, but why are they in my kitchen, have you seen the mess all over my clean floor!" Peggy fumed.

"McGregor was going to drown them, so I told him that we would have them, duck eggs are really good for baking you know," he said and smiled, his sweetest smile.

"But where are we going to put them?" She asked as the duckling that was following her around was leaving a nasty trail behind it, Peggy shook her head and let out a small growl.

"Tomorrow is Stan's day off, he's coming over to help me build a pen," He replied still fussing over the ducklings.

"What? Butcher Stan? Since when have you and he been friends?" Peggy asked.

"He was at the farm today, we got chatting, you know about London and Reg, and then he offered to help me," Bill said happily, Peggy nodded.

"Good, well you need to move them out of here, I'll have to mop the floor before I can cook the tea, oh Bill look at my floor!" she cried. Bill chuckled as he walked out to the pantry and grabbed an empty box, placing each small duckling inside. He lifted the box and walked towards the lounge.

"Er, where do you think you are going with them?" She asked, Bill, sighed.

"You want them out of the way don't you!" he said and took them to the lounge anyway.

Over dinner and over the noise of the latest family additions Peggy and Bill were chatting about their day.

"Oh, I almost forgot!" Bill said, wide-eyed and full of excitement. Peggy put her knife and fork down on the plate and waited. "I have been offered a job at the farm," he said so matter-of-factly.

"But I thought that you couldn't do manual labour?" Peggy said, sounding almost disappointed.

"It's just as well that I have been offered the job of farm manager then isn't it!" He roared with jubilation. Peggy jumped up in the air and then ran to him, throwing her arms around him as she did.

"Oh Bill, that's wonderful news!" she said and kissed him.

BOB

Bob walked into the house after a hard day's graft, he was absolutely knackered! He went straight to his room, to grab himself some clean clothes, then walked to the bathroom and began running a hot, foamy bath.

As he lay, enjoying the warm water there was a knock on the door.

"Robert, is that you in there?" Martha asked, he stayed silent, and she knocked again.

"I say, Robert is everything all right?"

"Robert isn't in here," he called out in a posh voice.

"Oh, I do apologise, how dreadful of me, anyway, do carry on, I shall leave you in peace," she said and then he heard her scurry along the hallway to his room, where she knocked on his door and said the same thing. Bob quickly jumped out of the bath, dried himself and got dressed. He opened the door only slightly and watched as Martha had given up on the plight to find him and walked back down the stairs, he quickly ran along to his room, dumped his work clothes in the corner and then ran down the stairs. He walked to the lounge and peeked in, she wasn't there, so he quickly poured himself a drink and sat in front of the fire, making it look like he had been there for ages.

After a few minutes, she entered, smiled at him as she poured herself a sherry, and then sat opposite him.

"I feel so foolish," she sighed.

"Why, what's up?" Bob asked trying his hardest not to laugh.

"I thought that you were in the bath, so I knocked on the door, I think that it may have been the new guest that checked in this afternoon, he's a barrister you know," Martha explained as she blushed at the very thought. Bob nodded intently.

"I mean how utterly ridiculous of me, he must think me such a buffoon!" Martha continued. "I expect that my name will be nothing short of mud all over the Inns of Court tomorrow!" she sighed. Bob could no longer stifle the laugh and it burst out of his mouth like a deflating balloon.

"Robert isn't in here," he said as he laughed, Martha gasped.

"It was you, all the time, I have been fretting ever since the awful experience, honestly Robert sometimes the practical joker in you is simply just too much!" Martha fumed as Bob howled with laughter.

"I was just proving a point!" Bob said and wiped the tears of laughter away from his eyes.

"And your point is exactly?"

"That I am Bob, not Robert!" he said and burst out laughing again.

"Funny, very funny, sometimes you can be such an arsehole!" Martha said, causing Bob to gasp.

"Martha! Language!" Bob said and chuckled as Martha burst out laughing and sipped her sherry!

After dinner, he walked to Mags's house. Cyril had arrived at Martha's, so Bob grabbed the opportunity for some alone time with Mags, he had it all planned. He popped into the off-licence and brought a bottle of wine and some chocolate, thinking they could cosy up in front of the fire, he was almost skipping as he turned the corner of Mag's street. He straightened his collar, then tapped on the front door. Within seconds Mags had answered it and jumped up at him with the front door still open. "Mags, the neighbours!" Bob said as he walked into the house carrying her and closed the front door, then he ran with her into the lounge, about to throw her onto the sofa, when he noticed Reg and Alice sitting on the sofa!

"What are you two doing here, aint you got homes to go to," Bob said disappointedly, then looked at Reg and scowled. He had already told him at work what he planned to do if Cyril was to visit Martha that evening. Reg awkwardly shrugged and then looked at the floor.

"They were at Alice's house, but her dad came back from the pub early and caught them at it!" Mags said and squealed with laughter.

"Oh no, what, he actually caught you at it? Reg you old rascal!" Bob said and then howled with laughter.

"It's not funny!" Alice snorted. "God only knows what the neighbours were thinking when Reg was chased outside by my old man with his trousers and y-fronts at his ankles!" Alice said as she began to cry. Reg tried to comfort her by putting his arm around her, but she shrugged him off.

"Where was your mum Alice?" Mags asked as she passed her a hanky.

"Bingo," she sniffed and then wiped her tears.

"I take it that you won't be going for Sunday dinner then?" Bob said as again he stifled a laugh.

"No, my dad said that he better not show his face anywhere near," Alice sniffed. Bob glanced at Reg who was blushing.

"What are you going to then?" Mags asked.

"Elope," Alice replied.

"Eh?" Reg said bewilderedly.

"We have to Reg, I have missed my monthly, we're going to have a baby!" Alice said and then burst into tears. Bob looked awkwardly at Mags.

"Right, well, we're going to pop up the shop, leave you two to talk it over," Bob said and gestured to Mags, who jumped up off of the armchair and walked out of the door.

"Blimey! Alice is pregnant!" Bob said and shook his head in disbelief.

"I told her to be careful, with you know," Mags said trying to be discreet as she grabbed hold of Bob's hand and they walked to the park. They sat down on the bench. "Bob, there's something that I have to tell you," Mags said and gulped. Bob's eyes widened.

"You're not… are you?" He asked as he looked at her tummy.

"No silly! We're more careful than them two, no Mr Edelman has offered me a promotion, it's a year's training then he wants me to set up my own factory," she said.

"That's wonderful Mags, well done, see I told you that you were brilliant didn't I," Bob said exuberantly.

"There is one more thing," she added apprehensively.

"What, what is it?" Bob asked anxiously.

"The factory is in Kent, so it would mean moving there," she replied nervously.

"Oh I see, does that mean that the wedding is off then?" He asked looking down at the ground. Mags placed her hand on his leg.

"Only if you want it to be, I mean, I'll understand if you don't want to come with me," she said, hoping beyond hope that he would come.

"Of course, I want to come with you, I couldn't imagine life without you, I love you more than life itself," Bob said quietly. "I just wasn't sure that I was invited," he added. She took his face in her hands.

"I have never been happier since the day that you walked into my life, I love you with all my heart," she said sincerely. He threw his arms around her and held her as tight as he possibly could without crushing her!

They took a slow walk back to the house and chatted about their future, how very exciting it all was, a new beginning for both of them!

The mood inside the house had changed and when they returned, Alice and Reg were sitting cuddled up together on the sofa.

"You wanna go careful, you've already been caught in the act once today," Bob said and laughed as they walked into the lounge, warming their hands in front of the fire.

"Very funny Bob, such a comedian," Reg said and shook his head.

"So, have you two worked out what you are going to do?" Mags asked as she sat in front of the flickering flames of the fire. Alice smiled the biggest smile and nodded.

"We are going to Scotland, we'll get married and live up there, Reg can go back to the butchers," Alice said cheerfully. Bob glanced at Reg, whom he believed was not sharing the same sort of enthusiasm as Alice.

"When? When are you planning on going?" Mags asked.

"I'll see this week out at work, and then we'll head on up there," Reg replied.

"But where's Alice going to stay until the wedding?" Mags asked, that's one of the reasons that Bob loved her so much, she was always sensible, and she always looked at the bigger picture. Reg looked at Alice and shrugged.

"Hold on a minute," Bob said and walked to the hallway, returning a few minutes later. "Sorted, she can stay with Peg and Bill until the wedding, I just phoned and asked," Bob said and grinned at Mags.

"Oh Bob, you are such a darling," Mags cooed. Reg looked unsure and it wasn't until Bob thought about it that he understood why.

"Right, well we had better leave you two beauties, we've both got an early start in the morning," Bob said as he stood up. They said their goodbyes and began the walk back to Martha's.

"Reg she will be fine with Peg, she has no problem with Alice, they got on like a house on fire," Bob said and nudged him.

"I hope that you're right Bob," Reg replied with more than a hint of uncertainty in his voice.

CHAPTER 22

Alice stayed with Peggy and Bill for three weeks while they arranged a swift shotgun wedding. It was a small but beautiful day and Alice looked gorgeous in the dress that Shona had made and designed for her, with the help of Mags's advanced tailoring skills. Bob and Mags had booked a week off and spent the week with them.

That all seemed such a long time ago, Peggy was thinking as she opened the duck pen and let her darlings out. The stench from the pen was awful, so Peggy went straight to work and began to clean it out. She walked back inside the cottage and into the warm kitchen where the oven was warming everywhere nicely, the aroma of cakes baking was wonderful, and she took in a deep breath as she put the kettle on to boil. She closed Carrie's cookbook and placed it back on the shelf, she had been tempted to bake one of the recipes from the Grimoire but thought better of it! She made a pot of tea, looked at the time on the clock, and then put out three cups and saucers out in readiness. 9.30 on the dot there was a knock on the front door. Peggy answered and Mrs Tanner and Shona followed her through to the kitchen.

"Oh I say, what a wonderful smell, what are you baking?" Mrs Tanner asked as Peggy handed her a cup of tea and a bottle of her usual dandelion tea.

"Bonfire cakes, it's an old family recipe," Peggy said as she passed Shona her cup of tea and then checked the time. She opened the oven door and felt the cakes, happy that they were adequately cooked she grabbed her oven mitt and took them both out placing them on the hob.

"Could I have the recipe, you see I am taking over the café, my dear mother is too old and frail to continue," Mrs Tanner asked.

"Of course Mrs Tanner, hang on and I'll write it down for you," Peggy replied as she grabbed the recipe book from the shelf and walked out to the hallway in search of pen and paper.

"Please, call me Annis," she called out as Peggy returned with pen and paper.

"That's a lovely name," Shona said as she placed her cup back onto the saucer.

"Aye it's the Gaelic version of Agnes," Annis replied and smiled. Peggy had finished writing the recipe and gave the piece of paper to Annis. "Thank you so much, Peggy, I'll do this as a bonfire week special," she said as she folded the paper and placed it into her handbag. "Are you girls doing anything special for bonfire night?" she asked as she drank her entire cup of tea in one gulp!

"Aye, I have family travelling up from London, Bill has permission to do a small display at the farm and build a bonfire, they have so much scrap wood knocking around that it gives them a chance to get rid of it all," Peggy said and smiled, she was so excited and was finding it hard to contain, not only was Bob and Mags travelling up today, but also Martha, she hadn't seen her for two months and she missed her so, she had become Peggy and Bob's surrogate mum.

"Lovely, well I must go, I have to collect wee Heather from school and take her to the opticians," Annis said as she stood.

"How is wee Heather, would you like to bring her to the display?" Peggy asked.

"Oh, she's fine, growing up too quickly for my liking, what time are you starting?" Annis said as she edged towards the door. Peggy frowned and looked at Shona. "The fireworks?" she added as she opened the front door.

"Seven I think, I'll ask Bill when he gets home and I'll give you a call," Peggy shouted as Annis was about to close the door.

"Cheery bye," she called out as she walked quickly down the path.

 Peggy sat opposite Shona at the table.

"And to what do I owe the pleasure, sure it's Thursday today," Peggy said and poured then both the last of the tea that was in the pot.

"Aye I know, but I have something to tell you," Shona said excitedly. Peggy leaned forward in anticipation. "My dad has a contact in Paris, he came over and stayed at the house, this morning he asked if I would like to go to return with him and work in his fashion house for a year!" Shona screamed. Peggy screamed out, jumped up and grabbed hold of Shona dancing her around the kitchen.

"Oh Shona, that's wonderful!" Peggy said as she danced her around again. "When are you leaving?" Peggy asked as they both returned to their seats.

"Pierre is leaving on Tuesday, so I guess it will be then," Shona replied.

"Pierre eh!" Peggy said and laughed, Shona, tutted and tapped the back of Peggy's hand.

"I will miss you so," Peggy sighed and looked at an incredibly happy Shona. Shona grabbed Peggy's hand and held it tightly.

"I feel happier leaving you now, you know since Bill has changed, and I will come and visit," Shona said and smiled.

"You promise?" Peggy asked.

"Cross my heart," Shona replied.

Later that afternoon, Peggy had finished getting the rooms ready for her guests and she walked down the stairs with her arms full of laundry when the front door opened, and Bill walked in. "You're back early," she said as he took the bundle from her and walked into the kitchen.

"Aye, I have just got back from the infirmary," Bill replied as he put the laundry out into the basket in the pantry.

"The infirmary, why what's happened?" Peggy asked anxiously as her heart began to race.

"Young Smithy got caught in the tetherer," He said as he filled the kettle.

"Oh my goodness!" Peggy exclaimed as she placed her hand over her mouth.

"It's alright, there was no permanent damage, just cuts and bruises, he's a lucky young fella though, it could have been a lot worse!" Bill said and shook his head.

"How did it happen?" Peggy asked and smiled as Bill passed her a steaming cup of coffee.

"The boy was not paying attention, the machinery stopped, so he climbed out of the tractor, and began to meddle with it, rather than leaving it and coming back to the office, something had become jammed and as soon as he released it the bloody thing started to move, and he became caught up in it. I was checking the fencing in the next field and heard him scream," Bill said, clearly shaken by the whole event.

"You poor thing," Peggy said and held his hand.

"Oh, I'm alright Peg, he hasn't had to stay in so that's good," he said and smiled, then he looked at the clock. "Blimey, their train is due in half an hour," he said. Peggy smiled.

"Aye that it is, Reg is picking them up," Peggy said. Bill nodded.

"I wonder if he would run me in the van to collect the fireworks?" Bill said.

"Ask him when he drops them off, he and Alice are coming for dinner tonight," Peggy replied, then walked out to the garden to call the ducks in.

It was complete chaos when they all arrived! Peggy showed them to their rooms, she was a little embarrassed when she showed Martha and Cyril that they were sharing a twin room. Martha looked at Cyril and grinned.

"I'm sorry that we cannot give you a separate room, but we only have three bedrooms," Peggy said awkwardly.

"It's absolutely fine Peggy, it's awfully quaint, and just look at that view!" She said as she looked out of the window and pointed.

"Well, I hope that you will both be comfortable, I'll leave you to unpack," Peggy sighed with relief as she walked to the door.

"It's all right Cyril, we can push the beds together," Peggy heard Martha whisper as she closed the door. Peggy ran down the stairs sniggering and ran straight into Bill, she wasted no time at all in telling him what she had just overheard. Bill roared with laughter, then tutted and shook his head. "She's a sly fox, that Martha!" he said as he laughed.

Peggy had cooked a huge meal for them all and they all seemed full-up and content as they moved from the dining room into the lounge, Bill had lit all of the fires, and Peggy was happy to be using the dining room again, she remembered back to when they used it last, it was when Abe, Michael and Molly were, Carrie had appeared and smiled, how Peggy missed them all so much, she was thinking. Because it was just the two of them, it seemed such a waste, heating the room just for supper, so they didn't really make use of the room that much.

Bill had handed out the drinks and Peggy looked around the full room and smiled, how Carrie would have loved it, how she would have adored Bob and Mags, and Martha! Peggy thought to herself as she smiled. Bill tapped her hand, he could see that she was reminiscing.

"So tell me, Peggy, how far is it to Loch Ness from here?" Martha asked.

"It's about an hour and a half drive," Reg jumped in and replied.

"Oh, I'd love to go and see the monster," Mags sighed.

"We'll take you into town girl, you'll see a few of them there!" Bob said and roared with laughter, and so too did Bill and Reg.

"I could ask Dougal if we could borrow the school minibus for the day," Reg said once he had stopped laughing. They all nodded in agreement. "Remind me in the morning to pop and see him," Reg said to Alice. Peggy looked at Alice endearingly, she seemed to take to rural life, she thought, Martha must have read her thoughts.

"How are you finding life up here in Bonnie Scotland Alice?" Martha asked. Alice looked at Reg and smiled.

"I love it, Martha, the people are so lovely and friendly, and I love being close to Peggy, she really looks after me," She said and smiled directly at Peggy, Peggy smiled.

"As always, she is a wonderful specimen of a human being, don't you all agree," Martha said and jiggled her empty glass at Bill. They all nodded and agreed, Bill got up and poured Martha, yet another drink.

The following day, Peggy, Bob, Mags, Martha, and Cyril took a walk into town, Bill was supposed to have the day off, but after the accident, he was a man down. They wandered in and out of the small shops, and then Peggy suggested that they go to the café for a drink. Old Mrs Campbell was behind the counter bossing Annis around like a servant girl, and as they all walked in Annis rolled her eyes at Peggy. Peggy ordered the drinks as the others sat at two tables. "How did wee Heather get on at the opticians?" Peggy asked Annis as she hurriedly served the drinks under the watchful eye of the dreadful Mrs Campbell.

"Oh fine thank you, Peggy, she has a wee squint that's all," Annis replied as she put the remainder of the drinks on another tray. "The wee bugger won't wear her glasses though," she said and chuckled.

"Why don't you bring her over next week, I think I might have something for that," Peggy said, Annis smiled and nodded.

"Aye I will, thanks Peggy," She replied as she passed the two trays towards her.

"Bloody mumbo jumbo, a good clip round the ear is what that lass needs," Mrs Campbell grumbled as Peggy carried one of the trays to the table, she returned and looked at Annis who was shaking her head at her elderly mother, Peggy chuckled and grabbed the other tray.

They had finished their drinks and Peggy placed the empties onto the trays and took them to the counter. Mrs Campbell sat on a stool and wiped her brow.

"Are you not feeling too well?" Peggy asked as she put the second tray down on the counter.

"Old age is all," she grumbled.

"I might have something for that too," Peggy said and looked at Annis chuckling.

"What like a shot of laughing gas!" Bob whispered as he walked past and overheard the conversation.

Annis burst out laughing, Mrs Campbell shot her a look.

"Haven't you got work to do, I can see this place going to rack and ruin when I go," she said and shook her head, Peggy raised her eyebrows and looked at Annis.

"I'll see you and wee Heather tomorrow then," she said as she walked towards the door, the others were waiting outside for her. Annis nodded and hurried into the back kitchen on the orders of her mother!

Saturday evening came around quickly, and Peggy had been rushed off of her feet all day, preparing food. Reg and Alice arrived at three in the afternoon, Reg had brought boxes full of sausages. Mrs Dooley, who was a girl guide leader had kindly agreed to lend them the grill that they used on camps to cook the sausages and baked potatoes, and then Reg began transporting everything to the farm, where Bill and Bob were setting things up. Martha and Cyril spent most of the day out walking and exploring, Martha seemed to be in her element.

They all arrived early and sat down on the hay bales that Bob had put out earlier.

"I say, this is wonderful, what an absolutely idyllic lifestyle," Martha sighed as she sat beside Cyril on a bale and looked around the farm. Alice had made posters and put them all over the town, inviting the locals to come to the display, and now many began to arrive. Peggy and Mags were cooking and serving the food, Bill and Bob were lighting the bonfire, and Reg and Alice were serving drinks.

Peggy was grabbing another handful of sausages when she heard a familiar voice.

"I'll have two sausages and a baked potato," she heard, slowly she stood to be faced with Jean bloody Douglas! "Actually, if she's cooking I don't want anything, I don't fancy food poisoning!" She snorted. Mags looked at her and frowned.

"Don't be so rude!" Mags said angrily.

"I can do as I like, I don't have to answer to a dirty Londoner like you!" Jean roared, now getting the attention of everyone who was there. Mags said nothing, she looked at Peggy wide-eyed. Peggy walked around from behind the grill to be nose-to-nose with Jean.

"You are not welcome here, now go away before I let her at you," Peggy growled through gritted teeth. Jean shoved Peggy so hard that she flew backwards into a gathering of people, who luckily caught her. Annis was one of them, she ran at Jean and shoved her, and she flew backwards into Mags who had run out from behind the grill. Mags jumped up and grabbed her by the face, she pulled her fist back and punched her in the face, causing blood to explode from her bruised and swollen nose.

Stan walked over to the now gathered crowd and pushed through, he grabbed hold of Jean and marched her to where her brother was sitting.

"I suggest that you take her away from here before she gets really hurt. One day Jean Douglas, you will learn to keep that filthy mouth of yours shut!" Stan bellowed and pushed her at her brother, who turned and saw that all the local men were now standing behind Stan, in unity. He grabbed his sister by the arm and dragged her to his car, then they pulled off at high speed forcing the tyres to screech.

"Sorry about that everyone, if you would now please walk to the bonfire, Bill is just about to light it," Stan said, the crowd cheered and clapped then walked to the huge bonfire. Bill walked around and saw that Heather had made a guy and brought it with her. He walked to her, grabbed her by the hand and walked her to the bonfire.

"Are you ready?" He asked, she nodded, her eyes glistening with excitement. She handed Bill the guy, which he threw to the top of the bonfire and the crowd cheered as the guy began to burn. Peggy walked over to Bill, he placed his arm around her shoulder. "I'm sorry about Jean," he whispered in her ear.

"You have nothing to be sorry for," she whispered back and then kissed his cheek.

The night was filled with 'oohs and 'ahhs as Bill and Bob detonated the fireworks. Peggy, Mags Martha, and Alice stood together, and arm in arm they watched as the beautiful fireworks exploded into the dark night sky.

"I must say that this has probably been one of the best nights of my life," Martha said once they had returned to the cottage and were warming themselves by the fire drinking cocoa, the others all nodded in agreement, well all except for Mags who was frowning.

"Yeah, except for that horrible cow at the food stand, who was she Peg?" Mags asked, Peggy, looked at Bill, who nodded.

"That was Jean Douglas," Peggy said and looked at the floor ashamedly.

"It was not!" Martha shouted. "If I had known that I would have given her a bloody good hiding myself!" she scorned and looked at Peggy.

"Well, I am even happier that I punched her on the nose then, cheers everyone," Mags said and lifted her cup into the air.

"Cheers!" they all said in unison and laughed, Bill looked at Peggy and mouthed sorry, she smiled at him and shook her head.

Chapter 23

Normality had resumed at the cottage now that the London lot had left, Peggy had done all the jobs that were on her list for the day and was wondering what on earth she was going to do until it was time to prepare the evening meal. She turned the radio on, only to turn it off, she had no interest in how to effectively clean your oven! She quietly walked through all the empty rooms, the distant echoes of the voices that filled them, still resounding. She walked over to the sideboard in the dining room and lifted Carrie's framed photo. She held it close to her heart and sighed, how she missed her, she thought as tears began to sting her eyes.

Now that she had found Bob, Peggy felt as though her work was as much as done, she had built a good reputation amongst the community, and she and Bill were happy, and relatively well off, but she still felt as though there was something missing, something important. She was staring out of the window, where Carrie would sit and enjoy the sunshine, and very soon became lost in the memories that had begun to flow through her mind like a stream trickling forward to become something much greater.

How she listened as Carrie spoke of turbulent times, how she had carried the burden, and whatever crossed her path, be it good, or bad, she would continue on her plight relentlessly. Peggy could not imagine having to cope with the heartache and loss that Carrie had to endure, yet she had a purpose, to extend and protect the magical bloodline, to keep the Grimoire safe for future purposes, and above all else sacrifice everything that she loved in that pursuit.

Peggy felt useless, she had no magical powers, she didn't have the gift of insight, and the best that she could do was create healing potions (following Abagail's instructions from the Grimoire!) and see pictures within the old soggy remains of tea leaves! She sighed out loud, then her thoughts were rudely interrupted by the sound of her ducks quacking frantically. She ran to the kitchen and opened the door. She stepped out into the garden and came face to face with a large red fox, who clearly had sights on her ducks as his dining preference. The frantic ducks waddled to stand behind Peggy, making an awful racket as they did, the fox, however, remained cool and calculated as it stood in a staring contest with Peggy.

"Now you'll do yourself well and leave my wee darlings alone Mr Fox, they are not for animal consumption!" Peggy said sternly, the ducks had now quietened and were huddled in a group at her ankles. The fox continued to stare, and then it began to growl as it bared its sharp teeth, Peggy was trembling now, and even though she feared that the fox might attack her, there was no way on this earth that she would let it touch her ducks! The fox crouched, in an attack position and before she knew it, the fox lunged forward at her. She raised her hand in the air and shouted, what she shouted was non-comprehensible, and she had no idea where it had come from, but, and this is a big but, the fox jumped back, whining, and cowering, then Peggy could have sworn that it bowed it's head at her before it ran to the back of the garden, its tail between its legs and jumped over the high wall. She sat on the grass and comforted the ducks for a while, then she walked to the wall, peering over to make sure that the fox had cleared off and was not lying in wait for her to go back inside. She could see no sign of it, but she was still shaken by the whole experience, so she decided to round the ducks up and lead them to the safety of their pen.

Happy that her darlings were now safe, she walked back to the cottage and jumped back as she walked straight into the path of Alice, who was clearly distraught.

"Whatever has happened?" Peggy asked anxiously as she ushered Alice into the kitchen and guided her to a chair.

"I keep getting these awful pains Peggy, and this morning I lost some blood," Alice cried, her hands trembling. Peggy took her hands into her own, trying to calm her. "You don't think that I am losing the baby do you Peggy?" she sobbed, now bordering on hysterical, Peggy knew that she needed to calm her down.

"Come into the lounge," Peggy replied shaking her head, trying to reassure her. "Now lie yourself down there," she said gently as she led Alice to the sofa, Alice nodded and did as Peggy had asked. Peggy inhaled deeply, closed her eyes, and quietly meditated, just like Michael had taught her, enabling her to enter a higher state of consciousness. She looked at Alice who was still silently weeping and stroked the hair away from her face, in a bid to comfort her.

"I am going to place my hands just above your tummy," Peggy said and smiled, Alice nodded. Peggy could feel the energy running through her body, into her palms and out through her fingertips. She held them just above Alice's enlarged tummy and closed her eyes. She could see in her mind's eye, Alice, and Reg's baby, she could see its tiny heart beating away, ten to the dozen, and then she saw her as a wee lassie, running up and down their small yard. Peggy opened her eyes and looked at Alice, who looked like she was going to explode in anticipation of what Peggy was going to say. Peggy smiled, "She is absolutely fine Alice" Peggy announced and then quickly slapped her hand over her mouth when she realised that she had given the sex of the baby away. Alice grinned, as wide as a Cheshire cat.

"So she's a she?" Alice said excitedly as she wiped the residual tears away from her flushed cheeks. Peggy rolled her eyes and then nodded.

"Oh, Peggy, how wonderful, thank you!" Alice said as she sat up and threw her arms around her.

"Now you wait there for a wee minute, just relax, I won't be long," Peggy said as she trotted out to the garden shed. She quickly opened the chest and took out the Grimoire, which she placed on the worktop while she closed the chest and to her complete amazement the pages began to flick back and forth, completely independently. Once they had stopped Peggy looked at where they had remained open. It was a recipe for an elixir, she wasted no time and quickly scribbled the ingredients and instructions down, kissed the Grimoire and placed it back in the chest, she ran as fast as she could back to Alice, who was in the same position as she had left her, still grinning from ear to ear.

"I can make you something to put in your tea at night-time," Peggy said and waved the piece of paper at Alice, "I just have to nip out and collect a few things, now do you want to wait here for me, or should I call Reg and ask him to collect you?" Peggy asked.

"I'll wait here if that's all right," Alice said and sighed a most contented sigh.

"I won't be long," Peggy said as she hurried out to the hallway, donned her coat and scarf, and walked out of the back door. She climbed the wall behind the cottage and ran through the field behind until she came to the gate, which led down to the small stream, she knew that there was a fine willow tree there which elegantly draped over the water. She came to it and bowed, again, just as Michael had taught her all those years ago.

"Please may I take some of your bark to help my friend who is with child?" Peggy asked, looking all around, hoping that no one would see her. She saw the tree nod, she bowed again, took a nail file from her pocket, and chiselled at the trunk, taking just enough of the bark to make the elixir. She thanked the tree and hurried back to the cottage. When she returned, she checked in on Alice, who was now in the kitchen waiting for the kettle to boil, and then she went back to the shed. She prepared the elixir, bottled it, and took it back to the kitchen, handing it to Alice who had filled the teapot and put out the cups.

"Put three drops in your last cup of tea, before you go to bed, no more and no less," Peggy said and smiled. Alice held the bottle close to her heart.

"Thank you so much, Peg, I don't know what I'd do without you," Alice said and smiled, an affectionate smile. Peggy rubbed the top of her head and then sat opposite her at the table. They seemed to have been chatting for ages when the front door knocked, Peggy answered it and smiled when she saw Reg, she was glad that Alice didn't have to walk the long walk back to the town.

"I guessed that she would be here," Reg said as Peggy led him through to the kitchen. Peggy refilled the kettle, while Alice told him all about the scare and then what Peggy had done. Peggy poured them all a cup and returned to her chair.

"She's the best is Peggy," Reg said affectionally and winked at Peggy.

"I know, why don't you and Bill come for dinner tonight?" Alice suggested excitedly, she just wanted to repay Peggy for all of her kindness. Peggy frowned.

"I thought that I told you to take things easy young lady," Peggy scorned. Alice chuckled and looked at Reg,

"I will be taking it easy Peg, you see, I've been teaching my Reggie how to cook, he makes a smashing Spaghetti Bolognese, don't you Reggie," she said and smiled, Reg chuckled and nodded, then rolled his eyes at Peggy.

"Spaghetti eh! Bill loves Spaghetti," Peggy lied and chuckled to herself, remembering back to when Peggy had it on their first trip to London, then she remembered the parmesan cheese and screwed her face up.

"You don't serve it with Parmesan do you?" She asked wearing a look of complete and utter disgust, making both Alice and Reg laugh.

"No chance, loathe the stuff!" Reg replied as Peggy exhaled with relief.

"In that case, we would love to," Peggy said as she drank her tea.

"Come on then Allie, let's get you home for your afternoon nap," he said as he finished his tea and placed the cup into the sink.

"I'll drop by and pick you up at seven, is that a good time for you both?" Reg asked as Alice stood and hugged Peggy, still clutching onto the elixir. Peggy nodded and they both left.

BOB

He was busy tying the steel for the foundations of a large block of flats, he was working so hard and really missed Reg, he was like a workhorse, Bob was thinking to himself as he grabbed another load of steel and dragged it to the spot where he was working, then he heard the gaffer calling him.

"Robert, could you come up here?" Mr Sendle called out. Bob tutted, threw the steel onto the ground, and mumbled as he climbed the ladder out of the pit that he was enforcing. "It's not like I aint got anything else to do, I've got no labourer, nothing, doing the work of three men all by myself!" he muttered as he reached the top and walked over to Sendle and the man that he was standing with, who as Bob got closer released that his face was familiar, he couldn't think where, but he had most definitely seen this bloke before,

"Ah, here he is, my number one!" Sendle said, Bob, huffed and then smiled.

"What's up? It's just that I've still got a ton of steel to tie before the sun goes down," Bob replied with just a hint of sarcasm in his voice.

"Yes, quite," Sendle replied, feeling slightly embarrassed, Norris was an influential figure, and he didn't want him to think that he was skimping on his workforce.

"Robert, this is Mr Norris," he said and pointed to the man beside him, who looked like a teacher or professor or something, Bob was thinking. Bob nodded, wondering what the hell all of this had to do with him. "Actually, let's go to my office, there are a few things which I wish to discuss," Sendle said and looked at both men for approval, Norris smiled and nodded, Bob on the other hand sighed and tutted.

"Like I said, I've got a shit ton of steel to put in," Bob replied and shook his head, it was only yesterday that Sendle was complaining about deadlines, Bob was thinking. Sendle appeared to be deep in thought. Sendle grinned and looked at Bob.

"We have three more men joining the workforce tomorrow, so you may as well finish for today and pick up where you left off tomorrow," Sendle suggested. Bob reluctantly nodded, the temperature was dropping rapidly at night, and he didn't want all the hard work that he had already put in spoil, but Sendle was the boss, Bob was thinking as they walked towards Sendle's chauffeur-driven car and climbed in. Bob was slightly embarrassed, his work trousers were filthy and were sure to stain the posh upholstery, he was thinking. As they drove through London towards the centre Bob was watching Norris, the more he looked at him, the more familiar he seemed to become.

Sitting in Sendle's posh office, Bob was looking around at all the extravagant furniture and ornaments, blimey, he thought, they must pay well in the secret service, I mean look at Martha's house, that must have cost a fair bob or two! Sendle handed Bob a scotch and sat down behind his huge oak desk, Bob and Norris were on the other side in two fancy chairs.

"Now then Robert, Mr Norris has been a friend and business associate for many years, and he has approached me about building a new venture for the, er, company that he runs," Sendle said awkwardly and looked at Norris, who nodded.

"We need some assistance building our new offices, they are underground and there have been a few issues with the foundations," Norris said, his voice gentle and incredibly well-spoken. Bob nodded, waiting for elaboration. Norris cleared his throat.

"Yes, we have a team of workers, who although incredibly experienced in working underground, simply cannot get to grips with the sedimentary rock on which London is built," Norris continued, still Bob nodded, then looked at Sendle.

"Tomorrow, I will take you to the site, where you can assess the foundations and see if your expertise can offer any form of a solution," Sendle said and smiled.

"But I thought that we had some new men starting tomorrow, how are we gonna sort them out if we are swanning around the city," Bob said. Sendle shook his head.

"That is not for you to worry about Robert, you leave all of that to me, now as we have concluded our business for today, you have the remainder of the afternoon to do as you wish," Sendle said almost shooing Bob out of the office.

"Oh, all right then," Bob said as he was being ushered to the door.

"I will send my car for you at eight-thirty sharp!" Sendle said as he closed the door as Bob walked out. He walked through the office block watching the office staff as they went about their daily business, all the while, thinking to himself that there was no way he could ever work in that sort of environment. As he stepped out onto the pavement he wondered what on earth he was going to do with himself for the rest of the day. Mags was at work, and he didn't fancy going back to Martha's, she and Cyril had become inseparable, and were all loved up, forever dancing around the living room, no matter what time of the day it was! That was it! He was going back to work, Mags wasn't expecting him til seven.

He finished what he had set out to do that morning and was pleased with the result. If nothing else, he was meticulous in his work, and everything had to be perfect. He climbed into his car and drove back to Martha's, once there, he would have a quick bath and then head on over to Mag's house, she was cooking for him tonight and he couldn't wait, she was the best cook, he was thinking as he parked up and ran up the steps.

"Is that you Bob, we are in here," Martha shouted from the lounge as he crept through the reception, he rolled his eyes and then walked in.

"All right?" he said as he popped his head around the door, most of the time he was terrified of what he might see!

"Yes darling, change of plan tonight," Martha beamed, Bob frowned.

"What do you mean? Mag's is cooking me a pie for dinner," he replied, Martha, chuckled and shook her head.

"No darling, we are going out for dinner, the four of us, to discuss your wedding plans," Martha said excitedly.

"Does Mag's know about this?" Bob frowned, he was so disappointed, he was really looking forward to a nice night in, just the two of them, good food, listening to some cool music.

"Well of course she does, it was she who suggested it!" Martha scoffed. "Now, run along and smarten yourself up, you haven't got long you know," Martha replied and shook her empty sherry glass at Cyril. Bob shook his head in dismay and slowly walked up the stairs to get ready.

CHAPTER 24

The next few weeks flew by, Christmas was fast approaching and the very thought of it filled Peggy with warm anticipation. It had all been discussed and arranged at the bonfire gathering. They would all spend Christmas at Martha's, and they were staying from the eighteenth of December until the twenty-seventh when they would all then travel to Scotland for Hogmanay.

Martha had a friend who had a hotel in Edinburgh, and she had booked rooms for them all, it was going to be wonderful, Peggy was thinking as she inhaled deeply, she was steaming the Christmas puddings, and just the smell of them made her all the more excited. The back door opened, and Bill walked in, Peggy looked at the clock. "Is everything all right?" she asked as she checked the water in the pans, then filled the kettle.

"Aye, why?" Bill asked as he kissed her cheek and took off his work coat.

"It's only three-thirty," she replied and smiled.

"I know, we are well ahead of schedule so I gave the lads the afternoon off, I thought that there was no point in me hanging around twiddling my thumbs, when I could be home with my darling wife, in front of a roaring fire," he replied and walked up the stairs to change. Peggy filled the teapot and then walked to the lounge to light the fire, she usually wouldn't light the fires until five, there didn't seem much point when she spent the majority of her time in the kitchen. Very soon the fire was roaring, so she walked back to the kitchen, waiting for Bill, and as she waited the telephone rang. She hurried through the hallway and answered it.

"Peggy?" she heard.

"Shona is that you?" she replied.

"Aye, I can't really hear you, can you speak up," Shona shouted.

"How are you? How's Paris, and how is Pierre?" Peggy shouted, she had so many questions that she wanted to ask, she hadn't seen or heard from her for weeks!

"Old news, I am working with Albert now," Shona said and chuckled.

"Albert! Albert who?" Peggy again shouted.

"Not Albert, Albearrr" Shona corrected her with her French pronunciation.

"Ooh! Sounds very French," Peggy said excitedly.

"Oh Peggy, he is wonderful, that's why I am calling, we are coming back for Christmas so you can meet him then," Shona said elatedly.

"Oh no! We are spending Christmas in London," Peggy replied disappointedly.

"Oh, how long are you going there for?" Shona asked miserably.

"We are coming back on the twenty-seventh,"

"That's ok then, we are not leaving until the third of January," Shona said, her voice more cheerful now.

"We are spending Hogmanay in Edinburgh,"

"Really where?"

"Hang on, I'll see if I can find the name of the hotel, I did jot it down when Martha called, give me a sec will you," Peggy said and placed the receiver on the table as she shuffled through the mountain of notes that were piled high, she found it and quickly picked up the receiver.

"Shona," nothing, the line was dead. "Shit!" Peggy exclaimed as she slammed down the receiver as Bill walked through to the kitchen.

"What's wrong?" He asked as he lifted his cup and drank his tea.

"That was Shona, she is coming back for Christmas, she wanted to join us for Hogmanay, and I was trying to find the name of the hotel when she must have got cut off," Peggy sulked. Bill took hold of Peggy's hand.

"Peg, just drop the name and address off at her mum's house before we leave," he said and chuckled.

"Oh, Bill what would I do without you," Peggy sighed and laughed.

"Go and get yourself comfortable in front of the fire while I put the ducks away," he said as he moved her towards the door.

"I can't, I'll need to get supper ready soon," she replied as she lifted the now steamed puddings from the pans.

"No you don't, tonight I am treating us to fish and chips," he said and winked.

"But Bill, that means that we will have to walk into town to collect them," Peggy said not relishing the thought of walking into the town, the wind was blowing fiercely, and the air was icy cold.

"No we don't, Stan is going to drop them off at six," Bill said as he closed the back door behind him, Peggy sighed a contented sigh and walked into the lounge, throwing the sofa cushions on the floor in front of the toasty fire.

BOB

He thought it was a bit strange when they first went to assess the foundations that none of the workforce were there, for such a big job it really should have been round-the-clock shift work, and now he knew why!

He didn't bother to drive to work, there was never a parking space to be had, which was not surprising really, what with Charing Cross station being situated right beside the Strand, so instead, he caught the underground.

And there he was just another morning standing on a packed tube train, with dozens of strangers all doing the same thing, he looked at the lady, wearing a tailored suit and wondered what her story was? Maybe she was a high-flying executive, or a politician maybe? He studied her for a while then had a funny thought. What if he struck up a conversation with one of these strangers, and they asked him about where he worked, would they believe him? He doubted that very much, if someone had told the same story to him, he would laugh in their face, he thought and chuckled.

It took him back to his first proper day there. He arrived and walked to the concealed entrance, just as Mr Norris had shown him, beneath the station. He took out the stupid-looking medal and placed it over the same medal which was embossed into the thick metal door, which opened, and he walked through. Now, what he witnessed next, made him question his sanity, a small man, no more than about three and a half feet tall walked over to him and held out his hand to shake, Bob thought that he was losing it and had to look twice!

"Hello there, you must be Robert," the man said, Bob was speechless, just standing with his mouth gaped open. "I take it from your reaction they never told you," he added, Bob slowly shook his head. "My name is Alius, I am the foreman," he said and waved his hand around, Bob took hold of his hand to shake, but felt as though a current of electricity was shooting through his hand and up his arm, he quickly pulled his hand away and shook it to relieve the lingering ache. "Hmm, magical blood," the dwarf said and looked at Bob suspiciously. Bob frowned not having a clue what this little man was talking about, and then another appeared.

"Robert this is Darlia, he is the miner elder," Alius said as Darlia held out his hand to Bob, who was now in a state of shock. "He cannot shake, magical blood," Alius said to the other dwarf.

"Right, just hang on a minute, let me get this straight, are you all like this?" Bob asked and pointed to the fact that they were so much smaller than his five foot ten well-built frame.

"Yes that is correct, we are dwarves," Alius said, while Darlia nodded in agreement. Bob burst out laughing.

"What is this, is someone on a wind-up? I feel like I have just walked onto the set of snow white!" he said as he laughed. Both dwarves were most offended by his remarks and scowled at him fiercely. Footsteps could be heard walking through the echoey tunnel and Mr Norris walked out.

"Ah, Robert, nice and prompt I see," He said and smiled over the top of his glasses.

"Michael, this is simply not on! This man has just ridiculed us, we won't stand for it you know!" Alius shouted, making Bob laugh all the more. Then the penny dropped, he knew he had seen Norris before and now he knew where.

"Michael, that's it, that's where I have seen you, from the photos in Carrie's chest!" Bob shouted and pointed.

The train stopped with a jerk, forcing Bob from his daydream as he looked out of the window to see the word EMBANKMENT displayed, he realised that he had reached his stop and quickly disembarked the train. He walked amongst the swathes of fellow travellers as they hit the escalators and then the exit gates, he checked the time on his pocket watch, which he carried everywhere, it was all right, he still had plenty of time, he thought as he walked back out into the daylight and walked towards the concealed entrance.

He had become quite used to the dwarves now they were all so hard-working, and he liked them all, they would have such a laugh on every shift, and they all seemed enthralled at how Bob worked. He walked through the long tunnels until he came to the point where the new dig was starting. As always Alius was there, ready and waiting.

"So boss, how are we doing this today?" Alius asked as Bob took out his nips. Bob spent the next ten minutes explaining the procedure to Alius when the rest of the gang arrived, one of whom Bob did not recognise. They all greeted Bob and set to work immediately. Bob walked over to the new one and tapped him on the shoulder.

"You're not one of the usual suspects are ya?" Bob said. The dwarf turned and smiled.

"Indeed I am not, I am here to oversee the progress," he replied as Darlia walked over to them both.

"Hans! What are you doing here?" he asked.

"I have been sent to check on the progress, how are you, friend?" Hans replied.

"Very well indeed, we have learned so much from this young man, and I can see that we could acquire many more contracts in the city, now that he has shared his expertise with us," Darlia said and smiled at Bob, who was now embarrassed and blushing.

"Wonderful!" he said and held out his hand to Bob. Darlia cleared his throat to gain Hans's attention.

"Magical blood," he said just above a whisper.

"Really! Now I wonder…" Hans said as he ran his fingers through his beard.

"I believe that you knew his grandmother," Darlia said as his eyes lit up, he knew that Hans was always weary of Carrie, and some of them believed that he was actually scared of her!

"And whom was your grandmother may I ask?" Hans looked at Bob.

"Carrie," Bob said and winked at Darlia. Hans's face turned a deeper shade of scarlet and he choked when he heard the name, once he had recovered he stood back and took a long look at Bob, weighing him up.

"And do you share your grandmother's fierce temper?" Hans asked nervously, Bob began to chuckle, the dwarves had told him all about Hans, and how Carrie would call him fingers, simply just to annoy him.

"Well, only when people upset me Fingers," Bob replied making Darlia and the others snigger in the background. Hans rolled his eyes and shook his head.

PEGGY

She packed three suitcases full of clothes, Bill walked into the bedroom and shook his head. "Martha does own a washing machine you know Peg," he grumbled as he lifted the first heavy case to carry down to the front door.

"I know, but this is going to be special Bill," Peggy replied as she struggled with the second one. The phone rang and Bill answered, he chatted for a few seconds then hung up the receiver. Peggy looked at him.

"That was Stan, he is coming to collect us because apparently, Alice has packed that many cases that we won't fit in Reg's van!" Bill said and shook his head. "Women!" he muttered under his breath as he climbed the stairs to grab the last case, Peggy chuckled.

"Is he on his way now?" she called up the stairs.

"Aye, oh bloody hell!" she heard.

"Bill, what's happened?" Peggy shouted, relieved when he appeared at the top of the stairs hobbling and limping.

"I dropped this bloody case on my foot, what have you packed in it, the church roof!" Bill scorned as he limped down the stairs. Peggy ran up and relieved him of the case, chuckling as she carried it down the stairs with ease. She could hear the horn of Stan's van and looked at Bill.

"Come on then, Stan is here," Peggy said waving her arms around, then she ran through to the kitchen to check on the ducks. Bill was adamant that he was not putting their pen inside, but Peggy refused to go anywhere unless he did!.

"Now you be good won't you, we'll be back soon," she said as she kissed her finger and rubbed each of the ducks on the head.

"Peg, come on!" Bill shouted.

"Oh and Merry Christmas my wee darlings," Peggy said before she turned and ran to the front door.

The whole way to the station, Peggy was grilling Stan, checking that he knew what to do with the ducks, he looked at Bill and sighed.

"Peg I know how to take care of ducks, I am a butcher," he said smirking and looking through the rear-view mirror to gauge her reaction.

"Hey! There had better be four of them there when I get back!" She scowled, as Stan and Bill laughed.

They arrived at the station, Reg and Alice were already there waiting for them, with their huge mound of luggage. "Jeez, I thought that Peg had overdone it," Bill said and shook his head, Stan laughed.

"Thank you so much, Stan, you will take care of my darlings and the cottage won't you," Peggy said as she hugged him. Stan chuckled.

"Your wee darlings will be safe as houses with me Peggy especially if they like a good party," Stan replied and laughed.

"Don't say that Stan, she won't go!" Bill said and shook his head as Stan and Reg laughed.

"Go and have a wonderful Christmas and I'll see you all when you get back," he called out as Reg and Bill searched for trolleys for the cases. The cab pulled up outside

Martha's house and both Peggy and Alice gasped with delight. There was a huge Christmas tree in the lounge window, the biggest that Peggy had ever seen! And above the door were boughs of beautiful evergreens, draping down and blowing gracefully in the gentle breeze. Peggy looked at Bill and grinned in sheer delight.

"Oh Bill, I have a feeling that this Christmas is going to be wonderful!" Peggy sighed as they climbed out onto the pavement and were met by a shrieking Martha who was standing at the open door!

Peggy helped Alice to climb out of the cab, the pavement was slippery from the ice, they held hands and slowly and carefully walked up the steps to Martha's open arms. "Don't worry, we'll get the luggage," Bill shouted sarcastically. Peggy chuckled.

"Ok darling thank you!" she said and laughed as Martha threw her arms around her.

"Peggy darling I have missed you so, Cyril and I spend every evening chatting about you," she said in Peggy's ear as she retained her grip on her.

"Ahem," they both heard, Peggy turned to see Reg waiting patiently to gain access with two heavy cases.

"Sorry Reg darling, how are you?" Martha shouted as she released Peggy and grabbed hold of Reg. Peggy took the opportunity to slip inside unnoticed as Martha played her best role, the hostess with the mostest! Peggy shivered when she walked into the large foyer, then gasped when she noticed yet another huge tree at the bottom of the staircase, it was beautifully decorated, with incredibly unusual ornaments, which Peggy was admiring, Alice noticed and walked to Peggy.

"They are beautiful aren't they Peg, I wonder where she got them from?" Alice asked as she touched a spiral glass bauble.

"Oh, those ones I got when we were working in the middle east," Martha said as she walked past them towards the stairs. Alice looked at Peggy and raised her eyebrows.

"I didn't think that they celebrated Christmas in the middle east?" Bill said as he struggled with a case towards the stairs.

"It's your usual room Bill, now come along you are holding everyone up, and no they most certainly do not celebrate Christmas, I found these at a charming Bazaar," she said answering his question, straightening the bauble that both Peggy and Alice had disturbed.

Bill struggled past them all and tutted at Martha's remark, making his way up the staircase, Reg hot on his tails with one of Alice's many cases. Martha stood on the fourth stair and clapped her hands to gain everyone's attention.

"Well, hello my darlings and welcome to our magical family Christmas, I have many delights planned for us all, but I completely understand that you all must be exhausted from the long journey, so this evening, if you freshen up, we will have a nice, relaxed meal and an early night, ready for tomorrows planned events," She said her voice dancing joyfully. Bill turned to Reg as they both waited behind her, he rolled his eyes making Reg laugh.

"I saw that Bill!" She roared making everyone howl with laughter as Bill blushed profusely.

Chapter 25

Peggy grabbed the last case and took it to her and Bill's room, throwing it on the floor before falling onto the bed. "I could really do with a hot bath, I can't seem to be able to get warm," Peggy said as she sat up and shivered.

"You unpack and I'll go and run you a bath," Bill said as he kissed her head and left the room. Peggy smiled as she stood up and grabbed the heaviest of the cases, throwing it onto the bed.

"Look who I found skulking in the hallway," Bill said as he returned, Bob jumped out from behind him and raced over to Peggy.

"Here she is, my lovely Peg," he said and threw his arms around her. She laughed as he spun her around, then pulled a face when he put her down. She looked him up and down, he was filthy, and he reeked of metal!

"You could have changed first," Peggy said and fanned her nose with her hand.

"Don't be like that Peg, I've missed ya, wanted to come and see you as soon as I got back," he said and hugged her again, rubbing his smelly clothes in her face. She jumped back and frowned. "Oh all right then, I'll go and run me bath now, then we can have a good catch-up after," he said and grinned.

"You can't, I have just run the bath for Peg," Bill said as he grinned at Bob, who hugged him, then looked at Peggy.

"Ah, but here's the thing," he said as he edged towards the door. "It depends on who gets there first don't it," he said and ran out of the door towards the bathroom.

"Bob! Don't you dare!" Peggy shouted as she collected her clean clothes and towel and ran after him. He beat her to the bathroom, ran inside and slammed the door shut. "Bob, please, I can't get warm, and I really need a bath," she pleaded from the other side of the door. Martha walked along the hallway, she had heard them both from the reception. She gestured to Peggy to follow her and soon they were outside Martha's suite. Martha opened the door and gestured for Peggy to enter.

"Here darling use mine," Martha said as she opened a door, to reveal a huge free-standing bath in her huge bathroom. It was the first time that Peggy had ever been inside Martha's private suite, and it was exquisite, Peggy thought as she looked around at the plush furnishings and extravagant ornaments.

"Are you sure?" Peggy asked, not wishing to intrude, Martha's generosity had stretched enough, and Peggy was not one to take liberties.

She ran the water, and thoroughly enjoyed soaking in the big bathtub, she didn't spend as much time as she would ordinarily like, and once she had washed she climbed out and dressed quickly. She walked back to her room and was shocked that neither Bill nor Bob was anywhere to be seen. She had expected them both to be there waiting for her, but no, they had obviously gone down to see the others. She folded her clothes and placed them on the chair, checked herself out in the mirror, and happy with her reflection, she went to join the others.

They were all in the lounge and Martha and Cyril were handing the drinks out. Peggy entered and smiled as she saw Mags chatting with Alice, she looked for Bob, who was in conversation with Reg and Bill, all of whom were hysterically laughing. She walked to Martha and handed her the tins that she was holding, Martha looked at her wearing a puzzled expression. "Christmas puds," Peggy said and chuckled.
"Wonderful! Cyril, be a dear and take these to the kitchen for me," Martha asked and smiled at a much rounder Cyril than Peggy had remembered.

"Cyril is looking well," Peggy said and smiled, Martha frowned.

"What you are so eloquently trying to say, is that he has put on a few pounds," Martha said still frowning.

"Well, maybe, but it suits him, don't you think," Peggy said affectionately. Martha watched as Cyril returned and chatted with the boys, she had a look of deep fondness about her and was in an almost dream-like state as she turned her gaze back to Peggy who was now laughing.

"What?" Martha asked as she blushed.

"You're really quite taken with him aren't you?" Peggy said as she continued to giggle.

"Nonsense! We are simply good friends and companions," Martha sniffed.

"Really! It's all right Cyril, we can push the beds together," Peggy whispered in her ear as she laughed. Martha gasped, now blushing even more, then too began to laugh, and very soon they were both howling with laughter.

"Share the joy," Bob said as he joined them both and watched as still they laughed incessantly. Martha looked at Peggy frowned and shook her head.

"Private joke darling! Come, everyone, dinner is served," Martha called out as she looked at the door and nodded to an older woman who was beckoning to her. Peggy looked at Bob as Martha walked away.

"Who is she?" Peggy asked, not recognising her from previous visits. Bob shook his head.

"I dunno, never seen her before in me life," he replied as smiled as Mags and Bill walked to join them.

"But you live here, do you never speak to Martha," Peggy asked.

"She is Martha's new housekeeper, Mrs Briggs," Mags said and frowned at Bob, who looked at her in complete astonishment.

"And how the heck did you know that?" Bob asked.

"Because she introduced me to her when I came in!" Mags replied and they all began to descend to the dining room.

That evening Peggy, ready for bed slipped beneath the crisp clean sheets and sighed, it felt so good to lie down, she thought as she nestled her head into the softness of the feather pillow. Bill climbed in beside her, grabbed the newspaper and opened it.

"You're not going to read that all night are you?" Peggy yawned. Bill flicked the newspaper to straighten it and then looked at Peggy. "It's just that Martha said that we all needed to be in the dining room for seven thirty tomorrow morning, and you know that you become Mr Grumpy pants when you haven't had enough sleep!" Peggy mumbled as she turned over and pulled the covers over her head to shield her from the bedside lamp.

"What do you mean, I become Mr Grumpy pants, bloody cheek," Bill chuckled as he folded the newspaper and turned out the light.

The following morning they were all in the dining room at seven-thirty sharp, waiting for their breakfasts and an update on the planned events. Peggy smiled when she saw Lucy bringing out the breakfasts, she liked Lucy a lot, they used to have such a laugh when Peggy was earning her keep there, oh how times had changed, Peggy thought to herself as Lucy put down her and Bill's breakfasts.

"Hello, Peg, how are you love?" she asked and smiled.

"Grand thank you, Lucy, how's things with you?" Peggy replied.

"Oh you know, mustn't grumble eh," Lucy said and tutted as she walked back towards the kitchen.

"How come you got yours first, surely we should have been served first as we actually live here!" Bob scorned as he watched Bill tuck into his full English.

"Bob, don't be so impatient, besides Peg and Bill are guests!" Mags scorned and tapped the back of Bob's hand.

"But I'm hank Marvin Mags, listen, me old derby Kelly is groaning, can't you hear it," He said and dropped his lip, making Peggy laugh. She handed him a slice of her toast.

"Here eat it quickly before you waste away," Peggy said, looked at Mags and tutted.

"Spoil him you do!" Mags said and chuckled. Bob grinned as Lucy returned to the table with his and Mag's breakfasts, then just as he was about to tuck in, Martha appeared.

"If I could have your attention please," she called out, Bob reluctantly put his fork down and tutted, making Peggy, Bill, and Mags laugh.

"There will be a bus arriving at eight-thirty sharp to take us all to the West End, where we will spend the morning Christmas shopping, then on to lunch at the Savoy, followed by a matinee performance at Her Majesty's Theatre," Martha announced excitedly. Peggy looked at

Mags and squealed with elation, Mags did the same thing. Bob looked at Bill and frowned.

"Couldn't think of anything worse," he grumbled under his breath.

"Aye, I'm with you on that one Bob," Bill agreed.

"Don't be so bloody miserable!" Mags said and looked at Bob.

"Well, you know me Mags, I hate shopping!" he huffed.

"Well, it will give you the opportunity to buy me something nice for Christmas won't it," Mags said and winked at Peggy.

"Yes of course it will my love," Bob said sarcastically and rolled his eyes at Bill.

Bill's hands were hurting after two long hours of trudging in and out of the many shops on Oxford Street, carrying multiple bags of gifts that Peggy had brought. They walked out of Selfridges and Peggy squealed as a snowflake landed on her nose, "Shall we grab a coffee?" She asked Bill who looked as though he was losing the will to live. He nodded frantically, so she walked in the direction of the many coffee houses and the wonderful aroma that was filling the crisp air. She looked across the road and noticed Mags, who was waving and shouting from an outside terrace, Peggy waved back and then spent ten minutes trying to cross the wide traffic-filled road, without getting run down.

Bill threw the bags down and slumped into the empty chair beside Bob.

"Why are we sitting outside, in case it had escaped your attention, it's bloody snowing and bloody well freezing," Bob said as he exaggerated a shiver.

"It adds to the fun don't it, it's not often that we see snow, now stop moaning Bob, honestly," Mags said and huffed.

"I hope that you got Mags lots of lovely gifts," Peggy said to Bob, who rolled his eyes.

"Well, I couldn't, could I, she has been with me!" he replied.

"We could go together while the girls have their coffee, I need to grab some gifts for Peg," Bill suggested. Bob grinned and nodded.

"Bloody good call Bill," he said as he stood and kissed Mags, Bill kissed Peggy and very soon they were lost amongst the swathes of angry shoppers.

Peggy and Mags managed to have two coffees before the boys returned and when Mags spied Bob walking towards her, his hands full of bags she looked at Peggy and chuckled.

"Looks like we could be in for a grand Christmas Peg," she said, Peggy watched them both pushing through the vast array of people, their arms laden down with bags, "Come on, we'll miss the bus, and we don't want to be late for luncheon at the Savoy darlings!" Bob said imitating

Martha's posh voice, Peggy and Mags howled with laughter.

Peggy opened her eyes and looked at the clock on the bedside table, it was seven-thirty, she nudged Bill and swung her legs out of the bed, while Bill moaned as he checked the time.

"Why are we getting up early today?" he asked, he just wanted one day when they weren't traipsing around London, looking at this and that, going to shows, carol concerts, he was knackered and certainly not used to it, and his knee was aching from all the bloody walking!

"Because my love, it's Christmas eve, and I promised Martha that we would help out today, she has more guests arriving today," Peggy said as she brushed her hair. Bill mumbled and grumbled as he climbed out of bed.

So once the breakfasts had been cleared, Peggy, Mags and Alice set to work in the kitchen. Peggy and Alice were making sausage rolls, and Mags was making mince pies for the carols around the tree later that evening. Bob, Bill, and Reg were out picking up the meats from the butchers and the veg from the grocers. Mrs Briggs walked through into the kitchen and placed the heavy box that she was carrying onto the table, making all three girls jump from the sound of the thud! Peggy looked at her curiously and smiled.

"Buffet food," she said and began to take pork pies, large joints of cooked hams, and cheeses out from the box.

"Would you like us to give you a hand when we've finished?" Peggy asked much to the disgust of Alice, who had been so overcome by tiredness that she and Reg had spent much of their time there staying at the house.

"Oh that would be lovely Peggy dear," Mrs Briggs sighed feeling so relieved, she could have done with some extra hands and couldn't believe it when Martha gave Lucy the day off, of all the days, thank goodness she hadn't given her tomorrow off, what with twelve hungry mouths to feed! She was thinking to herself as she took out a mountain of platters and began to fill them with the contents of the box.

It was late afternoon when they had eventually finished and Peggy was happy to slump down beside Bill on the sofa, her feet were killing her! Alice had abandoned ship by lunchtime and gone up for her afternoon nap! Then Peggy remembered that she still had a few gifts to wrap, she looked at Bill and sighed.

"What's wrong?" He asked anxiously.

"I still have gifts to wrap!" Peggy fumed, making Bill chuckle.

"Well have your coffee first, I'm going to give Stan a call after, make sure that everything is ok," he said and winked, Peggy nodded and sipped the delicious coffee.

She felt quite revitalised after her coffee and was now in her room and set to work on the wrapping, she turned on the radio and smiled as it played her favourite Christmas songs as she wrapped. Once she had finished, she stood up and walked to the window, everywhere was covered in snow, and still, it was falling from the sky, the sky was now dark, she had become so engrossed in the music and the atmosphere, that she had lost all track of time, she quickly glanced at the clock. It had just gone five, which meant that she still had time to get ready for the carol concert that Martha had arranged in the lounge, she was thinking as she opened her wardrobe and began throwing clothes onto her bed. She picked out the red dress and quickly changed into it, Bill walked as she was half-dressed.

"Now that's a sight for sore eyes!" he said and laughed.

"Saucy bugger!" Peggy replied and threw a towel at him. By a quarter to six, they were both ready, which was a miracle for Peggy, Bill was thinking, usually, Peggy would spend an hour on just her hair!

"Did you manage to speak to Stan?" Peggy asked as she took Bill's arm, and they walked down the stairs. Bill smiled and nodded.

"Aye, your wee darlings are fine, and guess what?" he said and grinned.

"What?"

"Stan has a lady friend going for dinner tomorrow,"

"No way! Who, do we know her?"

"Oh aye we know her all right," Bill laughed.

"Well, who is it?"

"Annis,"

"No way!" Peggy gasped.

"Is wee Heather going too?" Peggy asked, disappointed that she was missing out on all the local gossip, Bill nodded, and Peggy's heart melted just a little, they both deserved a little happiness, she thought as they walked into the lounge to join the others. The choristers had already arrived and were warming their voices and eating mince pies. Martha walked to them with the usual tray filled with glasses of sherry, they both politely refused, both of them detested the stuff! Then Bob walked over to them with a port and lemon and a pint, which was most appreciated!

"Have you warmed your vocal cords up?" Bob asked as he sipped from his pint. Peggy shook her head and Bill frowned.

"Have you heard her singing?" he asked and shook his head, Peggy shot him a look.

"Ah, never mind sis, I must have taken all the singing talent!" Bob said and sniggered.

"Aye I'm sure that you did, and I'm sure that Dean Martin is quaking in his boots!" Peggy muttered under her breath.

"Now, now, didn't anyone tell you that jealousy is a terrible thing," Bob said and nudged her as he laughed.

The front doorbell rang, and Martha shot out of the lounge to open it, which was unusual as she usually sent Cyril, Peggy was thinking.

"If I could have everyone's attention, I would like to introduce our new guests," Martha shouted as everyone looked in her direction, well everyone except for Peggy who was moaning to Mags about Bob and his big head, Bill nudged her, still she took no notice.

"Peg," he said, she turned and looked at him.

"What?" she asked irritably.

"Look!" he said and pointed in Martha's direction, she peered across the room and gasped, dropping her drink, she ran through everyone and stood there, tears running down her cheeks, it was Molly and Michael! She threw her arms around Molly and held her for the longest time, sobbing as she did, she thought that she would never see either of them ever again! Then once she finally let go of Molly she turned to Michael, who held his arms wide open, and she fell into them.

"What are you both doing here?" she asked breathlessly as she wiped the tears from her cheeks. Martha had now joined them.

"All the time that you are here, in my place, nothing or nobody can harm you, I have known Molly and Michael for years, and since Bob has been working for Michael for a while now, I thought that it would be a wonderful surprise for you Peggy," Martha said and smiled.

"Oh, Martha! Thank you!" Peggy cried and then turned to Bob who was shaking Michael's hand.

"You never told me," she said to Bob. He zipped a pretend zip across his mouth.

"I was sworn to secrecy," he said and winked as Peggy shook her head in disbelief.

"Peggy, have you met Hans?" Martha asked as Hans stood out from behind Michael. Peggy gasped and placed her hand over her mouth as she looked at the dwarf. She pointed at him.

"Fingers?" she asked, Hans, frowned and nodded!

CHAPTER 26

It was without a shadow of a doubt, the most wonderful, magical, excitement fuelled Christmas eve that Peggy had ever experienced. Only to be surpassed by the surprise appearance of Molly, Michael and Hans, there were a few moments during the evening when she found herself overcome with emotion.

The choir were gathered around the huge tree in Martha's lounge singing the 'deck the halls' beautifully and enthusiastically, and Peggy looked around the room, she smiled when she saw Molly chatting to Alice and Mags, and then her gaze turned to Bob, who was standing beside Reg, Bill, Cyril and Michael as they all sang out in the best tenor voices, making Peggy chuckle, she looked around and then saw Martha, sharing a bottle of sherry with Hans, which they both seemed to be enjoying a little too much! Peggy was thinking, then in the corner of the room, something caught her eye, and just away from the tree and the choir stood Carrie, Polly, and Jo, hand in hand, smiling as they watched in awe, the festivities that were taking place. Peggy waved at Wee Polly who was looking directly at her, and she grinned and frantically waved back, Peggy looked over at Molly, trying desperately to gain her attention, but she seemed far too engrossed in the conversation that she was having with Mags. She laughed, then happened to glance over in Peggy's direction, who in turn looked at the three spirits and pointed. Molly looked and gasped, smiling widely as tears appeared in her eyes, and then they vanished. Molly stood and walked to Peggy, throwing her arms around her, and holding her tightly, as tears ran freely down her cheeks.

"Shall we go and grab some fresh air?" Peggy asked, Molly, nodded as she desperately tried to hide the fact that she had become so emotional, Peggy grabbed her by the hand and led her out to the reception area and then opened the front door. They both stepped outside and watched as the fragile flakes of snow, fell gracefully and silently from the sky, landing to create an even thicker carpet of white over everything. Molly turned to Peggy and smiled.

"Oh, Peggy! My dearest Peggy, it is truly wonderful that Martha managed to arrange this, I was getting to the point where I felt I might disintegrate into boredom, things just no longer the same," she sighed and touched Peggy's cheek.

"What's wrong Molly, you seem really sad?" Peggy asked, seeing a side of Molly that she had never seen before, Molly was always the rock, the one to pick up the pieces and reassure everyone that everything was going to be all right.

"I miss Carrie so much, there were things that I could share with her, that only she understood, I miss my Jo, and above all else Peggy, I miss you," Molly said as she wiped the tears away quickly for fear of them freezing on her cheeks.

"Why don't you leave the guardianship and come and live with me and Bill?" Peggy asked, now genuinely worried about her. Molly smiled and then shook her head.

"Once you have made the pledge, there is no going back, that's what made it so difficult for Abe, he was never meant to fall in love with Carrie, but he did, and there was nothing that he could do to change that, which is why he tried his hardest to distance himself from her, I never truly understood that until now, and in fact, thinking back, I have been far too judgemental of him in the past," Molly said gently.

"You're not on your own Molly, we have all been guilty of that," Peggy said and placed her arm around Molly's shivering shoulders.

"I know that my time in this realm is drawing to a close," Molly said as she stared into the snow-filled sky.

"Don't be daft, you have years left in you," Peggy said and chuckled, Molly however did not.

"I hope not Peggy, my work is done, all the people that I love have gone," she replied sadly.

"Well, in that case, let's make this Christmas a Christmas to remember!" Peggy said and grabbed her hand to lead her back into the warmth of Martha's beautiful home. Molly looked at Peggy and grinned.

"I wish it could be different Peggy, I wish that we did not have to separate," Molly sighed as Peggy pulled her inside and walked to the drinks cabinet.

"Now, what will you have?" Peggy asked.

"Oh, go on then, I'll have a glass of red," Molly replied as Martha walked to join them both.

"Peggy darling, could you grab me the other bottle of sherry?" Martha asked, Peggy, looked at her wide-eyed.

"You have only just opened the other bottle," Peggy said, nearly choking.

"I know, it's those choristers, my goodness they can really put it away," she said and gestured to the carol singers, who had now finished their concert and were chatting with the guests. She looked at Molly and tutted as she grabbed the second bottle of sherry from Peggy and headed back towards Hans, who was now looking a little worse for wear!

A little later Bill emerged from the kitchen with yet another cup of coffee for Hans, who was beginning to feel a little better. Peggy sat down beside him and smiled.

"I have heard so much about you," Peggy said as she thought about Carrie's expression when she talked about Hans, it was always full of sentiment.

"All good I hope," he replied as he gratefully accepted the coffee from Bill.

"She held you in such high regard, she did truly class you as one of her only friends," Peggy said and smiled at Bill as he sat down beside her.

"That is most kind of you to say, sometimes I found Carrie incredibly hard to read," he said as he thought back to a memory. "You know, I remember a time when Carrie and your father were hiding out, he was only a small child, but he was so brave, he truly wanted to look after his mother," Hans said and then sipped his coffee. Peggy nodded she remembered Carrie telling her all about it.

"You should never have been offended that she called you fingers, she saw it as a term of endearment," Peggy said and grinned, a smile grew upon his face, and he turned to look at Peggy.

"Really!" he replied as he blushed. Peggy nodded frantically,

"She told me so!" she replied and winked at Bill, who placed his hand on her leg.

"Here they are, the best people in the world," Bob slurred as he sat down with Peggy and the others. Peggy looked at Mags, who was steadying him, and she raised her eyebrows.

"How much has he had?" Peggy asked and laughed.

"Too much!" Mags scorned.

"Don't be like that, my Mags, my darlin', love of my life," he slurred again looking as though he was going to slide sideways off of the chair.

"Right, come on you, let's get you up to bed!" Mags said as she struggled to get him to stand.

"Do you want some help?" Bill asked and stood up, Mags nodded gratefully, so together they led him to the stairs.

"We're off to bed now, night night Peg," Alice said and yawned.

"Goodnight both of you, sleep well," Peggy replied.

"Yes I think that I will retire now also," Hans said as he jumped down from the chair. "I will bid you a good night young Peggy," he said and bowed.

The following morning Bill nudged Peggy, she rubbed her eyes and looked at the clock, it was only six-thirty, she rubbed her eyes again and looked at Bill disapprovingly.

"Why?" she asked as she threw her head back onto the soft pillow.

"Merry Christmas, my Peg" he whispered in her ear and then kissed her cheek. She sat bolt upright when she realised what day it was, then threw her arms around him.

"Merry Christmas Bill," she said as she held him tightly, silently thanking the earth for restoring him to his former self, she loved him so much!

Martha had already told them to be in the dining room for half eight, so once they had exchanged gifts they dressed and then walked down the stairs to join the others.

The dining room was a hive of activity, the air was filled with excitement and the scent of coffee and freshly baked bread, Peggy inhaled deeply as she and Bill sat at the table, grabbed a basket of warm bread and scooped spoonful's of Martha's homemade jam liberally on top.

Peggy looked around at them all. Molly looked as though she had been crying all night, her eyes were swollen and puffy, Michael seemed to be pre-occupied, forever looking at his watch, Martha most definitely had a hangover, which she made quite apparent when she greeted them at the door and spoke in a very gentle voice, ordinarily her voice would boom above all others! Reg and Alice looked happy as they held hands over the table, Alice holding her hand over the top of her precious cargo, every now and then. Bob seemed to have recovered from the heavy drinking very well as he sat at a table with Mags, Cyril, and Hans, sharing stories and making them all howl with laughter! Then she turned to look at Bill, who was looking at her across the table.

"That's why I love you so," he sighed as he put another piece of bread and jam in his mouth. Peggy frowned.

"Well, go on, don't keep me in suspense," she said and laughed. Bill finished eating his mouthful, and then slowly wiped the remnants of jam around his mouth with the crisp white napkin. Peggy tutted and scowled at him.

"Because my darling, you are always concerned about the happiness of others, I have watched you, you treat them all like your ducks," he said and rubbed the back of her hand.

"That's because I love them all, just like I love my ducks and just as I love you," she said coyly and blushed.

Later that day Martha called into the kitchen for Peggy, who rushed through to the dining room.

"Be a dear and help me carry things through to the lounge," Martha asked, Peggy, smiled and grabbed the box of cutlery.

"Are we not eating in here?" Peggy asked as she looked around the now half-empty dining room. Martha shook her head and tutted.

"Of course not! It's Christmas day, and on Christmas day, we dine in the lounge darling," Martha replied and grabbed a stack of plates. Peggy followed her into the lounge, where there was one huge table laid out beautifully, with foliage centrepieces and candles. Peggy leant a hand laying the places for dinner and once they had finished they both stood back to admire their work. Martha smiled, as Peggy counted the place settings.

"Martha, we have laid one too many," Peggy said as she recounted.

"No darling, I just don't like odd numbers," She said as she chuckled. Peggy returned to the kitchen to continue helping to cook. Once all the food was in the large ovens warming, Peggy, Mags, Lucy, and Molly all ran up to their rooms to change, and within minutes they were all returning back down the stairs. As Peggy reached the bottom the front door knocked.

"Peggy could you answer that for me, I'm on the telephone," Martha called out from the reception. Peggy walked to the door, opened it, and staggered backwards when she saw who it was.

There he stood his arms open wide, bags of gifts at his feet, she jumped into his arms and held him, tightly, so tight that he was struggling to breathe, and when she finally released him, she stood back and looked at him, still gasping with disbelief.

"Can I come in, it's bloody freezing out here?" he said and exaggerated a shiver. Peggy grabbed some of the many bags and walked beside him into the reception.

"I thought that I would never see you again," Peggy gasped.

"One last time, and we have the wonderful Martha to thank for that, she has pulled out all of the stops!" he said and hugged Peggy once again. Bill walked out to see what was going on, he looked at Abe apprehensively, they had parted on bad terms and Bill wasn't sure if Abe was still harbouring bad feelings towards him. Abe looked at Bill and frowned, Peggy noticed this and gulped, this could really put a spanner in the perfect Christmas scenario, Peggy was thinking, when Abe pointed at Bill, laughed, and then walked towards him with open arms, both Peggy and Bill were at that moment filled with relief!

So after they were all completely and utterly stuffed after the overindulgence of the wonderful Christmas dinner, and were sitting around the table, chatting, laughing, and sharing stories with one another. Peggy was thrilled to discover that Abe, Molly, and Michael would be joining them for the Hogmanay celebrations in Edinburgh, for her, it was a dream come true. From the table, she witnessed just how natural and comfortable Bob was with them all like he had never suffered the detachment from them in his early life as if he had always been a part of their lives, and how happy he was to be within their close-knit circle. Mags was the same. She blended in as though she had known them all, all her life. This made Peggy truly happy.

Peggy watched Martha and was in complete awe of the woman who, had taken Peggy under her wing, when she relentlessly searched for Bob, how she took Bob under her wing and set him up with work, how she deleted his previous life and protected him from the bastards that had held him for so long, and now she had brought them all together for one last celebration, what a truly wonderful gesture, she gave them all the best gift that anyone could possibly ask for, and at that point, in her own mind, Peggy pledged that one day she would find a way to repay her for all of her unwavering generosity and kindness.

They shifted the tables back to the dining room, laid out a huge tea table in the lounge, filled with sandwiches, pastries, pickles, mince pies, yule logs and no end of tasty treats, then sat around the fire playing charades. By the end of the evening, Peggy was so full that she feared she might burst, and as if Molly could read her thoughts, she looked at Peggy and chuckled.

"Carrie would be so proud of the amount of food that you have eaten today!" she said and laughed. Peggy howled with laughter, as too did Abe. He paused from his conversation with Hans, momentarily and watched Peggy affectionately.

"I am so proud of you Peggy, there is not a single man in this land that could say that he has a more wonderful granddaughter than I," he said and raised his glass. Peggy stood and cleared her throat, to gain the attention of them all.

"If I may say a few words," she said awkwardly.

"Peggy, Peggy!" Bob, Bill, and Reg began to chant, making her blush and chuckle at the same time.

"Firstly, I would like to say a most heartfelt thank you to Martha, who has made this the best Christmas that anyone could have asked for, you are one of the most amazing people that I have ever had the pleasure to meet Martha, and every day I count my blessings that you have become such a huge part of our lives, and a true family member, so, if you could all raise a glass to Martha," Peggy said and held up her glass.

"To Martha the marvellous!" Bob shouted making them all laugh.

"To Martha the marvellous!" they all shouted in unison. Martha blushed and looked at them all coyly as she poured herself a drink.

"Now then, to Molly, I am the happiest woman alive, in the fact that I have been given this very special time to spend with very special and my most favourite people, Molly you have stood beside me through my darkest and happiest moments, you were not only Carrie's rock, but you were Michael's, Abe's and mine too, and for that, you should be very proud, you are a wonderful woman Molly, don't ever forget that, To Molly!" Peggy roared as she raised her glass.

"To Molly!" they all shouted.

"Now I don't want to go on all night, so I will wrap this up now, Mags, I couldn't wish for a better sister-in-law, Bob obviously has the best taste, Alice and Reg, I love that you live close by and have become our closest friends, in fact, I would consider you both as part of our family, to Abe, my Grandad, I now and forever will love you with all my heart, despite your faults," she said as everyone roared with laughter, including Abe.

"To my wee Robert, there are no words to express how happy I am that we have been reunited, even though you drive me up the wall, I look forward to making many happy memories with you, and last but by no means least, to my Bill, thank you for being you, please join me and raise your glasses to everyone," she said teary-eyed as she raised her glass in the air.

"TO EVERYONE!" They all shouted.

CHAPTER 27

As they sat in the compartment of the train travelling to Scotland, Peggy looked out of the window in amazement. She had never seen as much snow! She became lost in her thoughts and began to giggle as she thought back to boxing day and their excursion to Richmond ice-skating rink. She hadn't laughed so much in such a long time.

Martha, Molly, Michael, Cyril, and Abe all headed to the bar, as too did Alice, Reg didn't think that it was a good idea for a woman in her condition to be falling over on ice! Which just left Peggy, Bill, Bob, Mags, and Reg. Bill was insistent that he wasn't doing it, because of his past injuries, but she kept telling him that he was being a baby, and to save face he finally agreed. As usual, Bob was full of himself and even though he had never ice-skated before, he presumed that he would skate like a pro!

They all pulled their skates on and of course, Bob was the first to step foot on the ice. Mags followed and skated off confidently as Bob clung to the sides of the rink for dear life, Bill looked at Peggy in horror as he watched how nervous Bob was, he was always confident, and this was so out of character. Peggy chuckled and grabbed Bill's hands, leading him onto the ice.

He smiled as he put one foot in front of the other and began to glide, Bob was watching intently then followed Bill and did the same. Peggy surprised herself, she had never done anything like this before, she was clumsy enough on two feet, never mind having blades on her feet and ice beneath them! She was thinking but she got the hang of it almost immediately, and very soon she had caught up with Mags as they both skated around the rink beside one another. Reg simply could not get the hang of it, so he took off his boots and joined Alice in the bar.

Mags nudged Peggy and gestured to her to look to the centre of the rink, where Bill and Bob were holding onto one another, stranded in the middle and unable to move. Peggy burst out laughing as they skated towards them.

"It's not funny Peg, we are going to fall," Bill fumed, which made Peggy and Mags laugh all the more.

"Mags, stop larking about and grab hold of my hand will ya!" Bob shouted.

"But Bob, I thought that you were going to skate like a pro!" Mags said and skated away.

"Peg, come on, you're not going to leave us stranded are ya?" He pleaded, Peggy, laughed and skated away to follow Mags. They did three rounds of the rink, then skated over to the marooned men, as they both attempted to teach them how to move without falling on their arses!

Peggy looked at Bill and watched him fidgeting in his seat, which made her chuckle.

"Aye, you can laugh, it's not you with the bruised bottom is it!" he sulked and pulled a face as he attempted to get comfortable. Peggy glanced at Mags, and they could hold it in no longer as they both roared with laughter!

The train journey seemed to take forever, and Peggy sighed with relief when the train pulled into Edinburgh station, she really needed to stretch her legs. They all disembarked and headed out to the taxi rank.

Inside the hotel Peggy, Mags and Alice were looking around in awe. It was absolutely stunning! The décor was beautiful, and the furnishings were nothing short of sublime. The owner, a youngish Italian-looking man walked through the foyer and called out to Martha, who walked over and embraced him.

"Giovanni, it is wonderful to see you again!" she shrieked.

"If I could have your attention!" he called out and they all looked in his direction. "My name is Giovanni, I am the proprietor of this establishment, and you are my very special guests, very soon, our porters will arrive to show you to your rooms, and once you have all had the opportunity to refresh yourselves, I would be very happy if you would join me in the bar for welcome drinks," He said and bowed, Peggy turned to Bill and raised her eyebrows, he smiled.

"Where are the bloody porters, I'm dying for a jimmy," Bob said as he danced on the spot, Mags frowned.

"Look there are toilets over there," she said and pointed.

"I can't though can I? What happens if the porters turn up while I'm in there, I won't know where the room is will I?" He said still dancing.

The fun-filled days were shooting by incredibly swiftly and sitting in the beautiful dining room having breakfast, Peggy was finding it hard to believe that it was New Year's Eve already! She chuckled as she watched Bill tuck into his runny egg, the yolk dripping down his shirt, leaving a yellow trail. She looked around for the others, Martha and Cyril were staying in Giovanni's suite with him and his beautiful wife Mia, Abe, Molly, and Michael were sitting at the table next to Peggy and Bill, but there was no sign of Bob and Mags or Reg and Alice.

"Abe, have you seen Bob this morning?" Peggy called over. Abe shook his head.

"I saw them climbing into a taxi when I came down for breakfast," Molly said and smiled. Peggy nodded, then looked at Bill and frowned.

"I wonder where they have gone?" Peggy asked, Bill, shook his head and continued to eat.

"You know something don't you?" She asked suspiciously, he wouldn't look at her, so she knew that he was hiding something, again Bill shook his head, and was quietly relieved when a waiter walked to their table and passed Peggy a piece of paper, which she read and frowned.

"What? What does it say?" Bill asked,

"I will be back in a wee minute," Peggy said and stood up,

"Peg wait, what did the note say?" Bill asked again,

"If we are keeping secrets Bill, well," she huffed and walked into the foyer towards the huge reception desk, Bill was twisting his neck to see where she was going, but a coach load of guests had just arrived, and he could see nothing.

A few moments later Bill could see Peggy walking towards him, wearing the biggest smile. "Well, would you look at who I have just found skulking in the foyer," Peggy squealed and stood aside to reveal Shona and a very tall man, Bill jumped up and threw his arms around Peggy's best friend, then held his hand out to the man that Shona introduced as Alberrr!

"Would you like me to show you around the place?" Bill asked Albert as the two girls nattered away like a pair of old gossips.

"I, er, would like zat very much," he replied, Bill, smiled and walked around the table to kiss Peggy on the cheek, even though she was now oblivious to the fact that he was even there!

It wasn't until they both come up for breath, that they noticed that the restaurant was now empty, and the staff were giving them looks as they were laying the tables in preparation for the lunchtime sitting. "Oops!" Peggy said and laughed as she and Shona stood and walked out arm in arm to the foyer.

They sat on the large, luxurious sofas that were scattered all around the foyer, Peggy was wondering where on earth Bill had got to, when she heard his deep booming voice, then he and Albert came into view, walking towards them at the very same time that Bob, Mags, Reg, and Alice walked through the main doors. Peggy stood so that they would notice her, and they all headed in their direction.

"Where have you been?" Peggy asked, and both Bob and Bill began to reply. "I only have one pair of ears!" Peggy said and tutted. They stood for a few seconds trying to do the polite thing, Peggy was losing her patience and then began rolling her eyes.

"I was showing Albert around, I mean I did tell you, but you were engrossed in conversation," Bill huffed, Peggy smiled and kissed his cheek.

"And we, er, we went out for a walk, didn't we," Bob said and looked at the others for verification.

"Why did you need a taxi, if you were going for a walk?" Peggy asked suspiciously.

"King Arthur's Seat!" Mags shouted and smiled at Bob, who chuckled and winked at Mags.

"Yeah that was it, we went to King Arthur's seat," he collaborated with Mag's story and nodded, grinning like a Cheshire cat. Peggy shook her head, she did not believe a word of it, they were clearly hiding something from her, and she would find out what! She was thinking to herself as she scowled at them all.

"Blimey Bill, I know what we're getting you for your birthday," Bob said and laughed, trying his hardest to change the subject. Bill frowned,

"Eh?" He asked wearing a puzzled expression.

"A baby's bib, look you've got egg all down your shirt, you mucky bugger," he replied and laughed, as everyone had a look and laughed.

"Well, if you would all excuse us, we are going to get ready," Peggy said as she stood and grabbed Bill's hand.

"Get ready for what?" Bob asked, Peggy, shrugged,

"Well as it seems that we are all keeping secrets from one another, you won't mind if we keep that information to ourselves, will you," She huffed and walked with Bill towards the lifts. Bob looked at Mags and pulled a face.

"Maybe we should have told her," She said quietly,

"Nah, she'll be all right," Bob said and looked as Abe and Michael walked to join them. Abe smiled.

"We are just popping out to see to some business, we will be back before the celebrations begin," He said and nodded to them all.

Peggy did well to hide the fact that she was absolutely furious, and they had a lovely afternoon wandering around Edinburgh with Shona and Albert. Peggy was so happy to have her best friend there, but this was all masked by an underlying sadness, Shona was moving to France indefinitely so that she and Albert could marry, and this made Peggy feel a little lost, nevertheless, she wasn't going to let it spoil the celebrations, so she put on a brave face!

Dinner was served to them in Giovanni's private suite, and the meal consisted of everything Italian, which Peggy loved, Bill, not so much. After dinner, they were served coffee and brandy before they joined the other revellers in the ballroom. Peggy kept catching a glimpse of Bob who was looking at her, he had a look of concern on his face, and then he looked at Martha, who nodded to him, he tapped his spoon on his brandy glass to gain the attention of everybody.

"Sorry, but I have got something to say," Bob said awkwardly. Peggy looked at him anxiously. "I, er, well, I don't really know where to start," he said, looking directly at Peggy, she gulped, so scared about what he was going to say next. "Well, it's like this you see, I've been called up for national service," he said and gulped. Peggy frowned.

"What do you mean?" she asked, not having a clue what he was talking about.

"At the age of eighteen, every young man is called up to serve in one of the armed forces and serve for two years," Martha said gently and smiled at Peggy. Peggy was still frowning.

"I have been drafted into the army, my post is in Germany," Bob said quietly.

"Germany! Martha, surely you can stop this, you know, with your contacts," Peggy asked despairingly. Martha smiled and gently shook her head. In sheer desperation, she looked at Abe,

"Abe, please tell me that you can stop it," she pleaded, Abe shook his head as he lowered his head and looked at the table, not wanting to see the despair in Peggy's eyes.

"Peg, I want to go," Bob said as he walked to where she was sitting and grabbed her hand.

"Why, what about Mags," she asked as the tears spilt down her rosy cheeks.

"I think that it'll do me good, it will be a good experience, and Mags is all right with it, aint ya?" Bob said and looked at Mags who smiled and nodded.

"But I thought that you wanted to get married," Peggy said trying her hardest to change his mind, Bob looked at the floor.

"We did get married, this morning," he mumbled.

"What?" Peggy cried, Bill, placed his arm around her shoulders. She turned to face Bill, her face full of angst.

"You knew, you knew didn't you," she seethed, Bill nodded shamefully.

"Why did you all keep it from me?" Peggy sobbed. Bob kneeled down and grabbed her hands which she swiftly pulled away.

"I didn't want to spoil your New Year, I knew that you would take it badly, so we just went to the registry office this morning and did it, we can all celebrate when I get back, you could even do one of those hand thingy's couldn't you, eh," Bob said desperately trying to make his sister feel better. Peggy stood and ran out of the apartment, out of the hotel and into the grounds, pushing her way through the many people that were there ready to see in the new year. She stopped when she came to a small wall which she sat upon and sobbed. She felt an arm slip around her shoulder, she looked up, relieved to see that it was Molly, she couldn't face the others, not yet.

"Peggy, they were only trying to protect you, I completely understand that you feel as though you were excluded, but my dear, if Bob had told you it would have spoiled the wonderful Christmas that we have all just shared with one another, he did it for you, as too did Bill," Molly sighed and wiped the tears from Peggy's cheeks, Peggy sniffed and nodded, Molly was right, she always was. Martha walked out and nodded to Molly, who tapped Peggy on the shoulder and walked back towards the hotel.

"We wanted you to have the best Christmas, goodness knows you deserve it, nothing and I mean nothing was done to spite you or exclude you, just to protect you my darling," Martha said as she pulled Peggy in for a hug. "Now wipe your tears away, don't spoil that beautiful face with puffy eyes and angry skin," Martha said and handed Peggy a hanky.

The clock struck twelve and the cheers could be heard for miles as they all headed out towards the garden for the firework display. Bob was on one side of Peggy, Bill on the other as they both put their arms around her shoulders. "Happy new year Peg, I have so much to thank you for," Bob. said and kissed her cheek.

"Happy new year my Peg," Bill said and kissed the other cheek. Peggy looked up into the night sky, the smell of sulphur filled the air as the bright colours lit up the sky, followed by the loud bangs and whizzes. She looked up as far into the sky as she could.

What now? She asked the universe.

ABOUT THE AUTHOR

Louise lives in Devon with her fellow writer husband and family. When they are not teaching at home, they love to roam the moors and the coastal paths, searching for new material!
This is the eighth book that Louise has penned, and she still has many more waiting to be written!

For more info go to: www.undertheoakspublications
Or follow Louise on Amazon, Facebook, and Instagram!

Printed in Great Britain
by Amazon

37920182R00200